V. Mahanenko

CONDEMNED

Lord Valevsky: Last of the Line

Books are the lives
we dont have
time to live,

Vasily Mahanenko

A Progression Fantasy Series
Book 9

Magic Dome Books

Condemned Book 9: A Progression Fantasy Series
(Lord Valevsky: Last of the Line)
Copyright © V. Mahanenko 2025
Cover Art © Lunar 2025
Cover Design V. Manyukhin
English translation copyright © Taylor Elise Margvelashvili 2025
Published by Magic Dome Books, 2025
All Rights Reserved
ISBN: 978-80-7702-338-2

This book is entirely a work of fiction.
Any correlation with real people or events
is coincidental.

Table of Contents:

Chapter 1 1

Chapter 2 17

Chapter 3 35

Chapter 4 53

Chapter 5 71

Chapter 6 87

Chapter 7 105

Chapter 8 122

Chapter 9 140

Chapter 10 157

Chapter 11 174

Chapter 12 191

Chapter 13 208

Chapter 14 224

Chapter 15 241

Chapter 16 260

Chapter 17 275

Chapter 18 291

Chapter 19 308

Chapter 1

"ARE YOU KIDDING ME right now?! What are you two doing here??"

"Your anger is unwarranted, Archduke Valevsky. From henceforth, Hearth will be the foundation of a fair and impartial court. A place above all others. A place with rights. You wanted autonomy, and you got it. And not only from the Zarak Empire, but also from the light and dark lands. This is the decree of Chaos. Neither the Light nor Skron will dare to dispute it. And neither will you. You must accept this fact, Archduke Valevsky. From now on, we will be here, whether you want us or not."

The Interrogator fell silent, indicating that there would be no further commentary. The representative of darkness sat down on the dark throne to the right of mine and became a motionless statue. On the left side, on a snow-white throne, was the Inquisitor. This one did not honor me with a single word. The Inquisitor and the Interrogator were two sides of the same entity, and since I had *Golden Dome of Protection* in my magic field again, only the dark component of Chaos would communicate with me.

"We'll see who'll dispute and accept what," I muttered, not even thinking of sitting down next to him. I had a study, where I spent most of my time. Sitting on the throne surrounded by the two most powerful beings of this world was not the wisest of decisions...

The shocking discovery of Hearth's newest residents fell upon me as soon as I returned home. The journey had taken me almost two weeks, as I ended up being delayed in Al-Khorezm for some time. The Inquisitor had rended the palace of Padishah Bayazid the Third to ruin. The Echo of Chaos, called to protect the Light, had demonstrated its power and wrath to the entire world. The clergy couldn't even drag all the converts to the capital, there were so many. Huge bonfires were erected right there in the palace and the dark ones were destroyed in droves.

And the fires in the capital were still blazing. In three days, all the servants of the Light of the Citadel, including the Pope, had passed through me. The Inquisitor wanted to determine one thing: whether any dark humans had access to the Citadel. There were twelve such people, including the head of the supply service, as well as two servants of the Light. They all were sent to the pyre. But this fate was not just reserved for the clergy. There were two more whose souls were subjected to the cleansing fire. The first of them was Padishah Bayazid the Third, who believed until the very end that the Citadel wouldn't dare take such a step. Of course, the richest man in the lands of the Light, the hope and support of the throne of the Shurghan Empire — sent to the stake. How could anyone even think such a thing? Well, they did.

The second was the Duke of Odoevsky. And I was the one to send him there. By my decree. My main and, in fact, the only condition for rooting out the spies and traitors among the clergy was that they gave me Count Fardi. The Pope met with me personally, trying to understand the reasoning behind such a demand and dissuade me from a rash act. The Duke of Odoevsky was found guilty of making his daughter a vessel of Skron and was subject to execution. But I was adamant: Count Fardi's fate must be in my hands. The Church of the Light made concessions. The Duke of Odoevsky, who had already lost all hope of salvation, was freed from the steel bracers that blocked magic, taken out of the prison cell and even delivered to the Citadel Square. Hope flashed in the Count's eyes, which didn't fade, even when he was told that from now on his fate was entirely in my hands. It was funny, but I did not hate this man, so I did not play with him. Yes, Count Fardi could have chosen not to follow his master's order to destroy my family, choosing rather to resettle us (although

I'm not sure my father would have agreed). He could have tried, at least. Or pretended. But he didn't, and instead what came to pass, came to pass. No one could change it. So I simply sent Count Fardi to the stake. Sure, I had the help of the servants of the Light, including their own accusations against him, but I did it personally. The only thing that brought me satisfaction was seeing the emotions change in the Duke of Odoevsky's eyes. It was so sweet to watch that hope fade. I truly felt that part of my family had been avenged. But not all of them. Not by a long shot.

So I returned home and was immediately hit with this bucket of ice water. From now on, Hearth would be home to the Inquisitor and the Interrogator. Moreover, the two strictly forbade Eleanore and Alia from informing me about the situation, with punishment for violation up to and including complete destruction of their exceedingly pregnant selves, so they were forced to obey. The portal was up and running again. The Inquisitor ordered the mechanoid to activate the arch, and the city's defender did not dare to oppose the will of the higher being. So this was the mechanoid's ultimate master. The Interrogator now resided in Hearth, but the Temple of Skron was in no rush to sort things out with my city. One understood the limits of its capabilities and did not want to get involved with Chaos. On the one hand, the presence of such guests was an ideal defense against any hotheads with big ideas, but on the other, Hearth was now becoming a center of pilgrimage for all the offended and disadvantaged. All those who were ready to sacrifice everything they had, just to achieve justice, at least as the higher beings saw it. Before, I thought that the Inquisitor's task was to protect the Pope and occasionally go to the dark lands. In fact, it turned out that he acted as a justice of the peace, making decisions on controversial cases. The price of such consideration was enormous, up to the life of the applicant, but all cases were considered without exception. Be it the emperor or the most destitute and impoverished peasant. A similar situation occurred with the dark ones: the Interrogator, when he was not running around the lands of the Light and punishing everyone left and right, was engaged in receiving and delivering the final verdict on disputes between clans. And now this whole crowd of people rushed into my city. My city! And without my permission!

The only joy I found in all this (except, of course, my own security) was that from now on, all resources for considering cases and summoning the Supreme Court were not sent to the Temple of Skron or the Citadel, but remained in Hearth. It was this condition that prevented me from exploding with anger within the first few minutes of my conversation with the Interrogator. Another small joy was that cases were only considered for four hours a day, and in specially designated rooms. Outside of my palace. But it became crystal clear that I no longer had enough hotels in the city, even before construction was completed. The Goose would have to fork out even more gold and make additional accommodations, and for all different strata of society. Great Light, give me strength for it all!

Leaving the entities alone, I went to my office. I just wanted to sit in silence and think about everything that had befallen me recently. But even here, I couldn't get a moment of peace: Eleanore intercepted me in the corridor.

"Max, Magister Meram…"

"Did something happen to him?" I sighed helplessly.

"Time, Max. Time happened to him. Come on."

Meram was lying in his bed, surrounded by sheer chaos. Sheets of paper covered in symbols were scattered everywhere. Not just one or two, not even ten or twenty, but several hundred expensive sheets had been crumpled or even torn into small scraps of paper. The former runescribe was furious that he couldn't do anything, so he took out his anger on the innocent paper. He had tried to figure it out before his strength left him completely, but he couldn't handle it. The *Author* skill had bested him.

He was still alive. He was breathing, in any case. They were forced, wheezing, straining breaths, but he was still breathing. It was a frightening sight to behold: he looked like a mummy who had dried out under the scorching sun. Blackened, flabby, helpless, with faded, unseeing eyes. I used *Heal* in an attempt to somehow improve his condition, but my magic sank into the old man's body like water into sand.

Eleanore shook her head. "It's no good. We've already invited several healers. There's nothing wrong with Magister Meram's body. It's in perfect condition. In as perfect condition as a three-hundred-year-old body can be. The seals expire tomorrow, and the remaining years will catch up with him. Max, this needs to end. He's your pupil. Make the right move."

"He didn't leave anything behind? No note, no message?"

"Nothing. He has spent the last twenty days sitting in this room, trying to decipher this skill. I must admit that he held up well. He hardly ever lost his temper. Systematically, step by step, he tested one theory after another. I couldn't have done that, knowing what awaited me if I failed. For this alone, we should respect him enough to set him free. He has earned it."

"He has," I agreed. The vyrma blade appeared in my hand and swiftly entered the flabby body unimpeded. Magister Meram, runescribe, who had somehow managed to dictate his own terms to both the light and the dark for almost two hundred years, was sent to meet Skron. The end of an era.

"Is there anything useful here?" I said, looking around the room.

"I don't think so. As far as I know, he couldn't get a grasp on the skill. At all."

"That's strange," I frowned and pulled up the *Author* skill description. There were no restrictions. Anyone could be an *Author*. But for some reason, Meram couldn't do it. I needed to think. I wouldn't want to waste more resources on something useless to me.

"Are you in Hearth for long?" Eleanore asked.

"I'd like to tell you that I'm staying forever, but I can't lie to you," I replied bitterly. "I have been given three months to destroy forces that no one knows anything about. I need to prepare. Kimal Sarento won the tournament?"

"As if anyone expected a different outcome. The undisputed and reigning—"

Eleanore suddenly fell silent and crouched down, ready for a fight. In front of us, about two meters away, a huge, bloody portal arch appeared, taking up most of the corridor. No reaction from the city's security system, as if it hadn't seen it.

"Step back," I said slowly, taking a step forward and blocking Eleanore from view. I could do crazy things, but Eleanore wasn't allowed, even with her full suit of mithril armor. A second passed. Another. No one appeared from the portal. No creatures, no tentacles, no other incredible nastiness. Just a bloody shroud that flickered in the middle of the corridor. I might have even thought it was a hallucination, except I wasn't the only one who saw it.

"Max?" she whispered. Not a shred of fear or horror. Her years in the rifts had taken their toll on Eleanore. She was ready to meet any enemy. But none showed.

"I have no idea what to do here. I wasn't expecting guests."

"But they are expecting you, heir," a strange

voice sounded out. It seemed to be coming from within my own head.

"Did you hear that?" I turned to Eleanore.

"Hear what?"

"Something's speaking to me. Evidently, I'm the only one who hears it."

"That's right, heir," the strange voice repeated. "You should go through the portal. No threat awaits you. We need to talk. Immediately, before you do anything stupid."

Before I could say a word or warn Eleanore that I was leaving Hearth, the portal was no longer next to me, but was inside me. The space floated to form a small room. No windows, no doors. The walls were made of dark, unprocessed stone, but I couldn't call the area a cave — the floor and ceiling were perfectly smooth, as if made of expensive dark marble. And the unprocessed stone looked too perfect to believe that it could be a natural for-mation. I still couldn't determine where the source of the light was, but the room was illuminated. And most importantly, in the center of this room stood two chairs, and one of them was already oc-cupied.

"Have a seat, heir." The figure gestured invit-ingly. Outwardly, he resembled a human, but for some strange reason he was translucent. As if he was made of the same material as the messages and notifications that flashed in front of my eyes every time I used my abilities. *Analyze* did nothing, nor did the other magic stones. My status bar was behaving quite strangely in general — almost all the icons on it had turned gray and become inactive. Only personal information and a few settings indicated that I was still dark. Although no. It turned out that my map was available, and available scales showed that I was in an unknown place. Even if I zoomed out as far as possible, there were no familiar lands in the surrounding area, nor was there the *Author* skill. The dictionary and the ability to form sentences were still there.

The figure could have been about sixty years old. He was dressed in the fashion of the highest aristocracy of the Zarak Empire, which significantly reduced his age, but his short snow-white hair, as well as his thick snow-white beard, gave him away. His face was vaguely familiar to me, but nothing more. I sat down opposite the master of this strange place and asked directly,

"Why did you call me 'heir?'"

"That is not what we are here to discuss right now. If you don't like 'heir,' I can call you a janitor. It doesn't matter to me. It's just a set of sounds that form a certain structure, but they don't carry any power. Heir, janitor, elephant, triangle — these are all just sounds. What matters is why you're here."

The ghostly master remained silent, but I didn't rush to ask why I had come here. If there was one thing I'd learned in the last six months, it was patience.

"You are working with Chaos," the projection finally said. I remained silent. It was silly to confirm or refute obvious facts. "Chaos gave you a task. The two Observers sit on either side of your throne. You bear the marks of both servants of Chaos. I had to work hard to reach you undetected."

"I suppose asking who you are is also pointless? The answer will also be just sounds?"

"You're a quick learner," he replied with a grin. "What will it give you to know that I am a sixth-generation interactive neural network? Or that my name is Yuri? These are just sounds that have no power behind them."

"So sounds can be imbued with power, and then they will cease to be sounds?"

"My capabilities are limited. You need to go to where one of my auxiliary cores is located. There, beyond the access boundary, we can speak of more substantive things, heir."

"Why have you sent me here? For what reason? You said that I'm working with Chaos. That means you're not Chaos."

"I am not," it agreed. "You know my name, you know what I am. But it's just sounds to you. They don't have any power here."

"Too many words. Or meaningless sounds. For what purpose did you bring me to — wherever this is? What is this place, and why have you brought me here?"

"You have the key, heir. You can go to the location where my auxiliary core is stored and receive answers to the questions that concern you. The location was given to you by the previous heir."

"Are you an ancient?" I asked, finally putting all the pieces together. The heir, the key, the strange names, the sadness in the voice at the knowledge that I was working with Chaos. It all sounded like what my grandfather had told me when he handed me that very key.

"I am a sixth-generation interactive neural network," the projection repeated. "Not an ancient."

"Okay, let's move on. Why do I need to go to ancient ruins?"

"This is your purpose. This is your destiny."

"Why should I blindly follow orders from unknown entities?"

"Because this is your destiny. You must use the key and get answers. You must continue the path you started. You must cleanse the planet. Damn it!"

The translucent figure shimmered as if caught in the wind, but quickly regained its calm.

"I've said too much. Chaos is constantly monitoring the structure of your knowledge. They know that I've met with you. But I had no other choice. Chaos made its move, giving you the appearance of protection. You could have taken a liking to its servants. This cannot be allowed. You must enter the ancient city pure. Do not give in to persuasion. Do not accept gifts. And do not even think about receiving *Tainted Blood.*"

"What is it?"

"It's something that will close the door to the city of the ancients to you. By accepting a gift from Chaos, you will lose your purity. The defense system will not let you through, even with the key."

"I still haven't gotten an answer to my question: Why should I follow your orders, sixth-generation interactive neural network?"

"You are the heir. The last heir bequeathed you a key. This is your path. The path of every heir. You must remain pure. You must cleanse the planet. You…"

The space began to float again, preventing the projection from finishing the sentence. When the world around me gained density again, I found myself in the same corridor from which I had been taken. Eleanore was gone, and the Interrogator was in her place. A very angry Interrogator, judging by his face.

"Follow me," the Chaos entity ordered. Turning around, not even bothering to check whether I was complying, he strode into the main hall. It was empty — even the servants had left. The Interrogator sat down on his throne and was silent for a long time. I realized that I was standing in front of the two entities like a guilty child, so I climbed onto my throne to sit between them.

"You wish to receive *Tainted Blood*," the Interrogator said after a beat.

"I still haven't been told what it is," I replied coolly without turning. I looked stolidly forward. I was getting sick of all this! Just when I started to think that I'd dealt with everyone who used me to achieve some of their own goals, other, even stronger entities appeared and continued to do the same. Couldn't I just live in peace? Just for a couple of decades!

"It was a gift from Chaos to those you call offworlders, so that they could take their place in this world. Could defend their right to exist. But they did not use the gift to its full potential. We were unable to understand its true nature. We believe that you can handle this."

"You want to give me *Tainted Blood*?" I tensed up. Too many coincidences per square meter. One incomprehensible creature warned that *Tainted Blood* should not be taken, another incomprehensible creature immediately wanted to foist it off on me.

"Transferring the gift completely is impossible. It will affect the balance of power and shake the foundations of our already shaky system. *Tainted Blood* is a level 0 ability. An ability with which you can fight Light or Skron. If you can withstand the true power of these entities. But there is a substitute. A special magic stone that carries a piece of *Tainted Blood.* With it, you will be able to handle third-tier forces. With it, you will be able to complete your task. To destroy the watermen and the undergrounders."

"Why not the ghosts? Troggs? Mechanoids? Or that unnamed sixth force, which for some reason no one talks about? Why the watermen and undergrounders specifically?"

"They're the weakest. They don't deserve to live. A waste of resources. Useless."

"When the offworlders disappeared, rune magic went with them. The lithoids dragged dark fire back into non-existence. What will happen if the watermen and undergrounders disappear?"

"Those in the light lands do not use their abilities. These two forces were the weakest after the lithoids, so they do not deserve the right to remain on the planet. We do not wish to breed two more forces in the form of Karina Fardi and One of the Temple of Skron."

"So forbid them from doing so, that's all it would take," I snorted, barely restraining myself from turning to the Interrogator.

"Balance must be maintained. The third tier must contain either four or eight forces. The system must reach equilibrium. Peace must be achieved in the world. You were given a deadline: three months. Two weeks have already passed, and you are not one step closer to fulfilling the task. The fee for summoning the Inquisitor must be paid in full. Anyone unable to do this will be destroyed. You must set out now. The road to the locations where these two forces are located is not close, there are no portals there."

"You mean no mechanoid portals?"

"Correct." The Interrogator confirmed another one of my suspicions. Skron had nothing to do with portal arches. The dark god had somehow taken over this ability and if we rid this world of mechanoids, instant long-distance jumps would also vanish. Converts would become obsolete. If One was eager to take the place of one of these forces, it meant that the dark pyramid was not the main master among the mechanoids. There was a

Zero somewhere. Something that controlled all of the mechanical brethren.

"But before you set out, you must obtain the *Tainted Blood* stone and several support stones to bring it to a sufficient power level. We cannot give it to you — this will upset the balance. You must obtain it yourself. You must go to the Wall of the Kaliman Empire. In three weeks, a Wave will fall upon it. It will be led by one who has touched Chaos. Received a piece of our power. You will have to destroy him."

"Destroy a being that is immune to vyrma, mithril and magical stones? Is this another joke?"

"This is all the help we can give you. You must figure out how to defeat him. You have the capability, but we are unable to tell you what it is. The Wave is in three weeks. If you fail, it will cover the entire Kaliman Empire. This is our decision. Go, prepare. You have little time."

Rising from the throne, I went to my office. I wasn't going to look back at these soon-to-be corpses. I had no idea how, but I would destroy them, or my name wasn't Archduke Maximilian Valevsky! But first I needed answers from the Abyss. It was time to start hatching my own plans.

Chapter 2

"THESE THINGS ARE NOT simply done on a whim."

"So now Father Locke decides what I can and can't do?"

For a while, I had to battle the former high priest of the Zarak Empire with my eyes. Usually, there was no winner in such games — a third party always interfered in the silent battle — but today no one dared to interfere with my conversation. Alia and Eleanore sat next to each other and, it seemed, were holding their breath. Our guest, whom I had pulled out of the basements of the nocturnal guild, was the first to flinch.

"You are within your rights. What do you want to know about the Fortress' treasury?"

"Everything. Starting from how to get there, ending with traps, security and shift schedule."

"You do realize that twenty years have passed,

right? A lot could have changed since then."

"That is why you must give me as much detail as possible. Go on. If you need to draw something, go right ahead. There are sheets of paper on the table."

I settled myself more comfortably in the chair, ready to absorb the new knowledge. I was not going to go running at the Interrogator's first beck and call. There were three weeks left until the Wave. According to the map, I could reach the Wall in five days, worst case scenario. Add another two days for unforeseen circumstances and I'd have two weeks to figure out how to oppose this being that contained a fragment of Chaos. I temporarily postponed my trip to the Abyss. While my emotions were seething, it seemed that only this force could give me answers, but when the first wave subsided, I realized that a second-tier force could not help me in the fight against this creature of Chaos. Especially a force that had been shunned from the world at large. I could get the answer from the Fog Stalker, but I couldn't stand before him with my current set of magic stones. Sure, my foundation was already at level thirty, which made me one of the strongest mages in this world, but this might not be enough to get answers. My last visit with a being capable of giving me these kinds of answers showed that the real answers begin with the thirtieth wave. I physically couldn't handle that now.

In fact, I had only one place left where they could help me — the vault of the ancients. I had the key, some incomprehensible sixth-generation neural network was calling me there, but it was the fact that I was being actively lured there that gave me so much anxiety. Everything looked too much like a move in a game played by the higher powers, in which I was a simple bargaining chip. My opinion was that I should let these powers play around on their own. Without me. An unpleasant situation arose when I had no answers, but then I remembered the man I pulled out of the cage of the nocturnal guild. If there could be answers in this world on how to defeat the creature of Chaos, or whatever the ancients had planned, then they were only in the Fortress treasury. And the Fortress specifically, not the Citadel — the ancient city was in the Zarak Empire, and not the Shurghan Empire.

So step number one was to visit the high priest. I would plan all my other actions based on what I found there. And given the time constraints, I couldn't carefully plot my plan for years. All I needed to do was walk through the doors, break everything in sight, and take what I needed. In short, what I do best in this world.

"That's everything," Father Locke put down the last sheet of paper on which he had sketched out a schematic structure of the labyrinth. "It's impossible to pass this level without the key."

"Thank you, you can go," I nodded, sending the guest out of the office. Father Locke looked at me strangely, but didn't argue. For a while, the three of us sat and silently sorted through the scribbled sheets.

"I won't say that this is complete madness," Eleanore, as always, began first. "I lived in the Fortress for eight years, I can say that it is nearly as heavily protected as Hearth."

"I'm more concerned about the labyrinth," Alia said, staring at Father Locke's last drawing. "The key, as I understand it, can only be in the High Priest's possession. Remember your trip to the lair of the Nocturnal Guild — you fell into a vyrma trap. The Fortress's treasury must be more protected than the assassins' lair. So it may turn out that the walls are reinforced with a mesh of metal. You won't be able to cut through it with katars."

"Mithril?" Eleanore looked thoughtfully at her hand, which was cloaked in an invisible glove made of Pharapho's flesh.

"Perhaps," Alia agreed. "But perhaps not. We still do not fully understand the abilities of this material. What if the servants of the Light found a way to strengthen the walls with magic stones? They are one level higher than the mithril gloves."

"So I'll get the key first."

"Max, I don't want you to kill the high priest, or harm him in any way," Alia said, lowering her gaze. "I've reviewed a lot while you were gone. I talked to Father Locke. Father Nor. I even wanted to talk to Kimal Sarento, but he was busy at the tournament. Yes, Father Urg leads back to the Nocturnal Guild. Yes, he is a terrible man. Dangerous. But he is my father. Even if he is not my real father. He is the one who raised me."

"The one who prepared you to become the next overseer of the Nocturnal Guild," I finished the thought. "I remember our conversation about how, if necessary, you could bring in assassins to solve the issue with the Duke of Odoevsky. At the time, it seemed like nothing more than empty bravado, but now I understand that in fact, you really did have access to the Council of Three."

"It's silly to deny the obvious," Alia agreed. "No one has ever told me this openly, but now that I have the opportunity to look at everything from the outside, I am almost certain of it. The only thing I don't understand is how Father Urg wanted to give me this role. After all, the coordinators are all high priests. A woman cannot become the head of the church. It's the law."

"The law, which Father Urg has blatantly ignored almost every day," Eleanore said, grinning. "Okay, let's say you can get to the treasury. What do you hope to find there?"

"If I knew for sure...but I should catch you up to speed first."

Telling the story of what had transpired over the past few weeks took a lot of time. I spared no detail and didn't conceal any information unless absolutely necessary. Marisa's kidnapping, my run to Al-Khorezm, the results, the purge of the Citadel, the death of Count Fardi, the payment to the Inquisitor, today's meetings. I was tired of keeping everything to myself and shaking like a sick dog with the burden of the knowledge. If I couldn't trust my woman and city manager, who could I trust in this world? Although, just in case, I took the notebook from Alia, so that unnecessary entries would not accidentally appear in it. The Citadel did not need to know what we were talking about. I even revealed that Kimal Sarento had become my pupil and what it had led to, as well as how to gain access to the Abyss. If something happened to me, and I couldn't rule it out — life was long, and the knowledge of how to reach this second-tier power would definitely remain. The girls had vyrma and mithril, and those adapted to darkness, so that solved that problem.

"Actually, that's why I want to get into the Fortress' treasury. To see if there's anything useful there against Chaos."

"If we just ask Father Urg directly?" asked Alia.

"I have neither the time nor the desire to weave the verbal lace necessary to persuade him to cooperate. And I don't want to meet with Father Urg now. I'm not sure I could restrain myself and not kill him on the spot. So I'll go to the treasury without the high priest's permission. If there are no answers there, I'll go to the city of the ancients."

"And you will do what your grandfather and that incomprehensible force that arose in Hearth expected of you," Eleanore noted.

"That's why the treasury first. I want to see what the clerics managed to get their hands on throughout their long history. The more I think about the ancients, the more I remember my meeting with my grandfather, the less I want to show up in their city. Although, I must admit, the *Author* skill would be useful. Somehow, both my grandfather and the sixth-generation neural network used portals. Since I am destined to go to the other side of the world, it would be logical to obtain such an ability. There's a lot to do overall, and not a lot of time to do it."

"Okay, Max, then I have another question. No less important than the coming Wave. What to do with Miralda and Marisa?"

"Do I need to do anything with them?" I was surprised. "I'll take Marisa to the capital today and hand her over to her father. Miralda is under the protection of Hearth. How is she, by the way?"

"She's worked through most of her issues, although she still shrieks at night. The night terrors will torment her for a long time. But that's not the point — until now, no one knew that Miralda was in Hearth. Today, Marisa and Miralda met in the courtyard. We don't have many places where young girls can walk. The cousins recognized each other. The guards separated them when Miralda tried to pull out Marisa's hair. There is no love lost between them and, I think, there never will be."

"Sooner or later, the empire would have found out who lives in Hearth. What difference does it make if it's now or in a few weeks? The Inquisitor will not allow Zurgan the First to openly show aggression, the city's defense system will not let in uninvited guests. In this regard, we are protected. We will solve the rest of the problems as they arise. The only thing I would not want is the presence in the city of all those who sympathize with the previous regime. I am talking about the Duke of Turb. Drive them out of the city. Let them live behind the walls."

"I understand, I'm not thrilled with the current influx of guests, and we don't need any revolutionaries here. Max, Miralda wanted to talk to you."

"That's definitely not necessary yet. Our last conversation did not go well, and I don't want to repeat it."

"She's changed. She's no longer the flighty girl who treated others with disdain. A month in a cage straightened her out."

"I believe you, but now's not the time." I shuddered at the mere thought of having to communicate with Miralda again and listen to all her demands that I drop everything and immediately seat her on the throne. Yes, our meeting was inevitable, but let it be three months now. Perhaps there would be no more need to negotiate. Because the forces of Chaos would have already killed me.

"Okay, I'll tell her that you can't find time for her right now. What about the connection?"

"A very good question. Haven't you figured out the armor yet?"

"No. Everything is too unusual and new. The Defender doesn't know anything, I'm not ready to ask the Inquisitor. Maybe it would be worth contacting the Fog Stalker?"

"I have three passages left," I sighed. "The communication issue is, of course, critical, but I hope to sort it out on my own. Without involving the Fog Stalker. By the way, here's one of the keys.

Keep it in the treasury. You never know what might happen."

I gathered the three hundred fragments of the key into one whole and handed the result to Eleanore. You can't put all your eggs in one basket.

"If not the Fog Stalker, then maybe we should ask the Abyss?" suggested Alia. "You have a lot of essences that I'm sure the Abyss would be happy to guzzle down. If the mithril armor allows you to maintain a communication link, then information about it probably appeared long before fifty years ago. Yes, the Abyss might not know about how to destroy the Chaos vessels, but I can help research this issue. Will you try?"

There was logic in Alia's words, so I placed the triangle given to me by the Abyss in front of me.

"To open the passageway, you need to set this thing down and arrange eleven essences around it."

"That's another point I'd like to discuss with you," said Eleanore. "We need a rift. From what I understand, Naira has embarked on the path of a rift conqueror. She is with her family now, but upon her return she will need to be sent underground."

"What for?" Her suggestion surprised me.

"First, she must learn to adapt to the darkness. We can't place the burden of that entirely on you. I'll also descend into the rifts to test the mithril armor. It is important for us to make our own group of rift conquerors. Secondly, we need to check the process of obtaining essences. We cannot rely on you alone. Everything that we can do ourselves, we must do ourselves. Close rifts, obtain essences, fight the dark ones, destroy the Fog of Pharapho. We will need to send messengers to the Temple of Skron with an offer to exchange. Surely they need something from us. It cannot be that they are entirely without need. It would not hurt us to know how to create rift creatures from essences that can exist under the sun. With their help, we can hunt the Fog of Pharapho. We do not have your dark mirror, but we can replace it with pets that exude darkness. I will do this myself, only after the baby is born."

Nodding, I laid simple essences around the triangle and space around us forming into the familiar cave where the white seraph resided.

"The Abyss welcomes you, human," it said. "What has brought you to my abode?"

"A few questions. Is it possible to create a connection using mithril armor?"

The white seraph remained silent, looking pointedly at the tray that appeared in front of him. Questions require payment.

"How much?" I didn't want to give any more than I had to, so I decided to ask the price up front. Because if I just started laying out essences, the Abyss might pretend that it still wasn't enough, and the answer would cost me everything I had.

"This is not a particularly complicated question, so we can limit ourselves to thirty krona essences."

"That's straight theft!" I said indignantly.

"Thirty essences for a textbook question?"

"One essence for the answer, twenty-nine for the fact that only I hold the textbook."

"You're not. There's also the Fog Stalker."

"To get an answer to your question, you will have to pass through twenty-five waves. In other words, pass through the other twenty-four waves all in a row, without receiving answers or items for them. If you are satisfied with such a fee for an answer, you can go to the Fog Arena. The Abyss knows its worth and does not agree to exchange for trifles."

"Alright thirty essences. How does one establish this connection?"

"An additional device is required," the white seraph fell silent, as if mockingly. I began to boil, and the voice of the Abyss took notice. He continued after a pause: "You create mithril from the armor of a Pharapho sergeant. Not the most ideal way to obtain Pharapho's flesh, but quite effective. Now, as I see, you have a full suit of armor. In order to obtain communication devices, you need to embody a ball of mithril with a clear understanding of what you want to obtain. From the amount of Pharapho's flesh that comes out of the bone armor, you can embody two communication devices at once."

"Just holding the thought in my mind that I need a communication device?" I asked incredulously. "No blueprints, recipes, or anything like that?"

"Blueprints and recipes are mechanoid inventions. Those whose entire life is strictly regulated and divided into components. You didn't need blueprints to create your armor, did you? You created it according to your inner understanding. The same with supplementary pieces."

"So remote connection isn't the only thing mithril armor can do?"

"Too many free questions, human. If you just want to talk, you can talk in your world. The Abyss is not interested."

I silently placed ten krona essences on the tray that appeared in front of me. I had plenty to spare.

"The mithril armor you created is a base. A foundation on which additional functionality can be added. You should have realized this earlier — I see you have an aura variator control system. Apparently, you have visited the Fog Stalker. How many waves did he demand you pass before providing you with a device for aura control?"

"Three. From twenty-third to twenty-fifth," I replied. "But the prize wasn't just an aura control device, but also creating an additional socket and installing an aura variator in it."

"That is the Fog Stalker's forte — it offered you a working, but extremely suboptimal solution. You had to pay for the socket, then for the variator, then for the device to control it. I do not argue — this method of controlling auras is perfectly within its right to exist. But you do not have steel armor, which is usually used to enter the Fog arena. You have adaptive Pharapho flesh, which allows you to ignore many restrictions. In order to control the size of your aura, you only had to create a ball of mithril and embody it in the required device. The result is the same, but without having to pass through three additional waves. If you wish to continue the conversation on this topic, you need to make an additional payment."

"I understand about the mithril, I am interested in something else. The Inquisitor and the Interrogator have arrived in Hearth, my city. From now on, they live next to me."

"Interesting news. What motivated the servants of Chaos to move?"

"The fact that my city is receiving not only formal autonomy, but also actual autonomy. That there will be no division into dark, light, and gray. Everyone has the right to come and receive a fair trial. But that is not my question. The servants of Chaos want me to destroy the watermen and the undergrounders. I was given three months to do this, two weeks of which have already passed. When asked how the expulsion of the two forces would affect the world, the Inquirer did not answer. He said that the light lands do not use their gift anyway. I need to understand what I have been signed up for."

"Expel two more forces? Chaos wants to stabilize the system by reducing the influence of the third orbit?" Some emotions flashed across the expressionless face of the white seraph.

"Is it possible? What will it affect?"

"Yes, such a possibility exists. The world will stabilize and the four forces that remained in the third orbit will gain additional power. Mechanoids, trogs, ghosts and humans will become stronger."

"Humans?" My eyebrows shot up. "What do they have to do with it?"

"This is not information I can freely disseminate. I named this power because you shared with me information about the current changes of the servants of Chaos. In fact, knowledge of the last power is on the same level as *Tainted Blood*. If you want to find out something about this, go to the Fog. But, from what I know, an answer to this question will require that you pass through all forty waves. I can only add one thing: this is not about all humans. You will have to look for answers elsewhere."

"How will the disappearance of the water and underground people affect it?" I returned to the original question, although the new information stuck with me. How were humans one of the forces of the third orbit? And why not all humans?

"The disappearance of the watermen will remove the magic of images from this world. The undergrounders are in charge of decomposition. The servants of Chaos did not deceive: the light worlds really do not use these abilities. Just as they do not use them in Kerux, which is adjacent to your empires. But it cannot be said that this magic is not used at all — in the Beral area, the dark ones actively use these abilities. Magic stones are not available to them. If these forces disappear, vast lands will remain without magical support. But this will not affect the light ones in any way."

"In order to destroy these two forces, I must have the *Tainted Blood* stone. At the moment, it is in the possession of one of these Chaos beings. In three weeks, a Wave will crash against the light lands. Do you know how I can destroy this being? How much will the answer cost?"

"Destroy a being that has touched Chaos?" Emotion flashed across the white seraph's face once again. "Human, I do not have the right to speak on this subject, even if you offer me hundreds of Rift Master essences."

"Fine then, don't tell me. Can you name the place where I could find answers to this question? I'm willing to exchange a metamorph essence for this information."

As confirmation of my words, I took out one of the rare little orbs. I had very few metamorph essences, unlike kronas, rapses and other small rift-beasts.

"The ruins of the ancients," the white seraph answered after a pause. "This is the only place I know where you are one hundred percent guaranteed to find the knowledge you seek. With a certain degree of probability, the information exists in the treasuries of the Temple of Skron, the Citadel, the Fortress and the Stronghold. But I cannot guarantee it 100%. That is all I have the right to tell you on this matter."

The essence migrated to the tray and immediately vanished.

"I have the *Author* skill. Do you know how I can use it?"

"I don't have that information either. This skill belongs to the very force that interests you. It is closed to me. It is closed to the Fog Stalker. It is closed to everyone, including Chaos. These are the agreements reached a thousand years ago."

"Of course, you can't tell me anything about them."

"You understand correctly, human."

"Even if I offer you this?" I pulled out the mechanoid core I had obtained from Seven from my inventory. The white seraph looked at the ball indifferently and answered,

"This item is useless to me, therefore uninteresting. The only beings that can use this item are the mechanoids themselves. It will make them stronger. Your time is up, human. The Abyss is always open for further communication."

The space spun, and a few moments later I found myself back in my chair. Alia and Eleanore were waiting for my return. The manager immediately noticed the unfamiliar object in my hand.

"Did you manage to find out anything?"

"It worked. I'll just need to exert twice as much effort as usual. And also, I need a meeting with the Defender. I want to see him in person, talk to him. This ball is an amplifier for the mechanoids. If I don't have any questions for the Defender, I'll give it to him. We need to fortify our city."

"Twice as much effort — is that your veiled way of saying that you'll need to process two bone armors without Kimal Sarento?"

"Yes, remote communication can be done with

mithril."

"Then let's go. The Defender is sitting in the treasury."

The mechanoid was astounding. Alia's picture hadn't even come close to reflecting the entire epochal nature of this creature. The bald hedgehog had made a lair for itself in the far edge of the treasury and was constantly clicking its numerous short thin legs, which were not in Alia's drawing. The Defender didn't speak out loud, but messages appeared before my eyes:

"The Defender greets the head of Hearth. All systems are in working order, no violators have been identified."

Speaking to the mechanoid didn't really yield much. He answered in the same way, emotionlessly, to the point, and kept repeating that his main task was to protect the city entrusted to him. The only emotion I got from it was when I demonstrated the mechanoid core and asked if it would strengthen the Defender. Its twitching said a lot. Yes, it would. And significantly. Because it was the core of the eighth most powerful mechanoid in this world. With it, my Defender would become not just strong, but ultra-strong. Not a single insidious force would be able to sneak into the city unnoticed.

We had to work hard to turn bone armor into mithril. I took the iridescent balls myself, turning them into the device I needed, and then integrated it into myself, Alia, and Eleanore. The connection worked perfectly, I didn't even have to use my hands. A new icon appeared on the status bar, and by selecting it, a list of available recipients appeared. Convenient. In the end, I had one more device left, which I decided to give to Kimal Sarento, not Naira. My dark wife went to the Bartolomeo Clan — she didn't want to be at the construction site without me. I had no right to blame her for this, as I was almost never at home. The only thing Eleanore told me was that it was highly likely that Naira would be the third woman to bear my child. But that was no certainty.

Finally, having finished all my business in Hearth, I said tiredly,

"Prepare the carriage, and Marisa. We are leaving for the capital. It is time to return the princess to her father and receive our well-deserved reward."

Chapter 3

"AND WHY HAVE YOU SET these pieces of junk at my feet, my mysterious mentor?" Kimal Sarento looked suspiciously at the two bone armors that I was dragging behind me. The porter brought in several suitcases, accepted his tips and ran off to do his business, but I didn't trust anyone else with the remains of the Pharapho sergeants. Dragging them in myself was inconvenient, but I didn't mind. Only when they were in my possession could I ensure they wouldn't be stolen.

"In order to set up a remote connection, my lazy and inattentive pupil," I answered. After some thought, I decided to give the fourth communication device I had created to Naira. Or rather, I asked Eleanore to give it to my only official wife when she returned to Hearth. If Eleanore was right and I had a third woman carrying my child (I would conduct a paternity test after the birth), then I needed to establish a connection with her. So I had to rework my plans once again.

"Is that so?" Kimal Sarento left the world behind for a few moments as he buried himself in his notebook. I was a little upset — the news that various devices for mithril armor can be created from bone armor had only resurfaced three days ago. That was exactly how long our journey from Hearth to Turb took — when you're moving as part of a huge delegation, you can't really pick up the pace. And, instead of getting acquainted with the new information, my student was doing whatever he wanted.

"Alright, say that is true," Kimal Sarento became serious after reading the new input data. "Why do you need two to create one connection? How many are left in total?"

"I'm tired of constantly losing my bracelet for detecting those who possess *Phantom*. The invisible ones in Hearth are no longer scary, but outside my city they can appear in the most unexpected places. Even now, here. Are you sure that your stone can detect owners of high-level *Phantom*? To be honest, I have serious doubts."

Now I knew how Kimal Sarento checked for invisible beings near him — for this he had a level fifteen magic stone, *Survey Area*, which informed the owner about the presence of living beings within a certain radius. The ability had to be used constantly, so such protection was not ideal and if someone's *Phantom* was at least one level higher, it would not be possible to detect them this way. My pupil surveyed the area, of course, but found nothing.

"That's what I'm talking about. Do you really think that the Church of the Light or the dark ones would be stingy with their resources in that way? I don't. That's why I decided to sacrifice these — there are only two bone armors left in Hearth. In case of emergency, if urgent repairs are needed."

"I think I'll have to agree with you now, my dear mentor who is losing valuables at a monstrous rate. We need to be able to constantly surveil the environment around us. The only point I'd like to bring up is suggesting changing the format of the input query. Why would you need a divide that determines whether or not someone possesses a certain magic stone? It would be a very limited — dare I say, completely useless device. But — if we slightly change the initial formulation..."

"Perhaps you should cut straight to the point, my talkative pupil who so loves the sound of his own voice?" Kimal's mode of communication was contagious. The more I had to interact with him, the more small peculiarities I adopted from him.

"You must hone your patience, my agile mentor. But now, perhaps, I will give in to your persuasion and stop communicating in hints. I propose we create a device that informs its owner about all living beings within a certain radius."

"Why?" I asked.

"A very stupid question. It's obvious that you

don't want to think, my lazy mentor. Wielders of *Phantom* are not the only creatures that can hide in the shadows or hide from view. The simplest example is the rift rapses. If that's not enough for you, what about the squadrons of high-level mages hiding just around the corner, waiting to attack when you least expect it? Or the undergrounders you were sent to finish off? The name suggests that you might be spending some time underground. Imagine walking along, not bothering anyone, and then suddenly bore-hole passages begin to form from all sides and waves of these creatures pour out. What if they are inert to the dark influence and you have to fight hand-to-hand? There are countless scenarios where you may need to know the exact location and, most importantly, the number of creatures around you. I can't list them all."

"You don't need to convince me of something I'd already come up with myself," I said, just in case. "The main question is where are we going to do it? I don't think there's a testing ground in the Golden Goose."

"Is there any point in staying in the capital, my time-constrained mentor? It seems like we need to run and do the impossible. You don't think I'll miss a unique opportunity to fight an equal opponent, do you? And I haven't been to the Kaliman Empire for a long time. I suggest we move right now. I've already handed over all the affairs of the magic academy, the decision to appoint Tarra Loyd as chancellor has been received, and explanatory work with her has been carried out. There's nothing else keeping me in Turb."

"But there are things keeping me here," I looked around pointedly, showing that it was highly likely that the walls still had ears. As if confirming my guess, there was a knock on the room door. Kimal Sarento, like me, did not have personal servants, so he went to open it, as my pupil.

"Count Sarento." I heard a familiar voice. One of Zurgan the First's assistants. "How fortuitous that I managed to find you at home. Tell me, is Archduke Valevsky with you?"

"As if you don't know," Kimal Sarento grinned. "When?"

"Today. Here are the invitations. His Imperial Majesty wishes to see you both. This is his personal order. What should I tell the Emperor?"

"What else can we tell him, but that we will certainly be there, on time. Nine o'clock? Not too late for dinner?"

There was no answer, and from the way the front doors slammed shut, it became clear that the emperor's assistant had left. Soon, a thoughtful Kimal Sarento appeared and casually threw a sheet of paper that had been folded several times onto the sofa.

"Do you have a suit?"

"A whole rack to choose from," I replied, flipping through the mithril armor outfit selections. The trip to the clothing store in Al-Khorezm had been a great success. From now on, I could transform my armor into several business suits for all occasions.

"Give me back the previous one," my pupil asked and walked around me several times, memorizing the details. Soon a similar suit appeared on him. "There is a training ground at the academy. I don't think the new chancellor will refuse us such a small favor. Let's go. First, we'll solve the issue with remote communication and our new device, then you can tell me about the next flight of madness you have planned. You have been scheming something, haven't you? Keep in mind, my mysterious mentor, I will not accept 'no' for an answer."

I couldn't help but stare at the letter I'd received. It stated that His Imperial Majesty had highly appreciated the contribution of Count Sarento and Archduke Valevsky in liberating his daughter and wished to personally testify to his favor at a private meeting today at nine o'clock this evening. The imperial monogram and personal signature indicated that Zurgan the First had not simply given the order to write the letter, but had personally reread and initialed it himself. If we were to approach the matter from a formal perspective, then this piece of paper should have been smoothed out and framed, showing it to all the guests. For this was evidence that the family, in this case two families, were among the favorites of His Imperial Majesty. But I wasn't going to do that — today I would have to try hard not to finish off the man who ordered the destruction of my family. It was too early — Hearth was not yet ready for an open confrontation with the Zarak Empire. First, I needed to visit the city of the ancients and learn those same bloody teleports that my grandfather and the sixth-generation neural network used to move around. I have determined four people for myself who must die so that my family can be avenged. Two have already been destroyed. The others I will get to later."

Tarra Loyd came out to greet us personally. The once gorgeous girl had turned into a gorgeous older woman. For her sixty years, Tarra looked fantastic. Maybe forty. But definitely one of the most charming and stunning beauties of the empire. Instead of feigned beauty, it was in her presence. While Kimal Sarento, as chancellor, had looked like a fat, contented cat who had gotten everything he wanted in life, Tarra Loyd truly fit the role of the head of a magic academy. Her look, her movements, her posture — everything gave her away as someone who was at the top of the food chain. The way she extended her hand to Kimal Sarento to greet him caused my chest to seize violently. Her feminine wiles were still intact.

"To what do I owe the pleasure of your unexpected return to your home turf?" Tarra asked, arching her eyebrow eloquently.

"Do I really need a reason to see you? What if I just miss you?" Kimal Sarento replied, and on a momentary impulse, he hugged Tarra Loyd. The woman was momentarily taken aback, her arms spread wide at her sides, but she quickly came to her senses and wrapped them around his back. For a while, the former and current chancellors stood hugging each other. Students passing by whispered, several masters who were also walking nearby looked away, but these two didn't care. What did anyone's opinion matter to them? Finally, Kimal Sarento was the first to break the embrace and stepped back. But Tarra immediately seized the initiative:

"Two conditions, Kimal. First, don't destroy anything. If you break something, you'll pay for the restoration. Second, I have to accompany you. I have no idea what you're planning, but all my experience is screaming in my ear that I need to be there to see it."

"We'll go to the first level of the rift."

"No problem. I've adapted all the way up to the third."

"So you're not even going to ask why we're here?"

"If you came here, that means there's no other place in Turb that would work for your purposes. I know there's a meeting with the Emperor this evening. I'm invited too. No, actually I have a third condition. More like a request. I'd like to hear a story over a glass of wine. I think your young mentor can find a way to occupy himself on the academy grounds while you tell me an amusing tale."

"And I have no other option?" Kimal Sarento frowned dramatically.

"None. And don't tell me you didn't bring a bottle of Kimal Sarento's world-famous wine. Knowing you, that's simply impossible."

"How can I refuse such a woman?" my student

spread his arms wide, admitting defeat. "No breaking things, let her watch, and then tell her a story about the goings on in this great, big world. What do you say, my silent mentor? Are you prepared to agree to such conditions?"

"As far as I know, there is a closed section of the library at the academy where students are not allowed. I will gladly wait for my pupil there. I promise not to steal anything."

"It begins," Tarra Loyd sighed. "Max, how can I let you into a place where not even all magisters have access? Walk around the grounds, look around, talk to your peers. When else will you get a chance to just be a young man without any obligations?"

"I'll have that chance in the closed section of the library. Do you want Sarento to tell you a fairy tale, or a fairy tale with some elements of reality sprinkled in? What are your thoughts on the lithoids? My student has much to say about them."

The strange look he cast me could have passed as surprise if I didn't know him better. I saw any information I could divulge about the lithoids as completely safe and harmless, but Sarento's reaction demonstrated that not everyone felt that way. I'd definitely need to comb through all the information I had on those blockheads. I needed to understand what was making Kimal Sarento twitch. In reality, there was nothing I needed in the closed section of the library. All the books were already in Kimal Sarento's notebook and had migrated to me during the integration. There was a lot of interesting stuff there, but little that could be used here and now. Nothing at all, really. The collected works of some ancient philosophers discussing the meaning of existence, the change of power to a republic, and other democratic nonsense. In all fairness, most of the tomes should have been burned as useless trash, but Kimal Sarento had been collecting these books for too long to do such a thing. They were valuable not for their content, but for their lifespan.

"Lithoids?" Tarra Loyd looked at Kimal Sarento, and he nodded. "Alright, you will have access to the closed section. I hope the tale of your adventures will be interesting and worth it, considering that I'm marking the very beginning of my tenure as chancellor by officially committing a crime. Let's go. We don't have much time — I still have to thoroughly prepare for today's meeting. My first official reception with His Imperial Majesty as chancellor."

We were able to uphold the first two conditions with no problems — we didn't break anything and we showed Tarra Loyd the way of transforming the bone armor into a floating mithril orb. Her audible gulp said a lot. Primarily, that she understood the degree of trust being placed in her. After creating the communication device, I thought long and hard about how I wanted to formulate my next request. Kimal Sarento was right — I needed a device that would not only determine the invisible people within a certain radius, but also inform me about all living creatures in the area, invisible or not. I had almost reached out to touch the orb before I realized that bugs and spiders were also living creatures. Did I really need to know that several dozen flies and mosquitoes were buzzing around? Not really. So I needed to adjust for a certain size range. But what should it be? What did I know about the undergrounders and watermen? Nothing, apart from the name. Maybe these creatures were the size of a carp or mole? So, there must be an additional setting for the size of living beings. From around a centimeter to several meters wide. If the creature was any larger, I'd definitely notice it.

Basically, I'd have to consult with Kimal Sarento, as well as Tarra Loyd, since she wasn't going anywhere. I needed to structure the query correctly. Loyd was helpful. After figuring out what I needed, she almost immediately produced the perfect syntax, which after five minutes of discussion, was accepted as optimal. Just in case, running this description through my head several times, I approached the iridescent orb and extended my hand to it. I clearly understood what I needed, and did not doubt for a moment. Two oblong objects appeared in my hands. I immediately pressed one of them to my chest, installing it on the mithril armor. For some time, nothing happened, as if the device was trying to find its place on my armor, after which a translucent projection appeared in front of me. It had several settings - you could set the transparency, scanning radius, size of the creature and even the color with which to highlight creatures of different volumes and masses. The system worked in three-dimensional space, with me marked as the central point, as well as the horizon line, so that I could understand on which side the subjects were located. The subjects themselves were displayed as rectangles, which corresponded to the height and average width of the creatures. Why average? Because otherwise, if a human spreads their arms to the sides, this would increase their perceived width significantly.

I turned the scanning radius up to the maximum. The mithril armor couldn't get through to the second level of the rift, as there were partitions in the way. But the walls weren't an obstacle for long, and soon I began to understand how many beasts were hiding on the first level. Only twelve had not yet been finished off by the students. I didn't know what was happening on the ground either, the ceiling was in the way, but I knew for sure that these two red rectangles standing not far from me were Kimal Sarento and Tarra Loyd. There were no invisible creatures in the surrounding area.

The second device went to my pupil. I was led to the closed section of the library, and after leafing through several dozen volumes, I was convinced that I would find nothing of interest or import here. Surprisingly, not all the books had been copied over into Kimal Sarento's notebook, but when I leafed through the copies that were missing, I understood why. Revolutionary texts written two hundred years ago. Delirium multiplied by madness.

In short, it was a useless waste of time that I could have spent trying to get into the Fortress's treasury. However, it wasn't only the closed section of the library that I was wasting my time with. After a while, I entered the wide-open doors of the imperial palace.

The herald, who was standing nearby, began to call like a madman, "Archduke Maximilian Valevsky!"

No one paid me any particular mind, as those present were otherwise occupied. Unlike official receptions, today the main hall of the imperial palace was an unprecedented spectacle. There were flowers, music, laughter, acrobats performing intricate tricks, and flames shooting up into the air from the far wall, where the fire swallowers performed. The courtiers and high aristocrats of the Zarak Empire were having fun, drinking wine, and mingling. The atmosphere was completely different from what I had seen on all my previous visits to the palace.

Putting on a stoic face, I stepped inside. The closed format of the meeting meant that I wouldn't have to stomp up to the throne and bow and grovel before the emperor. Put on a happy face and smile. It was enough that I showed up at the meeting. And there was no one on the throne — the emperor, if he was in the room, was walking among the courtiers, pushing everyone aside with his huge bulk. Or, he hadn't even deigned to honor this event with his presence, which was just as likely. What would he be doing here among this rowdy crowd?

"Count Kimal Sarento!"

My pupil followed me, but, like me, no one paid any attention.

"Does this happen here often?" I asked Kimal Sarento as he approached. A young man with a tray was running past and I grabbed a glass of white wine. I couldn't stand the stuff, but I didn't want to just stand there, not knowing what to do with my hands.

"On occasion." Kimal Sarento was radiant, as if he was in his element. He bowed left and right, managing to compliment the ladies and wish his best to the men. "Is something bothering you?"

"Alright, that's enough! I didn't come to Turb to hang around here!" I switched to communicating through the mithril armor. The system I'd created was perfect. The armor's second-skin quality guaranteed that our communication would remain private, while the helmet displayed to those around me that I had serious intentions.

Several noisy performers ran past us, deftly juggling balls. After watching them go, I returned to Kimal Sarento, but my pupil was already in full conversation with some lady and had totally forgotten me.

"So this is Archduke Valevsky?" the woman asked. Judging by the way she slurred, she already had more than one glass of wine in her. Kimal Sarento didn't even have time to introduce us before I doused the woman with *Heal.* Purely out of spite.

"Oh!" Her eyes brightened. She batted them for a moment, as if she had forgotten what she was doing here. As her gaze fell on me, she turned white and retreated, remembering that she had important business in another part of the hall.

"I consider your behavior beneath you, Archduke Valevsky!" Some guy immediately appeared next to us. Maybe twenty-five years old, no more. Young, nimble, zealous. The belated understanding came that the lady had been foisted on us for a reason, and Kimal Sarento took the first blow, managing to practically extinguish the conflict before it began, but then I intervened. Judging by how heavily my pupil sighed, I had messed up.

"Who are you and what do you want from me?" I asked wearily. A crowd had already gathered behind this nimble fighter, calling for justice, so everything had been planned in advance.

"I am Count Marius Razumov! You dared to use your dark magic on my aunt against her will! For such a…"

He didn't have time to finish as I brazenly interrupted him,

"So you think I should have let her die peacefully, right? Am I right in thinking that Count Marius Razumov wants to let his own aunt die?"

"What are you talking about?" he said. "What would she have died from?"

"Because she had an incurable disease that

would have had her standing before the Light in a week. I cured her. Or does Count Marius Razumov doubt my healing skills?"

"I..." Marius began to look around. No, this was not carefully staged, it was improvisation. Someone heard that I had come to the event and decided to square up with me. As far as I knew, those found at fault in duels called during such events were stricken from all further guest lists. That was why this young man had approached me. I didn't feel sorry for him.

"Next time, try to understand the situation before you throw accusations around, Count Razumov. You might be considered a fool who can't see beyond his own nose."

"What lofty words from a man who was almost exiled!" I heard the voice of Kimal Sarento, audible only to me. Snide and unpleasant. I did not react to it, so I turned away from the young Count Razumov and said,

"Gentlemen, please forgive me, I want to see the fire dancers. Their art has always fascinated me. There is something enchanting about it, don't you think?"

No one else seemed to think so, but they didn't follow me. I walked over to the far wall and watched the fire lords. Two were doing such strange things with the flame that I couldn't help but run *Analyze* on them, suspecting that some of their moves must require magic. But no, they were just ordinary people.

"You understand that this is just the first and

rather crude attempt to feel you out?" Kimal Sarento stood next to me. "There will be others."

"Why would they be trying to feel me out?" I asked in surprise.

"Because, my slow-witted mentor, I have already been advised to stay away from you. For today you will experience the full wrath of His Imperial Highness. He knows about Miralda, and right before the event, information came from the Citadel. The clergy informed the Emperor of the Zarak Empire about the fate of one of his closest associates, not forgetting to mention that the former Duke of Odoevsky was executed on your orders. And now our fat little friend is wondering whether to finish you off right away or first find out what Count Fardi managed to spill to the servants of Light. So enjoy the fire dance. One more thing — if we are separated, we will meet near your former estate. This is just in case our connection suddenly stops working. And remember: mithril armor is not a panacea. It can also be destroyed."

"Archduke Valevsky, what an unexpected and unpleasant meeting!" The voice ringing through the hall made Kimal Sarento fall silent. Turning around, I saw Count Vyazemsky Sr. During the time we'd been apart, he had become much stronger. His stones had reached level thirty. Next to him stood George, A.K.A. Count Vyazemsky Jr. I liked the young man. He seemed alright to me. Honestly. The way a true aristocrat should be upon receiving strength and power.

"I must say, I'm not particularly pleased to see

you either, Count Vyazemsky, but what can I do? Sometimes we must swallow our disgust, for the sake of the empire." I wasn't going to hide behind gilded words. They wanted to openly tell me that I wasn't welcome here? Great, this was my response! Your move, two-meter-tall giant. You think I'll retreat? Not today! Since His Imperial Majesty had decided to punish me, so be it. The only question now was who would punish whom.

Chapter 4

"HAS ARCHDUKE VALEVSKY forgotten himself?" Count Vyazemsky's voice was steely, but there was no stopping me. If His Imperial Majesty had decided to punish me, I wouldn't stand aside and meekly await my fate. I had no business with the people gathered in this hall. That was a fact. Not Count Vyazemsky, not Count Shub and not Count Kuzminsky. Regarding the latter, however, things were not so clear-cut, and he was not at this event, but I certainly had no desire to speak with the High Priest of the Zarak Empire. Father Urg stood apart from the others, surrounded by his retinue, and watched the spectacle with interest. Fine, let him watch.

"Archduke Valevsky believes that your presence at this event is among the greatest mistakes made in the Zarak Empire. Your place is in a prison cell. One full of scoundrels and other cowards who fled the stone monsters. Why are you here, and your mages are back there, lying on the battlefield? No one could even bury them, because nothing was left to bury. But not you, Count Vyazemsky. You are still here, sleek and very much alive, looking down on the others with arrogance, as if..."

"That is quite sufficient!" Count Vyazemsky barked, causing the people around us to recoil. "I have no intention of listening to absurd accusations from a man who..."

"Who destroyed all the lithoids?" I interrupted him. "My pupil and I, realizing the kind of casualties would be incurred if the lithoids were allowed to run rampant across the Zarak Empire, forgot any sense of self-preservation and penetrated the lair of these creatures. We destroyed them! All at once! Wasn't the all-powerful Count Vyazemsky interested in why the monsters pursuing him suddenly turned back? Did you really think that they were afraid of your soiled trousers? They rushed back to save their master, whom Kimal Sarento and I had to finish off. We finished it off, Count Vyazemsky, not this man standing before me who knows how to frown menacingly, flee the enemy and commit vile acts at every step, setting fanatics upon my city. I feel uncomfortable even breathing the same air as you, Count, but I am forced to do so, since His Imperial Majesty personally asked me to be present at this event."

"How dare you?!" The younger Vyazemsky

rushed towards me, but was stopped by his father's powerful hand. I liked George — all his previous actions had led me to believe he was a good person, in any case — but I couldn't go back now. Ensuring that Count Vyazemsky Sr. wouldn't have time to talk his son down, I once again poured oil on the fire.

"It's funny that you didn't try to stop Count Marius Razumov from speaking such blasphemies. Of course, I don't feel sorry for him, unlike your son. What a blow to the prestige of the family if one of the promising heirs is furthermore denied access to such colorful events as this. After all, there are so many harlequins and clowns here. Does Count Vyazemsky have something to say to me, or am I free to go about my business?"

"You don't have any business here, Archduke Valevsky. You must leave."

"Has Count Vyazemsky taken it upon himself to decide what business I have the right to conduct? Do you think you have the strength and resources for that?" I raised an eyebrow eloquently. The silence in the hall indicated that those gathered were hanging on our every word. Even the artists froze in place, afraid to make a sound.

Count Vyazemsky Sr. raised his head, pressed his lips together and exhaled furiously through his nose.

"It seems to me that you have nothing," I said, continuing to hammer nails into the lid of the coffin inscribed with the words "Valevsky's place in high society." No one would ever invite me to another event like this. True, I still needed to get out of this alive and, preferably, without spilling someone else's blood. Looking around at those gathered, including several dozen guardsmen who had suddenly appeared in the hall, I continued,

"The only reason you are still alive, Count Vyazemsky, who fled the battlefield in disgrace, is because the Inquisitor demanded prudence from me. He, through whose mouth the Light itself speaks, ordered me not to be the first to show aggression. He ordered me to wait for Skron's followers to reveal their true intentions. For them to reveal their true nature. Or does the completely disrespected Count Vyazemsky not know that Hearth is now a stronghold of the Light and that the Inquisitor sits beside my throne?"

"As well as the Interrogator!" called a voice from the crowd.

"As well as the Interrogator." I had no issue agreeing with the obvious. "His task is to let the dark ones know that Hearth is now untouchable. He is not interested in the affairs of the Light empires. They are handled by those who have the right to do so. Therefore, I have to ignore my desires and emotions in order to carry out this order. I am not displaying aggression, Count Vyazemsky. I am not starting fights. I am simply standing aside and watching the fire dancers. Do you have any questions left for me?"

Count Vyazemsky knew how to keep a straight face. Without saying a word, he turned around and walked away with a wide stride, keeping his son close so that he would not commit an irreparable mistake. The people began to whisper and the circle of alienation around me grew even larger, but I did not care. I turned my back to the crowd and gestured for the fire dancers to continue their interrupted performance.

"I see you know how to make friends," I heard Kimal Sarento's voice in my ear. He was standing next to me and communicating through the mithril armor.

"So I should have started a fight, killed Count Vyazemsky, and fallen into disfavor with the entire empire?" I clarified. "By the way, why is he still alive? Weren't you planning to destroy him at the tournament?"

"You won't believe it, but we were never paired in the brackets. Both Count Vyazemsky and Count Shubn lost to Count Kuzminsky. The old man turned out to be a dark horse with a surprise up his sleeves. We met in the finals, and I had to try hard to win. His defense turned out to be no worse than mithril armor. Run *Analyze* on him. We need to find out where Count Kuzminsky obtained such strength."

"I didn't see him here."

"He's not here. He is not a fan of these kinds of events. He's probably sitting at home and..."

"Archduke Valevsky, will you spare a few minutes for an old acquaintance? Or will you also frighten me with scary stories about the Inquisitor?"

Turning around, I saw Father Urg. The High

Priest had left the cover of his entourage and approached us, while still keeping some distance. I stared mutely at the man, urgently coming up with a plan of action. On the one hand, this man had helped me become who I am. This was an indisputable fact. If it weren't for the High Priest's will, I wouldn't have trained with the Evil Engineer. The man with whom my whole journey had begun. But Father Urg's true nature nullified any positive aspects about him. The outwardly good-natured old man was one of the most dangerous people in our empire, even outside of his status. *Analyze* clearly showed that Father Urg had no secret magic stones or incredible power. Heeding my own feelings, I decided not to demonstrate obvious aggression toward the High Priest.

"It's always a pleasure to talk to an intelligent and educated man." I nodded in greeting and stepped aside, inviting the High Priest to join me in watching the fire show. The performers began their amazing manipulations again, pulling out all the stops. Father Urg hesitated for a beat, but joined in, and for a while we stood silently watching the show. The exclusion zone around us was larger than it had been during the altercation with Count Vyazemsky.

"I would like to speak with you in a more relaxed atmosphere," the High Priest said at last. "From what I understand, you were planning to go to the Fortress tonight. I believe that before you put your plans into action, you should discuss them with me. I am sure that two, as you said, intelligent and educated people can always find common ground without destroying each other's property."

"Three," I automatically corrected. My head was occupied with other thoughts. How did Father Urg know that I was going to visit the treasury? Only a very limited circle of people knew about this, and I could trust my life to almost all of those who knew. What was the source of the leak?

"Of course, a mentor cannot forget about his pupil." The High Priest turned towards Kimal Sarento, who had prudently stepped aside so as not to interfere with our conversation. The fact that he could hear the entire conversation perfectly well was irrelevant. "Count Sarento, I would be happy to meet with you. I suggest we do this in an hour in my office. It seems to me that there is nothing else to do here. The Emperor will not be here today, we have already seen the artists' performance, and as I understand it, you are not interested in staying for the buffet. They won't have any of that magnificent wine that is made on your estate, Count."

"I am but a slave to his will," Kimal Sarento spread his arms out to the sides, showing his helplessness. "Wherever my mentor goes, I will have to go. If he decides that a meeting in the Fortress may be dangerous and unpredictable, so be it. Who am I to debate his decisions?"

"Dangerous?" the High Priest cast a pointed look at Kimal. "Count Sarento does not trust the Church of the Light and me, its leader in the Zarak

Empire?"

"I'm afraid that is my fault," I interjected. "A week ago, on the Pope's orders, I had to thoroughly comb through the servants of the Light in the Citadel, and, as sad as it is to admit, there were several dark ones among them. Even among the commanders. Not to mention the head of the supply service. Hence my distrust of everyone, High Priest. This has nothing to do with you. After all, I see that you have no business with Skron."

The crowd began to whisper again, which was really starting to get on my nerves. They were supposedly the highest aristocracy, the support and hope of the empire, but they were behaving like grannies in the marketplace, driven by an unquenchable desire to discuss what they had just witnessed.

"We accept your invitation, High Priest. We will be at the Fortress in an hour."

"Archduke Valevsky, you will remain here!" The Emperor's guards, who had filled the hall, stepped forward. The music died down again. The artists, as if they had agreed in advance, left the room in an orderly manner. The spectators parted, allowing the warriors dressed in full steel armor to step forward. I didn't flinch, enjoying the spectacle. Not a minute had passed before we found ourselves surrounded. At least they hadn't drawn their weapons yet.

"How am I supposed to understand this, Colonel?" The High Priest immediately singled out the commander among the guardsmen. The man did not back down.

"An order from His Imperial Majesty! Archduke Valevsky is to be arrested and escorted to a cell for high-born prisoners until further notice. The High Priest of the Zarak Empire is unaffected by these restrictions."

"So Zurgan is in the palace after all?" the High Priest's voice was filled with ice. "Good. In an hour, Archduke Valevsky and his student must be in my office. Such is the will of the Light. If they are not there, and I do not care at all why, the Fortress will declare *fadgur*. You have an hour, gentlemen. Make your decisions wisely and with a clear understanding of the consequences."

With these words, the High Priest pulled a red glowing wand from his wide sleeve and broke it in two. The glow died down, and for the umpteenth time today, a deathly silence fell over the hall.

"See you soon, Archduke." The High Priest nodded and left the room. The guards did not dare stop the head of the Church of the Light of the Zarak Empire.

"What are we talking about?' I asked Kimal Sarento. I considered it sacrilege to break the general silence, so I used our intercom.

"The point is, my mentor who knows how to get himself into amazing situations, that if the empire does not fulfill the demand of the High Priest, then the Church of the Light will declare a holy march upon it. A decision will be made that the entire top layer is compromised and the Inquisitor will personally begin to establish the guilt of each and every one. Literally, every single one. If anyone from the capital does not undergo this vetting procedure, they will be destroyed. I believe there is no point in explaining why a meeting with the Inquisitor is dangerous. Everyone has sins and this creature does not give a damn about excuses. He records only the fact itself and makes a decision based on logic known only to him. In my memory, *fadgur* has never been declared. Apparently, the High Priest has decided to remind Zurgan the First that the Fortress is not just a place where condemned soldiers live, but a force that determines the policy of the entire empire."

"What was with that glowing stick?"

"A sign that the Church of Light is in danger. If Father Urg does not break another green stick in an hour, the Citadel and Stronghold will receive a notification that *fadgur* has been declared in the Zarak Empire. Including the Inquisitor. The servants will cordon off the capital for twenty-four hours and will not let anyone out. Not even the Emperor."

"Now the only thing left to do is figure out why the High Priest suddenly took this step and why he was carrying that wand around with him in the first place. I doubt he has it on his person at all times."

"What a correct line of reasoning, my mentor who is now beginning to understand the world. You know, we can stand here twiddling our thumbs forever. Personally, I think it's time to act. Zurgan the First cannot fail to understand what the *fadgur* entails."

The logic in his words was ironclad, so I turned to the commander of the guards surrounding us and asked,

"Do you have any more questions for us, gentlemen? Or can we go to the Fortress?"

"The Emperor…" the commander said and stopped short. He had an order that he could not fail to carry out, but he also knew perfectly well what obeying this order would result in.

"Everyone, leave the hall!" A familiar, unpleasant voice was heard. The door behind the empty throne opened, and His Imperial Majesty waded into the hall. Zurgan the First was accompanied by an impressive team of guards, who managed to make their way among the highest aristocracy, shamelessly pushing people aside. Marisa followed behind. The princess looked well — returning home had clearly done the girl good.

The hall emptied rather quickly. Not even Count Vyazemsky remained, only a few dozen guards and personal guards. And, of course, me and Kimal Sarento. Where would we be without us?

"Zurgan, you look well." Kimal Sarento was the first to break the silence, addressing the emperor as if he were an old friend. "You seem to have a fresher look about you. Have you really taken my advice and started caring for your health?"

"Quiet, Kimal!" the emperor said, not taking his eyes off me. His gaze was heavy and devastating. Father Nor loved to look at me just like that.

In fact, that was why I didn't even feel a hint of embarrassment. The man standing next to me had ordered the destruction of my family. Ordered the destruction of the Valevsky clan, because he needed three rifts located on our lands. Could I kill him now? Yes, and without the slightest difficulty. I could unleash a level fifteen ousel on him and nothing would remain of Zurgan himself. But I wouldn't do that now. No! I wanted to destroy this man morally. Make him grovel before me. For this, I needed more power than I had now. Much more.

Zurgan looked at me for a long time and, what pleased me most of all, silently. I'm not sure I could have refrained from blaming the emperor for the death of my family if we had started a conversation.

"You're free to go," the fat man said, turned sharply and, with a speed uncharacteristic of his build, left the hall. The guards followed their master, and only the princess lingered.

"Father... His Imperial Majesty thanks you for my rescue, Archduke Valevsky...Father knows that you saved Miralda and are keeping her in your city. This is wrong, Archduke Valevsky. Power in the country must be absolute. That's how it was before, before you intervened."

"If it weren't for my intervention, you wouldn't be here now, Princess," I said. "I wouldn't have said a word to your father if he had killed Miralda Lertan. I have no warm feelings for that girl. But she was kept in a cage like an animal. Starved, defiled, broken morally. No person deserves that, so

I helped her. You must admit, it's stupid to give her up to be torn apart after I pulled her out of the pit your father drove her into."

"He did no such thing!" The girl flared up. "It was all the Nocturnal Guild! They…"

"My dear girl, there is no need to say things in such company. You'll receive no pat on the head for them later," Kimal Sarento intervened. "The deed is done, Miralda Lertan is saved and under the protection of the Inquisitor. Whether the Zarak Empire wishes it or not. Come, my protective mentor. The High Priest has given us too little time."

The carriage was already standing at the central entrance. A huge line of mismatched carriages crowded behind ours, but none of them dared to block our way. Father Urg's words had quickly spread throughout the capital. No one wanted to become the reason for calling the Inquisitor. Although it must be admitted that the guards did an excellent job — several particularly zealous fanatics lay on the ground mumbling. They had obviously demanded that we not go anywhere, and the punishment of the Light had descended on Turb. People could be very strange.

The Fortress hadn't changed at all since my last visit. But my chest tightened when I went to the central square. Once upon a time, there had been a bonfire there where they burned sister Alia, and this building used to house my cot when I was a doomed soldier. It seemed like all of this was in a past life, although, in fact, only four months had passed since I had left the doomed legion.

The High Priest was waiting for us in his office. When we entered, Father Urg was sorting through some papers, as if nothing special had happened. The head of the Church of the Light of the Zarak Empire spent several minutes on this, making us languish in anticipation. Finally, he put his intricate signature on the sheet, dripped some sealing wax onto it and stamped his ring to sign the document. One of the assistants immediately ran into the office and took the paper. The High Priest opened a drawer of his desk and took out a stick flickering with a green light. Having broken it, Father Urg threw the remains into the urn and said,

"Count Sarento, if you don't mind, set up a *Canopy of Silence*. I'm flattered to think that the Fortress is a protected place, but sometimes, even here, the walls have ears."

Kimal Sarento didn't argue, and soon a dome appeared around us, blocking out all sound. The High Priest reached into the table again and pulled out three wine glasses. A bottle followed. Judging by the way Kimal Sarento chuckled, the bottle was from his personal supply.

"Really, Count Sarento, did you think that I wouldn't be able to establish good relations with your family? Yes, they supply me with a very limited amount, but they still supply me. I want to note that your family definitely needs to think about increasing the territory of their vineyards. Nothing else can compare to your wine."

"We're not here to discuss my humble estate, are we?" Kimal clearly didn't like the High Priest's show of power. He paid no heed to how harsh his words may seem. He took out a corkscrew, opened the bottle and, wrapping it in cloth, filled the glasses.

"You are right, we're not here for that. But the topic, you must admit, is highly captivating. When you have some free time, I would be happy to discuss this issue with you. Max, this is for you."

A strange key, used to open barn locks, appeared on the table. Noticing my wary look, Father Urg decided to explain,

"You're going to the Fortress' treasury, aren't you? Knowing you, I can assume that you'll pass through all the protection like butter, destroying it as you go, and then we'll have to restore it. Given that many elements of our defense system are unique, and finding any analogues in the modern world is almost impossible, I think it will be easier for everyone. You'll go to the treasury, the Fortress will not lose a unique and protected place. I think it's the perfect solution."

"Our High Priest has his own man in Hearth." Kimal Sarento grinned and, taking the glass, inhaled the aroma with pleasure. "Father Urg, you understand that we will find him?"

"May the Light be with you, Count Sarento. Why do I need an inside man when all it takes to understand the logic of your further actions is to stop and think for a few minutes? Your main mistake, Max, is that you have too much humanity. Where it is necessary to show a bit of cruelty and kill all witnesses, you would rather save the man's life than doom him to even greater troubles."

"One of the three..." it wasn't hard to guess where Father Urg was heading.

"I had to have a serious talk with the one you didn't kill. I'm afraid that after this I'll have to find a new trio of leaders of the night guild. You saw the journal, Max. That alone is enough to destroy you. Not to mention that you pulled Father Locke out of the cage where I put him twenty years ago."

"But instead of killing us, you give us the key to the treasury?"

"Young man, do you really underestimate my ability to analyze information so greatly? You went to the event calmly, although if you were in any danger, your pupil would have been able to talk you out of it. Considering that Count Sarento himself went into the mouth of the overfed lion, neither of you was in any danger. Full mithril armor, I assume? And on both of you. Will you show an old man what it looks like? I've always been curious."

"The High Priest always has interesting information to share," said Kimal Sarento. I, in lieu of a response, transformed the armor from invisible to metallic and back. After a pause, my pupil repeated the same action, although he shot me a pointed look. As if to say, you should always have aces up your sleeve and not show all your strengths at once.

"Unexpected," the High Priest smiled. "You know, in preparation for today's conversation, I worked through several scenarios, but in none of them was there even a hint of trust on your part.

Perhaps transparency for transparency. I know that Count Vyazemsky conducted a series of tests with his mithril armor piece. The experiment ended with the complete destruction of the item."

"This is important information," Kimal Sarento said after a pause. "It's one thing to know that you are absolutely safe, another to know that your potential enemies have an understanding of how to destroy your defenses."

"Naturally," the High Priest chuckled and immediately became serious. "You did a stupid thing by following Zurgan's lead and agreeing to attend his event. As far as I know, you weren't supposed to come out of there alive. Even your close acquaintance with the Inquisitor wouldn't have stopped them. I had to remind everyone that it's not the Emperor who determines who is allowed to live and who should die. That it is the Church of the Light that supports the Light lands. True, now I'll have to write a lot of explanatory notes and prove to the new cardinals that I had no other choice. But these are all minor details compared to the result. It has been achieved, and you are both here."

"All that's left to determine is — why?" Kimal Sarento leaned back in his chair and looked at Father Urg. "What are you after?"

However, it was not the High Priest who answered, but me. Leaning back in the same way and sipping my glass of wine, noting the excellent taste, I said, as if it meant nothing,

"This particular matter is quite clear. Father

Urg wants to lose his official title once and for all."

Kimal Sarento almost choked. For some time, he looked from me to the High Priest and back, as if he did not believe what he heard and wanted to see at least some kind of refutation. But there was none. Father Urg paused for a long time and confirmed:

"That is correct. I am going to become pope, and you are going to help me."

Chapter 5

"THIS IS COMPLETELY UNREALISTIC," I declared, righteous in my words. "The world will never accept your resignation. They certainly won't place you at the head of the church."

"Why not?" Kimal Sarento quickly came to his senses and now thoughtfully looked at the beaming high priest. "The idea, my doubting mentor, is not without reason. Only a seasoned person such as Father Urg can lead an organization that puts the fight against darkness at the forefront. Innocent sheep will be gobbled up without a second thought. Our high priest would gobble them up himself. And it seems to me he wouldn't choke. Nevertheless, the main question remains: what do we stand to gain from this? This particular question is much more relevant to me than how it can be done at all."

"What about the loyalty of the future pope?" Father Urg arched an eloquent eyebrow.

"Offering us something we already have? A strong move. Too bad it doesn't always work. But you tried, I must admit," Kimal Sarento settled more comfortably in his chair and motioned for the high priest to continue.

"Actually, I assumed that you would tell me what you want."

"Father Urg, we've been working together for almost twenty years," Kimal Sarento said, flashing the high priest his usual grin. "I know very well that you have decided on a price you are willing to pay, and now you are looking for a way to somehow reduce it. Why all these attempts to dodge? Are you just that greedy?"

"What an ugly and manipulative ploy, Kimal. I expected something more sophisticated from you," the high priest sighed heavily. "It's not about what I can offer you, it's about what I've already done for you and how you'll pay for it."

"For us?" It was Kimal's turn to raise a skeptical brow. I wisely kept silent. When two such mastodons collide, other creatures should keep their distance. At least during the first few minutes of their brawl.

"Naturally. Isn't it the Church of the Light that has taken over the protection of the Sarento estate? I suppose you'll be interested in reading these documents."

Father Urg pulled out two sheets of paper and handed them to Kimal Sarento. His features sharpened as he read them. Even his usual grin disappeared. Nevertheless, Kimal Sarento managed to refrain from making any comments and simply handed the documents to me. An order from the emperor. A secret order. The estate of Count Sarento, in accordance with some law unknown to me, must be transferred to the use of the empire with all its contents. The only difference between the signed decrees was that in the second, the place of resettlement was determined. That is, the residents of the estate were not simply thrown out into the street, but were resettled to a place corresponding to their usual standard of living.

"It is unacceptable to have weaknesses, in our time, Kimal," the high priest said in a fatherly tone. "Your family, even if you pay no attention to it, is your weakness. Zurgan the First, as you can see, has remembered that. I had to intervene. The emperor did not comprehend this on the first attempt and tried a second time, when I had to personally inform him that your lands were the Fortress's zone of interest. Do I need to tell you how many resources and how much effort it cost me? Zurgan the First is an extremely unfriendly emperor. Envious and vindictive."

"Zurgan would never take this step," Kimal Sarento did not take his eyes off of Father Urg. "He knows the consequences this could entail."

"Do you mean to suggest that these are forgeries?" Father Urg asked, nodding to the papers. "I'm willing to submit them for verification. This is a real decree from the real emperor. A weak emperor, susceptible to manipulation, no matter how much he would like to think otherwise, but the true emperor nonetheless."

"You..." Kimal Sarento blurted out. The man leaned forward, but still managed to hold back his emotions.

"Don't make me out to be something I'm not, Kimal. It wasn't me who pressured Zurgan and forced him to attack your family. You have too many living enemies left. Influential enemies who have access to our well-fed emperor, among other things. So this is a rare case when I stood up for someone else's interests and set my own aside. And, as you can see, I kept my actions secret, in no hurry to inform you and demand some kind of reward."

"I need a name," Kimal Sarento's voice had a completely different tone than usual. "My family is untouchable."

"And are you so sure that I will now name the true instigator, and not simply someone the Church of the Light would like to quietly get rid of without getting their hands dirty? No, Kimal. The Fortress now controls your estate and provides protection there. No one will dare even to look askance in their direction anymore. Whether we come to an agreement now or not, this is how it will be for the foreseeable future. You see, I also don't really like it when outsiders get involved in these matters. I have nothing against blackmail, I often resort to it myself, but I prefer to use only what the person has done himself. Without involving his innocent relatives. However, it seems to me that we have gone too deep into this topic and have deviated from the main issue at hand."

"Unlike my fuming pupil, I'm interested in what exactly we have to do. Only by understanding the scope of the work can we estimate the price," I said. "Besides, the safety of my pupil's family can in no way affect the payment for my work. After all, I'll have to do the bulk of it, right? You weren't very keen on inviting Kimal Sarento to this meeting and, it seems to me, you improvised, pulling out of your secret chests everything that could influence his decision."

"What a perceptive and intelligent boy," the high priest grinned. "Kimal, your presence has had a positive effect on his development. Well, if you want to know how I can become closer to the Light, let's talk about it. The Temple of Skron has a mechanism that allows you to modify people, giving them properties that were previously unavailable. In order to become a pope, I need a piece of Light. I can get it by undergoing modification. That's all that is required of you. Get me the mechanism. I will do the rest myself."

"The Light will never accept a modified Pope!"

"He accepted a modified commander, right? And not just a commander, but the head commander. The second most powerful being in the Church of the Light, after the Pope."

"Okay, not the Light then. The Inquisitor. He'll know immediately that you've been modified."

"The Inquisitor is sitting in Hearth and, as far

as I understand, isn't going to leave. What does the pope mean to him? The creatures of Chaos don't care about worldly affairs. They care about the balance of power, not who is currently sitting on the snow-white throne. Actually, it was precisely because your city became the Inquisitor's haven that I decided to take advantage of the situation."

"What prevents you from directly contacting the Temple of Skron? That hasn't stopped you before."

"After certain events of which you are well aware, they stopped communicating with the light ones. Karina Fardi forbade it, and the misty servants decided to indulge her in this. It's strange, of course, but the situation is precisely that. I have no desire to wait for the conflict to be resolved. I'm no longer young, you safely buried the life-extending Magister Meram, and my ambitions have not gone anywhere. I have achieved everything I wanted in the Zarak Empire. Now I have other goals."

"But Father Urg believes that Hearth maintains contact with the Temple of Skron?" Kimal Sarento again intervened in the conversation. "Doesn't the high priest know that Karina Fardi has established a ban on visiting the lands of the dark ones? Neither I nor my frowning mentor are allowed to visit Kerux. The Temple of Skron is closed to us."

"But not the lands of the Bartolomeo Clan," he immediately corrected, showing that he was privy to all the world's affairs. "I believe that the temple servants will not refuse a meeting if someone from the clan warns them about it. For example, the notorious Adeline Sarento. I am sure that the Temple of Skron will listen to your proposal with interest."

"Especially after I destroyed Seven," I stated, and judging by the way the high priest frowned, this was his first time hearing about it.

"On the other hand, One still wanted to cooperate with us, for some reason," I continued the thought. "This means that before they kill us, they will listen to us. But what can we offer them that will interest the Temple of Skron? I have nothing."

"You have the Interrogator."

"He's just as useless as the Inquisitor. Just two carcasses that sit next to my throne and scare the people. He will never interfere with the communication between me and the temple servants. He limited himself to ensuring the immunity of Hearth from the forces of Skron. Not for me personally. And especially not for my loved ones. In order to communicate with the Temple of Skron, there needs to be a serious reason."

"Actually, that's where you come in." Father Urg shifted in his chair. "That's what I'm going to pay in fact you for."

"And now we've come to the most interesting part of our conversation," Kimal Sarento said. "All these beautiful words about saving relatives, lands, and so on — it's all just dust, high priest. You had a pretty way of throwing it in our eyes, but it's still a petty move. You know that the relationship between us and the Temple of Skron is quite strained. What can you give us about the mechanism? Something, it seems to me, the temple servants will be very reluctant to part with."

"This." Father Urg pulled several sheets of paper out of the desk drawer and handed them to us. "I was planning to involve only Max in the matter, so you will distribute the payment amongst yourselves. Whichever things are more important or necessary for whomever."

I looked through the list and had a hard time not immediately agreeing. Gold — heaping piles of gold, resources, magic stones, artifacts, the right to use devices for the production of potions, access to all the rifts of the light lands and, what bribed me the most, the transfer of ancient books written before Skron's arrival on our planet to our undivided use. The names of the vast majority of them meant nothing to me, but among the general list I found the line "Basic Dictionary." There were no details, but I had no doubt that this was the *Author* skill. The very one that old man Meram had failed to master.

"An amusing proposal. You can see right away that you've been thoroughly preparing for this. Are your ambitions to become pope really that grand?" Kimal Sarento asked, putting the sheets of paper aside as if everything listed was worth no more than the soot under his feet.

"I once believed that my task was to find someone who could cleanse the Church of the Light from the darkness that had settled in it," the high priest answered after a pause, looked at me and continued, "Even if that person considered me to be the darkness. Max was perfect for this role. A conqueror of rifts, a dark mirror, independent and angry at the whole world. A little more, and he could have become a paladin."

"Paladins are a myth," said Kimal Sarento.

"Not at all. In the entire history of the Church of the Light, there have been at least three paladins. Do you think that only the Temple of Skron wanted to upset the balance? The Citadel has tried throughout its history, raising humans within its walls who were completely immune to the darkness. Completely, Max. Even proximity to the true Skron could not destroy them. Just as Karina Fardi is a vessel for Skron, so the paladins were a vessel for the Light. I believed that Max would stay on this path and return the Church of the Light to its former glory. Destroy all the heresy, corruption and attempts to curry favor. But then something changed in Max. He turned off the path. Became independent. Became a figure. And then I realized that such a difficult task cannot be foisted onto another's shoulders. If I wanted to cleanse the Church of the Light of the infection that has settled within it, then I must do it myself. Personally. With my own hands. But the time was lost — the Light will not touch me anymore. I am too old, and my body will not withstand the changes. Most would retreat at this point. Most, but not me. I know what needs to be done. I know how to turn the face of the Light in my direction. To do this, I need to modernize my body. Make it strong. The runescribe is gone, but there are mechanisms of the Temple of Skron. They should help me gain the strength that will allow me to withstand receiving a piece of the Light."

"What a beautiful and tearful story," sighed Kimal Sarento. "Have you ever tried writing romances? Father Urg, you can hide behind beautiful words all you like, you may even believe them, but I, personally, am unconvinced. Becoming pope is a worthy goal. Considering what you said, maybe even feasible. But nothing will change if you gain a piece of the Light. Before you stands the current pope, as well as an entire army of new cardinals. Do not forget about the two high priests of other empires. Too many people thirsty for power. Many of whom are already marked by the Light. How will you do better than them?"

"The internal affairs of the Church of the Light do not concern you," Father Urg answered harshly. "I don't interfere in yours, and you don't interfere in mine. If I get the mechanism, I'll become pope. How is none of your business."

"And neither is the number of clergymen who will die in the process. Aren't you afraid that someone will risk bringing the Inquisitor in for investigation?" Kimal Sarento didn't let up. For a while, silence hung under the dome. Kimal looked at the high priest, who did the same in turn and it seemed to me that if I stood between them, I'd burst into flame from the fire flashing between their gazes. I went over everything I knew about Father Urg and with each passing moment I realized more and more clearly that his plan had many components that made it untenable. Wrong. A kind of plan that was unbecoming of this man. Because it wasn't a plan — it was insanity. Voluntarily undergoing modification to receive a piece of the Light and tremble in fear for the rest of your life, afraid that the Inquisitor might turn his gaze on you? That was not the Father Urg I know. The coordinator of the Nocturnal Guild was much more scheming than he wanted us to think.

Apparently, Kimal Sarento was thinking the same. Suddenly he asked,

"Okay, Father Urg, let's say you run all your competitors through the modification device and dump them on the Inquisitor. Quite a worthy deed for a future pope. In fact, all we need to do is provide you the mechanism, not provide you with access? But how will you get this piece of the Light? For some reason, I believe that in your case, obtaining it through the Inquisitor is no longer an option."

"There have already been cases in history when the snow-white throne was occupied by people without a particle of Light," the high priest answered after a pause. "If there is a precedent, then it can be repeated."

"Then why did you come up with this whole fairy tale about modernization? You know, I almost believed it. Did you really think that my humane mentor wouldn't help you if he found out that at least fifteen people would be killed when we got you the device? What do you say, my mentor, who has been in trouble with the Citadel more than once? Are you going to panic and throw a tantrum?"

"I will say that the high priest will need to add a few zeros onto the numbers indicated on those sheets. Plus, I do not fully understand the status of the Sarento estate. I do not want my pupil to constantly have to run off somewhere because his household is in peril. Especially as it is so far away. As I understand it, none of the books listed here are in the treasury?"

"The treatises of the ancients cannot be stored in the Fortress treasury," answered Father Urg. "The contents of this place are controlled by the Citadel. We only provide the space and security."

"I need more than just the treatises of the ancients. Their devices, maps, everything you have on them. I'm also interested in the question of where this all came from. As far as I know, when Skron appeared in this world, there weren't many places left where such items were kept. How did you get your hands on them? Will you tell me? Or will all these mysteries remain secret?"

"When I was the bishop of the southwestern region, I was lucky enough to find a very interesting archive. A cache. I still do not know who prepared it and for what purposes, but the information it contained included knowledge from the time before the coming of Skron. There were also magic stones there that no one had even heard of. Elixirs that improve parameters with no negative consequences for the body. Elixirs for expanding the magic field. Elixirs to increase the level of stones. There is the assumption — only an assumption — that this was the cache of the first emperor. Or someone from his inner circle. Thanks to this cache, I managed to become who I am today. As you can see, I am being entirely open with you."

"That's what scares me," Kimal Sarento chimed in. "Let's say, let's just say, you succeed and become the pope. What's to stop you from getting rid of the witnesses?"

"The Inquisitor," Father Urg answered simply. "As I said, he has now settled in Hearth. It is stupid to go against someone who has Chaos behind him. It is dangerous to your health. Besides, as practice has shown, it is better to be friends with Max. It brings more benefit and profit. So, do we agree? All we need is to increase the sum?"

"I also need a trade channel with the Kaliman Empire protected by the Church of the Light," I said, considering the prospects. "Emir Hadji and I had a rather interesting conversation that opened up some tantalizing prospects, but I'm uncomfortable with the fact that I don't have the opportunity to establish safe trade. No one must touch caravans from Hearth. And I'm not telling you this as the high priest."

"Good. If one of my units receives an order for matters related to Hearth, you will learn about it, and the customers will be eliminated. In that case, I also have a demand. Father Locke. I need him. I have my own scores to settle with him."

"I'm afraid I can't do that. If you had warned me in advance that you were the coordinator of the Nocturnal Guild and were simply carrying out an order from Count Vyazemsky or someone else, that would be one thing. My anger would have shifted towards the customer. But the night assassins slaughtered my people, destroyed what belonged to me, settled in Hearth and even tried to set their own conditions for me. Father Locke is the price for my trouble. As is Miralda Lertan."

"The girl is dangerous," the high priest reminded me, just in case. "In a year she will be twenty-one and will have the right to declare her claims to the throne. Is Hearth ready to confront the Zarak Empire?"

"Worldly affairs, as you recently said, should not interest the Church of the Light," I answered. "She simply had to be killed. You did not do this, and now she is under my protection. Even if I cannot stand her. And what to do next, I will decide in a year, when the time comes. By that time, if we succeed, the claims of Miralda Lertan will be supported by the new pope. He will give me Zurgan the First, just as the Citadel gave up Count Fardi. I have not forgotten who gave the order to destroy my family."

"It's good that you approach revenge without emotion. Kimal, I repeat, you have definitely had a positive influence on Max. Okay, give me the agreements. I need to make some corrections."

Father Urg quite cleverly corrected the values

indicated on the papers, increasing them all by almost one and a half times. If the numbers there were exorbitant before, now they had entered the realm of the absurd.

"Father Locke remains with you. As does Miralda. The Council of Three will receive a new order regarding Hearth. The Sarento estate will receive a special status as 'friends of the Church of the Light.' Not even the Emperor will dare confiscate the lands. Will that be enough for you to begin work with the Temple of Skron? I need the device as soon as possible. My life is short."

"That's not quite all. I want to get into the treasury," I decided.

"Why?" Not only Father Urg but even Kimal Sarento was surprised.

"Because a wise man taught me not to trust anyone, even this wise man. I want to see with my own eyes what is in this protected place, and only then agree or disagree with your proposal. Or is the high priest afraid that I might see something there that I will definitely want to pocket?"

His face remained calm, but that was answer enough for me. I definitely needed to get into the Fortress's treasury. And yes, Father Urg was being very disingenuous when he said that the Citadel was in charge of the contents of this place. I wonder if he was even telling the truth to himself?

"So be it," he replied after a pause. "On one condition: do not simply appropriate anything. If you need something, include it in your list of requirements. I will think about what can be removed from the list. I will not let you rob the Church of the Light. I still have to manage its affairs. Let's go. The sooner we start, the sooner you can go about your business."

"I will watch Father Urg's hands closely, my sagacious mentor," Kimal Sarento's voice was heard over the intercom. "I never thought the old man was so good at bluffing. There is something in the treasury that is somehow connected to you, and he wanted to keep it from us for as long as possible. Which is interesting in itself. But what is it?"

If I had known what we would find there, I would have thought twice about my list of requirements.

Chapter 6

"FATHER URG, YOU'VE PROVEN to be even more interesting than I thought," said Kimal Sarento. "To so beautifully lead your adopted daughter away from the influence of petty clerics — you must have nerves of steel. I admit, your actions impressed even me. What do you say, my silent mentor? You suddenly look quite frail."

"Alia didn't know," the high priest said. "The girl acted strictly according to the rules she was brought up on. She couldn't do otherwise — it would have been contrary to her nature."

"She will remain in Hearth. After what I have learned, I will not give her up to the Church of the Light." I turned to face Father Urg. He correctly read the emotion in my eyes. Despite all his strength and power, he retreated and with some elusive movement found himself behind Kimal

Sarento, hiding behind him as if behind a wall.

"Only the pope has the right to excommunicate hierarchs of such a high level. Even they themselves do not have the right," Father Urg said from his safe spot. "This is another point in our agreement. The child will be born in three months. You have more than enough time to get me the mechanism. We can both get what we want. As for the stone that you are clutching in your hand, consider it my gift. I will not be able to use it a second time anyway."

"You must admit, my enraged mentor: Father Urg will make an ideal pope." Kimal Sarento was definitely enjoying the situation. Of course, the high priest personally handed us such incriminating evidence! The magic stone *Wall of Rain,* as it turned out, was only elite. An ordinary gold eight-faceted gem. The thing was, in all my brief career as a rift conqueror, I had never seen such a stone. Even Kimal Sarento was astonished by the description. A wall of rain that follows the wielder. The mana requirements were outrageous, so it was hard to even imagine how many potions the assistants of the high priest had to pour into themselves. But the way Father Urg had treated Alia…I was speechless. It was that incident in the square that had led Alia to become so fanatically devoted to the church. After all, the Light itself had come to her aid, extinguishing the cleansing fire. When I realized what I held in my hands, only the presence of Kimal Sarento saved the high priest from instant death. I had one desire: to rip out his rotten heart and squeeze it in my fist so that the pieces flew all over the treasury. However, my no less shocked pupil managed to stop me. Then, Father Urg calmly explained the reasons for his actions, stating at the very end that if such a need arose again, he would do exactly the same. Because emotions always got in the way of these matters, and this was the only way to pull both me and Alia out from under the influence of corrupt bishops. Of which, as practice had shown, there were far too many in the Fortress.

My desire to explore the treasury vanished. Sure, there were many interesting items, ancient manuscripts, some artifacts, a bunch of rare materials, and more magic stones, the existence of which I didn't even know about, but all this no longer interested me. Squeezing *Wall of Rain*, I declared that from now on, it would be mine. I needed an object that would demonstrate to Alia the true nature of the man who raised her. To whom she strove to return. Father Urg did not dare to object, and soon we left one of the most protected places of the Zarak Empire. Perhaps I would have struggled to get in, even with my mithril armor. All the walls were lined with vyrma and were so thick that it evoked an involuntary sense of respect for the original designers.

"The only thing that can fight those beasts is another beast of that kind," I answered, gradually calming down. Father Urg was a dangerous, unpleasant, bad man, but his plan to cleanse the Church of the Light was clear, comprehensive and pragmatic. Inhumane, completely unsuitable for any concept of "goodness," but, as it became more and more clear to me, this word had nothing to do with the Light. Yes, initially the church was founded as a mechanism to fight darkness, Skron and any other plagues, but over time people distorted the foundation, turning the servants of the Light into what we had now. Everything needed to change, and radically, and only a person who did not squirm at the sight of other people's blood and was ready to end the lives of tens, if not hundreds of people, would be able to achieve this goal. Only a person like this would be able to eradicate all the darkness, all the servants of Skron. True, he would plant his own, no less bastardly people, but they would have at least some connection to the light. Who was I to oppose this? I had Hearth and I needed to keep developing it. If someone decided to challenge my right to my own city, there were always two representatives of Chaos. I needed to do something with them, too. But only in due time.

"So, is there anything else you wish to see here?" The high priest stepped out from behind Kimal Sarento and glanced meaningfully around the treasury.

"No." I looked at Kimal Sarento. "Write it all out in the form of an agreement, so that neither side can think of reneging on their obligations later. I need written evidence of our agreements."

"You don't trust the future pope?" Father Urg said, surprised.

"I don't trust anyone but myself. How much

time do we need?"

"I think a couple of hours should suffice." Kimal Sarento looked at Father Urg and nodded.

"We will need a guarantee that we can leave the capital unimpeded," I said and looked to Father Urg. I could no longer bring myself to call this man the high priest. Just as I would not be able to call him the pope, if he succeeded.

It was unlikely that any of the guards would be able to detain us, but we wouldn't want to leave corpses behind. The emperor agreed to let us go to the Fortress, but I didn't think he'd let us leave just like that.

"You will leave Turb under the protection of the Light," he assured.

We ascended to the upper floors. Kimal Sarento and Father Urg went to formalize the agreement, and I sat on one of the benches in the Fortress square and closed my eyes, exhausted. It was pitch black. The doomed soldiers and most of the servants of the Light were sleeping peacefully in their beds. Only a rare guard periodically approached me, but, noticing who I was, they immediately changed their trajectory. Archduke Valevsky, A.K.A. the Hunter of Darkness, was a household name, even in the Fortress.

I felt disgusting. One part of my consciousness demanded that I destroy Father Urg and cleanse the planet of this bastard once and for all, while the other insisted on the need for change. Insisted that a ruler should be guided not by the momentary desires and emotions inherent of youth, but by the future of his lands. If the Church of the Light started actually doing what it was founded to do, order would appear in the light lands. There would be no bishops who had sold themselves to Skron, there would be no kidnapping of children in order to turn them into supreme converts, the waypoints would disappear, the uncontrolled movement of dark and gray ones across our lands would stop. Was the current pope capable of providing all this? No. I'd seen him. He was an open, honest, bright man, filled with Light — it seemed he was brimming with it, right to the top of his head. He was a great, strong man, but out of touch with life. He hadn't even noticed that the head commander was a modernized man. The current pope trusted people and his surroundings too much. He even believed me, making me a monitor of darkness. All it took was pointing to a few high-ranking church officials and getting the Inquisitor to confirm. Having immense faith in people is good, but not with the current state of the church. We needed someone like Father Urg, no matter how much I wished it wasn't so. So the part of me that stood for faith and justice in all that was good needed to shut up for a while. I had to help this bastard. Whether I wanted to or not. The world needed to be saved.

Two hours later we were leaving the capital as part of a huge delegation. The guards at the gates did not want to let us through, but the personal appearance of Father Urg removed all obstacles. True, there was a huge detachment of the emperor's guards following us, but they kept their distance, not daring to come even a hundred meters closer to the caravan.

"From what I understand, my mysterious mentor, Hearth has taken the other side," said Kimal Sarento when we had driven far enough away from the capital.

"There are three rifts in the lands that once belonged to my family. From what I know, they are currently being actively and illegally developed. Even though Count Fardi is no longer alive, his people continue their work, sending resources to who knows where. First, I want to destroy the rifts so that not a single pebble remains behind. Second, I want to kill everyone I find there. Whether they are there by force or voluntarily makes no difference to me."

"There's no point in killing those who have already adapted to the darkness," Father Urg chimed in. The head of the Church of the Zarak Empire was moving along with us, guaranteeing our immunity. "However, I don't understand why you need such a trifle as this. The rifts that are on those lands are only level four. You should know this better than anyone else. Don't you have more important things to do than worry about something that can be dealt with by a few squads of doomed soldiers? We will seize those who are currently developing the rifts and send them to their well-deserved work."

Father Urg signalled and one of the escorts rode up to the carriage. Through a small window,

Father Urg gave him an order, and several people immediately rushed forward to convey his will to the bishop of the southeastern region. All those involved in the criminal development of the rifts in the former Valevsky lands must be captured, judged and sent to the Fortress. Their names would be written on the ledger of the doomed legion.

"You know a lot about the goings on in the rifts" Kimal Sarento chuckled.

"This is the basis of my existence," Father Urg said. He really didn't try to pull the wool over people's eyes. "The rifts are resources. Resources are gold. Gold is influence. My resources, my gold, my influence. The emperor claimed this area as his zone of interest, but times have changed. It is time to show the empire its true place."

"Do the laurels of the Citadel bring you no peace?"

"Among other things. The Shurghan Empire is an ideal example of how our world should be structured. The Church of the Light should be at the forefront, not trailing behind, picking up crumbs. This is the only way to defeat the darkness. If the issue with the rifts is resolved, I suggest changing our route. You must go to Hearth."

"No, we're going to the rifts," I answered, sparing no glance to Father Urg. The street was pitch black, dispersed by the light stones of the carriage and our escorts, but even this view was more pleasant to me than him.

"I would like to hear your rationale behind

this." His voice had become icy cold.

"We have three rifts, located in a triangle, and quite close to each other. This means that the strength of the Pharapho fog that will appear after the rifts are destroyed will be enormous. I need this fog and the resources that can be extracted from it. Is the Church of the Light ready to fight the spawn of Pharapho? I am going to completely cleanse these lands of infection. You can grab your people so that they do not interfere, but the rifts are mine and mine alone. As are the rewards of the Pharapho fog."

Father Urg chuckled meaningfully and, unfolding the map in front of him, began to study it. Kimal Sarento's voice immediately appeared in my intercom,

"Unfortunately, my challenge-loving mentor, we are very limited in time. We have only two weeks left to prepare for our encounter with the Wave, which will be led by a creature touched by Chaos. During this time, we need to get to the Kaliman Empire. This will also take a while. Should we be wasting time now on securing lands that are worthless to all of us? Sure, it would be nice to build up a good stock of bone armor. Checking whether it was possible to create mithril directly from the spawn of Pharapho is also good. But creating fog just for this purpose, and, from what I understand, a very high-level fog..."

"There will be no fog there."

"If there are rifts, then there are ruins in which fog will appear. This is an axiom. Or are you trying to break the laws of the universe once again?"

"There are ruins. As well as rifts that hide them from the rest of the world. But these are not simple ruins. Pharapho has no power over them. You wanted to visit the location of the ancients, right? Untouched by Skron or the Light? The place where the first emperor gained his power? There are three such places left on our planet, and one of them, by a funny coincidence, is located in the forests that once belonged to my family. Actually, that's why we settled there. My grandfather decided so. Evidently he wanted to keep it close."

"Then why destroy the rifts? Do they somehow interfere with your plan?"

"Rifts mean people. Natural, artificial, it doesn't matter. As soon as I destroy the three rift-masters, everyone will have to leave the area. The clergy cannot fight the spawn of Pharapho. We will have time to find the entry point and explore the ruins of the ancients without raising unnecessary questions."

"Alright, let's say this works out — how will this help prepare for the battle with the creature of Chaos?"

"My grandfather claimed that I'd be able to learn to use the *Author* skill in the safekeep of the ancients. I would be able to use the symbols of the ancients. That's one reason."

"If only you knew what to look for, and where." Kimal Sarento was clearly very skeptical of my idea.

"They're waiting for me in the city. A creature

that called itself a sixth-generation interactive neural network. It can help me gain the power with which I will stop the creature that brings Chaos."

"There is no information about this in the notebook," Kimal Sarento said after a pause.

"No. The notebook is controlled by Chaos. Or Skron. Someone who is responsible for the artifacts. The creature that came to me in Hearth used a strange bloody portal, inside which the artifact had no power."

"So you voluntarily go wherever this unknown creature invited you, without having the slightest understanding of what this creature wants from you?" Kimal Sarento clarified, just in case. "Even if, perhaps, its true goal is to acquire a new body? Yours, not yet spoiled by all sorts of modifications, would be an ideal choice."

"I don't see any other way to stop the Wave," I answered after a pause. "I'll have to take a risk. As always. The only difference is that this time I have a pupil who will help me get out of it if something doesn't go according to plan."

"So you have a plan as well?" Kimal Sarento said, his voice full of sarcasm. "Oh, wisest of mentors, share your wisdom with your pupil quickly, impart your great plan upon me!"

"Very funny. Any other suggestions? I'm ready to listen. How can we destroy a creature that has acquired a piece of Chaos?"

"Magic, my foolish mentor. Simple magic, albeit of a high level. The fiftieth, to be precise."

"The magic stones, if I'm not mistaken, belong

to the Light. Or are part of Skron. They are creatures from the first orbit. Chaos is above them. It's like poking Karina Fardi with a vyrma or mithril blade. Useless and ineffective."

"I would tell you, my young and ardent mentor, what you should have poked at Karina Fardi in her time to prevent all this from happening, but I won't. You know my opinion — it's not the best decision to risk everything when encountering the unknown. It would be better to stop the Wave, take the creature of Chaos and deal with it one-on-one. If magic doesn't work, drag it to the metamorph and make them fight. If that doesn't work either, then resort to the option with the ruins of the ancients. Any risk must be weighed and thought out. There aren't many creatures in this world that can withstand the blow of my lightning."

"I understand, but I have to refuse. First, we need to get to the ancient safekeep. If we destroy the creature touched by Chaos, the way to the ruins will be closed. Even with the key, I won't be able to enter. Because I'll be tainted. Polluted. No, my cautious student, I'll have to take a risk and enter the ruins now. Without the slightest idea of what awaits us there. I can go alone, I'm not dragging anyone along with me. But I must go."

"Time, Maximilian. All this takes time, which we don't have much of," Kimal Sarento said out loud, without using the intercom. Father Urg immediately turned in our direction, clearly not understanding why my pupil had suddenly said that phrase, and without any reason, but I shook my head.

"I understand. It's either this way or no way at all. I need these rifts. I need these ruins."

We spent the rest of the night in complete silence. In the morning, Father Urg headed back to the capital, leaving a large detachment of churchmen with us. An even larger detachment met us four days later, when we finally reached the former lands of the Valevsky family. My chest tightened unpleasantly as we passed the ruins — all that remained of my former home. Count Fardi's men had done a great job clearing the lands of any human presence. Villages, farmsteads — everyone had been evicted, the buildings all destroyed. The fields were already full of tall yellow grass. Everything looked deserted and abandoned.

Except for the three rifts. The servants of the Light acted quickly. When we arrived at the first rift, all the prospectors were already tied up and prepared to be sent to the Fortress. Among the rift conquerors, there were even several mages, quite good by the standards of the ordinary world. You couldn't just find level six magic stones just lying around in the road. Kimal Sarento pretended not to know these people, although the looks that the mages cast at him said otherwise. He knew perfectly well who they were and what they did, but he preferred to pretend that the situation didn't concern him.

"Great Identifier of Darkness, we managed to capture almost a hundred people from three rifts," reported the assistant bishop of the southeastern region. A rather unpleasant middle-aged man, with such a rat-like face that you wanted to fix with your fist. A face like that should have earned him a place in the Nocturnal Guild, not the Church of the Light. I had no doubt that this man was actively taking bribes and doing rather dirty deeds. The ingratiating look he gave me, how he fawned, how he inserted through the words "great" and "respected" was infinitely infuriating. I had to pull myself together so as not to destroy this slippery man on the spot. Father Urg would have to deal with this. It was his diocese.

"What else?"

"Your Radiance, the scale of people who have been deployed here is huge. These scum have never gone deeper than the third level. Only such a respected conqueror of rifts as the great hunter and monitor of darkness can handle the Warden, but these doomed soldiers couldn't get past it. They turned out to be unworthy, unlike you, respected Archduke. You were so very far-sighted in deciding to attack now — such a large team gathers once every two months, when the rift is again filled with resources and creatures. Usually, five or six criminals are on duty here, imagining that they are above the Church of the Light. We were able to obtain a good deal of loot, Your Radiance! Twenty full carts from unincorporated lands is an excellent result."

"Such small details do not concern me. Send people to the Fortress, take the resources and leave. The order of the head of the Church of the

Zarak Empire. Tonight I will destroy the rifts, and the fog of Pharapho will appear."

"Yes, Respected Monitor of Darkness." The cleric bowed. Kimal Sarento grinned, seeing my reaction — clenching my fists, I even leaned forward to slam this cleric into the ground. I think I understood why Zurgan the First chose the southeastern region. Since the local bishop had such an assistant, the bishop himself must be a similar type. Another bishop of Zwat, who actively cooperated with the dark ones? I'd have to check thoroughly. But when would I find the time to travel around the empire?

It took me only one night to close all three rifts. The illegal miners had culled the herds of riftbeasts. I didn't encounter any resources or a single dark creature on the first three levels. Except, of course, the Warden. The dangerous creature was protecting the level with the Rifmaster and was clearly not happy with my arrival. The fragments of *Amplify* fell into my inventory as usual, but they were no longer a joy. In order to strengthen *Devour*, I needed other resources. Those that were obtained from converts and creatures under the sun. I'd have to arrange for a hunting session at some point.

Nevertheless, I had to admit that for a short period of time, I felt happy. The trip through the rifts brought me back to the times when I was an ordinary member of the doomed legion. When everything depended only on me, my abilities and skills. On how I dealt with beasts. The only difference from all the previous trips through the rifts was that I finally got myself a guard essence. Four barrel-like creatures in each rift reacted calmly to my appearance in their cave (under my dark mirror, of course), but they got extremely excited when I tore the essence out of one of them. Yes, I got four yem, but the essence was much more important. I'd never gotten one before. Just as I had never fought with creatures emitting various auras before. Despite all their considerable size, the guards turned out to be monstrously fast. I had to use *Dash* to get close to the next victim. Mithril did the rest — the monsters' essences burst out without any problems. Now I'd have something to bargain with the Abyss. I still have many questions to ask.

"So there definitely won't be any fog?" Kimal Sarento asked just in case when I came out of the third rift. "By the way, I found the ruins. But I didn't find anything there. No protective fields, secret passages, scary monsters. Just ruined stones, almost completely covered with earth. Are you sure we've come to the right place?"

I didn't respond to such obvious bait. The point on the map that my grandfather showed me led straight ahead. Soon I could see stones. The trees had conquered the old city. Almost everything was swallowed up by the earth, and where the stones still managed to break free, greenery carefully hid them from the casual observer. If you didn't specifically look for ruins, you could easily miss them. Which was what my family did. I didn't think that anyone except my grandfather knew what was here.

I pulled out the key, which looked like an oblong plate made of flexible but quite strong material, and held it up in front of me. For a while, nothing happened, then a red dot appeared a few meters away from me. A beam came out of it, scanning me from head to toe. The beam paid special attention to my mithril plate, lingering on it for almost a minute. Finally, the beam disappeared, and an unpleasant message appeared before my eyes:

The purity criteria are not met.

Offworlder artifacts have been discovered. To continue working, clear yourself of foreign objects.

List of items...

Next, a fairly long list of what the ancients considered "impure" items unfolded. Starting from the mithril armor, disassembled for some reason into its components, ending with a *"particle of the essence of Light of the 30th level."* There were so many of the latter that I froze for a while, not understanding what was being discussed. Only the information about the level helped me figure out that we were talking about magic stones. The beam that had scanned me up and down decided to name the eight-sided gems in this strange way. Fortunately, the number of lines and levels coincided with the number of magic stones that were installed in my magic field.

I had to make a difficult, but quite expected decision — completely undress and take out all the magic stones. Both simple and exclusive. When I removed *Devour*, it was as if part of my soul was taken out and put aside. This stone had practically become a part of me. Handing over the items to Kimal Sarento, who stood aside and did not interfere, I lifted the plate again.

This time the beam analyzed me much longer. It lingered in the chest area, on the head, on the chest plate again, and when I had already decided that something had gone wrong, a red portal opened in front of me.

Access granted.
Welcome home, human!

Chapter 7

SPACE FLOATED FOR A MOMENT as a red mist, only to resolidify into a strange and amazing place. The ruins were gone. As was the forest. The status bar stopped working again, leaving only my personal information, the *Author* skill, and a map that showed in all scales that I was in an unknown place, in unknown territory. But all this was nothing compared to the buildings surrounding me. Enormous structures, significantly larger than the tower of the magic academy, rose up into the sky. The surface looked like it was made of mirrors, but it was unlikely that glass could withstand such a load. There were many buildings and they all looked different. Some were shorter, others were taller, some were thin as spires, others were massive and wide. There was not a single identical pair. I was on an open platform of one of these buildings, and one of the tallest. I looked down on almost all the others. The area resembled a small, well-kept garden, where caring gardeners carefully tended and pruned the shrubbery. A small fountain gurgled, and that was the only noise in this kingdom of silence. The city of the ancients looked beautiful, but seemed lifeless.

"All that remains of the original human civilization is memory," a familiar voice rang out, and an old man appeared a few meters away from me. The same one who introduced himself as Yuri, or the sixth-generation interactive neural network. "A memory of past greatness. A memory of those who left this world forever."

"And ended up in another?" I threw out a guess.

"We don't know for sure. The human soul is immortal, but humans never managed to figure out exactly how it moves through the world. Too early they stumbled upon the force that calls itself Chaos. Too early we became its slaves."

"I'd like a little detail, here. What is this force? How and why did people stumble upon it? How did this particular enslavement manifest? Or are you also unable to speak freely here, in this incomprehensible place?"

"This is one of three outposts that remain from the former greatness of the ancients. Chaos and its minions are barred entry here. None of their gifts work in this realm."

"So this status bar that is constantly in the periphery of my vision is a human creation?"

"Too many questions, Heir. You don't understand what's happening and you're clinging to words, trying to extract even a shred of truth. Didn't I tell you that all words are just sounds? Only the meaning matters. The essence. Everything else is vanity. I have a task for you, Heir. You must...

"Before you start making me work, I would like to hear a story. And also, my pupil is somewhere near the portal that leads here. I need him here."

"Your pupil does not have an access key, there are too many offworlder artifacts that he cannot get rid of, but most importantly, he used forbidden functionality to extend his life. He absorbed the souls of humans to delay his aging at their expense. He tore the unfortunate souls out of the cycle of reincarnation."

"From what I understand, I was also subjected to one of these seals. I was killed and revived."

"Those souls returned to the cycle, taking the fatal blow. You did not absorb them. Your pupil sealed the souls within himself forever, allowing him to appear forty years old despite his true age. He is almost a hundred and fifty years old."

"And how many souls did he seal?" I didn't even have any special emotions when I learned the true age of Kimal Sarento. Yuri was right: these were just sounds. But I did need to know what my pupil was doing right now. I knew I had no promise that Kimal Sarento was being completely open with me.

"The quantity is not important. One, ten, a

hundred — these are just numbers. What is important is the meaning."

"However, he is still alive and near the portal," I said. "You did not destroy him, despite what he did. Why?"

"You will need his help to fulfil your destiny. Besides, the imprinting of souls occurred at the moment of the expulsion of the lithoids. With his actions, your pupil has earned the right to continue living. But there is no place for him in the city. The impure have no access here."

"Okay, no means no. So start talking. I believe that now is the unique opportunity for me to learn the history of this world. What happened before Chaos showed up."

"Listen and pay close attention. There is no other place in this world where you can learn this…"

Humans proved to be quite an ancient race. Initially, our development was always spasmodic — each breakthrough was followed by a long period of stagnation, preparing the ground for the next breakthrough. This allowed people to get used to innovations and incorporate them into their lives. But the last few hundred years were marked by colossal breakthroughs that did not have a period of stagnation. It often happened that what was invented in the morning was already outdated by evening, because some innovation had taken its place. The amount of information that fell on the average person was so huge that many could not withstand the load, and this halted their development. But there were those who managed to adapt. Who were able to hold back the streams of information falling on them and understand it without losing the essence. They were the ones who created what I called the status bar — an adaptive mechanism for their weaker relatives. Allowing them to accumulate information, manage it, and provide it in the right form at the right time. A sort of invisible assistant, possessing all the knowledge of the world and successfully replenishing it as it appears.

So people were divided into two categories. Those who had a status bar, and those who did not need it. The true rulers of this world. They completely lost touch with reality. They felt like gods. Immortal. They developed a mechanism for interactive space management, known to me as the *Author* skill. They completely subjugated the laws of physics to their whims. But even this seemed not enough for them. They then turned their gaze to the worlds that were in other space-time spheres. Thus, a portal was opened through which Chaos entered our world. The entity that appeared was monstrously clever. It understood perfectly well that time was not on its side and, if it hesitated, people would come up with a way to banish it back to its realm. In fact, this moment spelled the beginning of the end for humanity, as it existed in that form. Almost all the geniuses who worked without a status bar were destroyed in the first seconds after Chaos appeared. But those who remained fought back. No, they could not destroy

Chaos, but they managed to cause significant damage. The creature retreated, but did not flee. It summoned assistants into the world. Its vassals. Thus eleven forces appeared in the world, rushing to destroy everyone they could reach. Humanity was threatened with extinction, and the geniuses took a terrible step: they decided to destroy the planet. Let humanity perish, but even the forces that appeared will not be able to avoid this fate. Mutually assured destruction.

And then Chaos decided to negotiate. The entity was wise and understood that it had fallen into a trap. The portal had closed, and it would no longer be able to escape to its native world. Humans were allowed to live, having adapted everything they knew before to the new requirements of the alien forces. They were divided between the entities, and a stabilizing contour of all their emerging forces was formed around the weapons of the ancients. Those same spheres that I already knew about. The system became stable and this continued for a whole thousand years.

"And humans became one of the forces as well," I reminded Yuri.

"The very same geniuses who didn't need a status bar," Yuri confirmed. "However, they forgot their roots. They forgot that this world originally belonged to humans, not to Chaos and its minions. They submitted. Yes, these geniuses still exist in our world, but they can no longer be called humans. They have become different. Dirty. Tainted. They must be destroyed, like everyone else who has come to our world. If the system is destabilized, the weapons of the ancients will be unleashed and the world will be cleansed of all alien forces."

"Along with all other living beings."

"Such is your goal! Such is your destiny! Eight hundred years ago, the first man pure enough to gain access came here. He was given power, but he used it at his own discretion. He broke the agreements, giving part of the humans to an alien force, and called it 'the Light.' Although these are nothing more than sounds, the true name of this force is different. Instead of destroying the lithoids, he sent them into oblivion. He did not fulfill any of the agreements. The system remained stable. The next heir also turned out to be weak and susceptible to the alien powers. It became clear that he, too, needed to be changed, and then you appeared in our field of vision. With your help, the offworlders and the lithoids were expelled. The system began to destabilize, but Chaos still manages to keep it from complete collapse. You must continue your campaign."

"It's strange, but this is exactly what Chaos wants too," I said, surprised. "For me to destroy the watermen and the undergrounders."

"Useless, worthless creatures who never managed to achieve true power. If only four forces remain in the third orbit, this will lead the system to become stabilized. Shaky, but still stable. Chaos knows this. However, if not two, but three forces are destroyed, no force in this world will be able to contain the weapon. It will gain freedom, and the world will be cleansed. This is your destiny, Heir. You must avenge humanity."

"By destroying it."

"This is the price of stupidity. Of madness. Of recklessness."

I didn't think it necessary to respond. The place where I had hoped to gain answers had gone mad over the course of a thousand years and lost all connection with reality. It wanted to bring forth a global catastrophe, simply to carry out the orders of those who were long dead. Maybe this world did not originally belong to Chaos, but it was already here, and we had adapted to living with it. If not for this force, the geniuses of the ancients would have opened a portal to another world, from which something much more terrible than Chaos could have crawled out. At least Chaos seemed like something with which you could negotiate. However, I did not voice this to the interactive neural network. It was not a living being. It was a mechanism with an algorithm embedded in it, demanding that the entire world disappear. And this device saw me as an executor of its will. Instead of these thoughts, I told it about what I'd learned from Chaos:

"As far as I know, two beings now wish to become stabilizing forces. Karina Fardi and the pyramid of the Temple of Skron. The forces will become nine again, and the world will gain stability."

"Yes, we know about that too. The Skron vessel and the echo of the mechanoids. You must stop them. Karina Fardi is insane. She does not understand what her actions may lead to. One is overly cautious. He will not do anything until he sees a result. If you stop Karina, the Temple of Skron will take no action."

"But are their desires practical? Could they actually become new ruling forces?"

"Yes. In order to become a new force, you need to find a master. Either Skron, as Karina Fardi did, or the mechanoids, as One is going to do. You need to take some of the forces for yourself and control them. You must stop the mad woman. She is dangerous."

"I have no way to stop her. The weapon I have is too weak for Skron's vessel, you forbade me to take *Tainted Blood*. How else can I defeat someone who has become the vessel of the dark god?"

"Not a god! A power occupying the first orbit!" Yuri roared so loudly that it made the building shake. "There is one God, but humans forgot about God when the aliens came!"

"Weapons, Yuri. We were talking about a lack of weapons," I reminded him.

"The place we are currently standing is an illusion. A copy of a city that once existed under this sky, an exact copy, but only a copy. Nothing material can be taken from here. And there is nothing here. However, I have something that might make you happy. Something that does not require physical embodiment. What you call the *Author* skill. Manipulation of space. Hear me, Heir!"

The icon on the status bar began to blink. Focusing my gaze on it, I opened the skill panel. It had changed significantly. New lines, tables, and data boxes had appeared.

"The essence of spatial manipulation is that you use individual words to form a sentence and embody it. The larger your vocabulary, the wider your possibilities for spatial manipulation. For example, take the words *Brick*, *Multiply*, *One hundred*, *Five* and *Row* and place them in the activation area. In order to find a word, you just need to imagine it. Your brain will give all the necessary commands."

Amazingly, it actually worked — as soon as I imagined a word, the dictionary scrolled through with imperceptible speed, stopping at the entry I needed. Having dragged everything that the sixth-generation neural network required, I mentally pressed the *Implement* button, and a small wall appeared not far from me. It had five rows and consisted of a hundred bricks. I approached and pushed the wall — it collapsed immediately. The bricks that I embodied were not bound together. Just identical rectangular blocks placed on top of each other.

"Here, in the virtual projection of the ancient city, there are no requirements for materials, but in the real world you will first have to determine where you will draw your resources from. You must indicate the source of the materials, how they should be installed, how they should be fastened, how they interact. Manipulating space is a difficult ability, but those who have mastered all its subtleties become dangerous beings."

"The being that was touched by Chaos and which I need to destroy wouldn't even bat an eye at these bricks," I muttered, not understanding the enthusiasm in Yuri's voice.

"If we're speaking in terms that you understand, then the creature touched by Chaos is a creature of the zero orbit. What you create with the help of *Author* are objects beyond categories. Magic does not affect them, no ability of this world does. Only physical strength. And this is only one example of what can be done with the skill. You need to experiment with queries. Form the most successful ones and save them in your memory. This way you can store not only sentences, but also entire texts. However, I must say that your dictionary is far from complete. The location you ended up in is the weakest of all that remained from the ancient people. Several heirs have already come here, and each of them received their share of power. You need to reach the other locations. To do this, I will give you an *Author* query for opening a portal. Ideally, you should get to it yourself, as the previous heir did, but we have no time for you to experiment now. Remember it!"

The query consisted of thirty words. At the same time, there was an extremely inconvenient limitation: I could only open a portal to a place that I had already visited personally. For this, an additional layer appeared on my map, highlighting such places in green. And these places, which saddened me most, turned out to be tragically few.

Especially in the lands that everyone was accustomed to calling the Kerux Metropolitan Area. Yes, now I had the opportunity to visit the lands of the dark ones without the portal of the Temple of Skron and the minotaurs, so Karina Fardi would not know that I violated her order, but I would not be able to do much with it.

"You can put this sentence in the quick access slot," the interactive neural network explained how to do this, and soon I had a rather convenient way to instantly return to Hearth. It only took a second to activate and another to jump into the portal. And from what I understood, this portal would work anywhere on this planet. Because it did not even relate to some zero-orbital force, but to the basic laws of the world.

"Now imagine the possibilities of this skill. You can upgrade space as you wish. You can create a homing spear that can pierce any armor. You can form a defense that no weapon or magic in this world can penetrate. You can become a force to be reckoned with. All you need to do is understand the dictionary."

"Aren't there any notes, tutorials or anything like that for beginners? With basic sentences?"

"They probably exist, but you'll have to find them yourself. They're scattered around the world in the form of artifacts that are practically no different from those that appeared with the alien forces. The place where we are now doesn't have such records."

"But you gave me the portal, didn't you?"

"This is the only sentence available to me. I had to free up some of the database to load the query and the ability to use it."

"I don't understand."

"You don't need to understand. These are all just words. What's important is the meaning: I cannot teach you. I can only give you a tool and one example with which you can realize all your desires. This was the will of the ancients, and it is not for me to change it. Now that you have a weapon against all the creatures of this world, let's return to the original goal. You must destroy three more forces of the third orbit. Then the balance of forces will be broken and the weapon will gain freedom."

I wanted to tell this monster who had lost touch with reality that not everyone in this world wanted to die, but I didn't. There was no point. Just as fanatics don't hear the voice of reason, this creature wouldn't understand my arguments. It would consider them nothing more than a childish whim. The world must be destroyed, period.

"If I receive *Tainted Blood,* will I be denied access here?" I brought up the point that had been concerning me.

"You will become unclean. Stained by alien abilities. Humans like that do not have access to the location of the ancients. If you do this, I will have to do the same to you as I did to the previous heirs who did not live up to expectations. I will have to deprive you of your reason. You will become dangerous and Chaos will destroy you. Either you will work with me or you will die.”

“But if I work with you, I'll die too, right?”

'This is your fate. This is the destiny of the heirs. This world needs to be saved, and you will help me with it.”

“Okay, what else? Do you have anything other than the *Author* skill and a nice fairy tale? How else can you help me?”

“I cannot. My abilities here are limited. The first heir received a dark mirror — the ability to reflect darkness. I see that you have the makings of it, but they are in an embryonic state, not saving you from the influence of Skron, the strongest of the aliens. You will have to develop this gift yourself. There is nothing else in this place. If you want more, visit two other cities of the ancients. The auxiliary cores of those places are much more saturated with information than this.”

“Maybe you can give me some hint on how to develop the dark mirror so that I am immune to the dark influence? I will still have to encounter Fardi, and she is Skron's vessel. I'm not sure I can survive close contact with her.”

“So make sure this encounter doesn’t happen. You have the ability to control space, Heir. Use it. Experiment. Create weapons. Create armor. I can't help you in any other way in this place. When will you leave to carry out your assigned task?”

“As soon as I deal with the creature marked by Chaos,” I replied. “In two weeks, it will arrive in the lands of the Light.

“You must not waste time, Heir!” insisted Yuri.

"By getting distracted by extraneous tasks, you forget about the main goal. The creature marked by Chaos will not help you destroy the three forces. Watermen, undergrounders and, perhaps, ghosts. They are quite easy to deal with even with simple magic. A person with the skill of space control will be able to destroy these creatures in a matter of days. Deal with this matter! Do not get distracted by secondary tasks! What is the point of saving people from the creature if both people and the creature will die soon? You must fulfill your destiny!"

"You've waited a thousand years, you can wait another two weeks." Now seemed as good a time as any to check the length of my leash. After all, didn't everyone's degree of freedom depend on the length of the chain around their neck? I was already convinced that everyone had one.

"By destroying this creature, you risk receiving *Tainted Blood*."

"Which will help me complete your task much more effectively. So what if the cities are closed to me?"

"I won't be able to communicate with you if you receive the gift of Chaos!!"

I read between the lines and realized that its true concern was that it wouldn't be able to influence me, but I kept silent again. I definitely needed this ability. But what was it? I asked the last question out loud, and Yuri explained,

"*Tainted Blood* is a special aura that surrounds its owner and generates destructive particles of Chaos in the blood of all creatures. No defense of this world can resist this aura. This is a zero-level weapon that Chaos actively used in the first years of its appearance on our planet. The aura affects not only those who surround the carrier, but also the carrier himself. In order to survive, you will have to accept Chaos into yourself, forever ceasing to be human.

"So I will have to acknowledge Chaos as my master?" I frowned.

"This will never happen. Chaos does not need new assistants, it has enough of those whom you are accustomed to calling Skron and Light. If you receive *Tainted Blood*, you will be forced to change. You will have to become a servant, but not an assistant. A weak-willed creature, fulfilling the whims of its master. Otherwise, you will die."

"And again — what difference does it make if it allows you to achieve your goal?"

"Chaos' goal, not mine! You will destroy two forces, but you will not be able to conquer the third, since you will be forbidden and you will have no right to disobey. No, Heir. Only by strictly following my orders will you be able to fulfill your destiny. Now go — my resources are not unlimited, and I have already spent almost all of my reserves on communicating with you. For some time I will be unavailable, but soon I will contact you again to find out how things are going. Keep in mind that if you betray me, I will not wait, as with the previous heirs. You will immediately lose your sanity. Do not even think of betraying me, heir. You have no right.”

The red portal floating nearby moved towards me, and soon I was standing in the middle of the forested ruins again. The key to the location was in my hands, and I had to make a huge effort not to throw it away like a poisonous snake.

“Judging by the face of my mentor, who cannot hide his emotions, the meeting did not go as you planned? Was I right? The force wanted to take over your body?”

“I'm afraid, my curious pupil, that everything is much worse than you could imagine. It seems that I need your help. For I can't think of a way to save myself and avoid the fate that the mechanism of the ancients has in store for me.”

Chapter 8

"I HATE THE PHRASE but — I told you so, didn't I? I did. This is the result of someone not listening to their elders and experienced comrades! Tell me, mentor, who constantly has adventure biting at your skinny and underfed behind, why did you go there?"

"For this," I said, activating the portal to Hearth with a wave of my hand. A red shimmering veil appeared a few steps away from me, illuminating the surrounding greenery with a gloomy light. Although what greenery was I talking about? Maybe the numerous firs and pines that grew in the forests. Everything else had long turned golden brown and was gradually falling to the ground. The piercing autumn wind made another attempt to envelop us in cold, but the mithril armor coped with such misfortune perfectly.

"Alright, fair enough," Kimal Sarento chuckled. Having walked around the portal from all sides, he asked: "Where does it lead?"

"Home. To Hearth. The central hall, to be more precise."

"Straight into the hands of the Inquisitor and the Interrogator," he grinned back. "You certainly do know how to find trouble where there shouldn't be any. Everyone knows that this portal is a creation of the ancients. Now imagine — the entities of Chaos are sitting there, not bothering anyone, a portal spawned from the technology of those they destroyed opens, and you pop out, happy as a clam. How are you certain they won't destroy you on the spot?"

"We can't know if we don't check," I said. "Are you with me? I need to talk to the Interrogator."

"As if I have a choice. You brought your pupil into the dense forests and now you want to escape? No, my cunning mentor, that won't work. If we encounter anything serious, we'll have to do it together.

"Let's hold hands, just in case. I'm not sure the portal will stay in place if I go through it. This functionality is still new to me."

Space blurred for a moment into a bloody mist to take shape as the central hall of Hearth. Kimal Sarento materialized nearby. The portal had considered us a single entity. I wanted to take a step towards the throne, but I could not move from the spot. Rather, I could move, but the blades of two huge swords rested against my throat, and I was not sure that the mithril armor would be able to protect me from damage. For on the other side of the swords were the Interrogator and the Inquisitor.

"Hello to you, too!" I said, taking a step back just in case. Judging by the fact that the red shimmer behind me had disappeared, the portal had evaporated. In my peripheral vision, I saw Kimal Sarento backing away with the dexterity of a dancer. But the creatures of Chaos paid no attention to him. Their swords were still pointed in my direction.

"You were in the ancients' location," the Interrogator said. Judging by the fact that there was no question in his voice, it was more of a statement.

"I was. I need to discuss something."

"In two weeks you will have to stop the Wave. Why are you wasting time on God knows what, instead of fulfilling the mission assigned to you?" The Interrogator ignored my words, deciding to stick to his guns. The only thing that changed was that the swords lowered. However, both echoes of Chaos remained glued to the spot, as if to say, 'One extra word or movement and you're finished.'

"Why do you want to destroy our world?"

From the way the Interrogator and the Inquisitor frowned, they clearly hadn't expected such an accusation. The Chaos entities even glanced at each other, as if silently communicating with each other, and I decided to supplement my accusation:

"I know that if the three forces from the third orbit are destroyed, the system will lose stability and collapse. The weapons of the ancients will be released, and our world will cease to exist. Why are the forces of Chaos so eager to destroy this world?"

"No one will destroy three forces," the Interrogator replied. "Only two, not three, need to be removed from the planet. This will stabilize the system."

"There are few ancient people left. Are you sure that old geniuses will not come up with some amazingly unique idea about leaving this world? To do what they could not do a thousand years ago? Are you so sure? Or do you believe in ghosts, troggs and mechanoids so much that you can guarantee that they will survive until the end of time? The offworlders also considered themselves untouchable. But we managed to deal with them without any help from you."

"The geniuses of the ancients will not take such a step. They care only about science."

"How is this not a scientific experiment?" I said, transmitting the words of Kimal Sarento, received through the intercom. My cautious pupil carefully avoided the Interrogator and the Inquisitor, not making even the slightest attempt to talk to them. "Now people know that their voluntary self-sacrifice will lead to nothing, but it is worth leaving only four forces on the third orbit, as temptation will appear. A year, two, ten. Sooner or later, one of them will get the bright idea to try and pull off such a trick. So I ask again: why do you want to destroy our world?"

"The geniuses of the ancients will not agree to

this," the Interrogator repeated, but even I could hear that his voice lacked the same confidence as before.

"You listened to the servant of the ancients, received its power, but came here. You have a proposition. Speak." The Inquisitor made no indication that he wanted to talk to me and wait for me to pull my stones out of my field. He began to broadcast and I listened to his last words as I was lying on the floor, where I collapsed, unable to resist the will of a creature with so much power. In fact, I did not hear the last words, since I was busy fighting for life, the question was repeated by Kimal Sarento when I began to move again and poured several *Heals* into myself. Damn it! Maybe Yuri was right after all. These two did exactly what they wanted. They had no limits, no brakes. If they decided to destroy Hearth, or indeed the whole world, no one would be able to stop them, ever.

"We need to restore the third orbit entirely," I wheezed, trying to get to my feet. It was going badly. The Inquisitor's words seemed to suck the soul out of me. Staggering, I nevertheless assumed a vertical position.

"It will take two forces. Chaos does not want Karina Fardi to be one of them. She is unpredictable and insane. She will become a terror and a bane to this world if she becomes one of the powers," the Interrogator declared.

"Then destroy her," I suggested. I felt extremely ill, but I couldn't show any weakness.

"We cannot. Karina Fardi has become Skron's

vessel. In order to destroy her, we will have to attract additional resources, which is unacceptable. You know what Chaos is doing. Any diversion of resources after the system has begun to destabilize will lead to a catastrophe. Apart from these two, there are no candidates in the world to occupy the third orbit. Your proposal is not viable. You must adhere to the instructions you have received. First, *Tainted Blood,* then the destruction of the two forces."

"It's time," said Kimal Sarento. "They're ready."

We had discussed at length how to get out of the situation I had been forced into. Chaos would turn me into its slave, the ancients would drive me mad and I would be taken out for good. A bleak prospect. I had two months left to accomplish everything, so it was time to write a will. But Kimal Sarento had a proposal that seemed completely crazy. It violated everything I had already learned about our world. And yet, it was entirely feasible.

"Okay, just answer one more question. What will happen to the balance if the new force appears not on the third orbit, as you planned, but on the second? Will this stabilize the system?"

"Only Fardi could reach the second orbit, but we won't let that happen. She'll destroy the world if she gets that much power."

"Why couldn't One reach that orbit?"

"Because the basis of his power is the mechanoids, the creatures of the third orbit. He will take some of their abilities, turning into an independent force, but these abilities will not be enough to ascend to the second orbit."

"Let's set this aside for now. You didn't answer: if a force appears on the second orbit, what will happen to the system?"

"It will stabilize completely. Two-three-six is the ideal ratio of forces to form a balance. But it will not happen. We will not allow Karina Fardi into the second orbit."

"So One must find a new master," I said, continuing my thought. "If the mechanoids are not strong enough, wouldn't the Abyss or Pharapho have enough strength? They can share some of their abilities with One, even while continuing to fight one another. This will not affect their confrontation in any way."

"What you're proposing is madness. Pharapho will never willingly agree to weaken himself. He will listen to neither you, nor us. None of us will be able to communicate with the Abyss — Skron banished it to a special place and does not want to share information on how to bypass his defenses."

"You gave me a deadline of three months to destroy two forces. Is this somehow connected with the fact that you no longer have the ability to contain the destabilized system? Or did you just pick a deadline out of thin air and decide to badger me?"

"You shouldn't care what our motivations are," the Inquisitor said, and I woke up on the floor once again. My nose was bleeding, and even several *Heals* didn't help my condition. I didn't have the strength to get to my feet. Nevertheless, I considered communicating with the forces of Chaos while lying down a sign of weakness, so with a groan I sat up, tucking my legs under me.

"That's not an answer. If this deadline is somehow related to your power or capabilities, that's one thing. If it's just something you came up with and it's not tied to any concrete event, I ask to be given the opportunity to communicate with the forces of the second orbit. I know how to get in touch with the Abyss. I need guarantees of immunity when I talk to Pharapho. Plus a translator, if he does not understand human language. If we act as you would like to, the planet will be doomed. Sooner or later, one of the forces will disappear, and then we will all die. There are no weaknesses in the plan I'm proposing. The system will stabilize, and you will have the opportunity to stop Karina Fardi. Deprive her of her powers. Keep her from entering the third orbit. You want that, right?"

The glance the Inquisitor exchanged with the Interrogator told me that this was not what they wanted. My words had fallen on fertile ground.

"Prove that you can communicate with the Abyss, and we can discuss the offer. Right now, it sounds like a bluff. The Abyss was banished many hundreds of years ago."

"It's done like this." I embodied the triangle I'd received from the white seraph, but the creatures of Chaos seemed not to see it. In any case, they paid no attention, continuing to hold my gaze. I took out ten essences and laid them out around the triangle. These, the two Chaos beings could see perfectly clearly. Their gazes shifted. Setting the last essence in its place, I activated the seal and disappeared from my palace. The last thing I noticed before the space acquired the usual forms of the white seraph's home were the frowning faces of the creatures of Chaos. It seemed that I had just postponed their order to destroy the watermen and undergrounders for an indefinite period.

"Greetings, human!" The white seraph appeared in his usual place. "Have you come for answers? Are you ready to pay?"

"I come with news. You sit here, unknowing. Meanwhile, the world has changed a lot in the last fifty years."

It took a long while to explain the key points about the current affairs of our world. I started with the destruction of the offworlders and lithoids, then moved on to Chaos' plans to destroy the water and earth dwellers, and ended with the order from an interactive neural network eager to wipe all life off the face of the planet.

The white seraph listened attentively, periodically asking clarifying questions.

Finally, I approached my main reason for coming: the idea of creating another second-order force in the world.

"Your story is fascinating, but I don't understand how it concerns me," the white seraph said. "Why should I give up part of my power? Don't tell me that it will help maintain the balance. You can destroy two more forces, and balance will be restored. Not as strong as before, but it will last for the next few thousand years. And then the weapons of the ancients will fizzle out. They, too, have a limited lifespan. Chaos knows it. I know it. Now you know it, too. Two thousand years, and the world will not need saving."

"You shouldn't pose such rhetorical questions at me," I grinned. 'My task was to demonstrate to the Interrogator and the Inquisitor the possibility of communicating with the Abyss. Chaos is responsible for the balance, so direct all your indignation at them. When I return, they will provide me with the opportunity to communicate with Pharapho. I'll go and warn your sworn enemy that for him too, the new division of power awaits. Then I'll pass Chaos's offer on to you and wash my hands of the whole situation."

"So you decided to act as a mediator? Why?"

"Because I don't like what I see going on around me. Some want me to destroy two forces, and for that they sent a creature touched by Chaos. The others want to wipe all life off the face of the planet, because all of it is foreign to this world. Both sides have issued some pretty hefty threats, so I'm trying to respond as best as I can."

"*Tainted Blood* will close your path to the ancient's creations," the white seraph said, confirming my suspicions. "And you will become a slave to Chaos. Weak-willed, not daring to contradict any of its whims."

"Is there an alternative? How can I avoid both?"

"The questions have begun, human, but I still don't see any payment."

"What do you think about this?" I held out my open palm, flaunting the guard essence. For the first time during the conversation, the white seraph twitched, the essence flew up from my palm, but I was quick, managing to intercept it before it flew away towards the Abyss vessel.

"It's not that simple," I had to send the essence back to my inventory, as it was trying to break free from my clenched palm and jump into the hands of its creator. "You used to set a price. You gave me crumbs of information and claimed that these crumbs were worth a whole mountain of entities. But in fact, it always turned out that I could have gotten the information I received from you elsewhere for a much more reasonable price. I don't like that you use me as a free way to restore your strength. Either we continue to work on mutually beneficial terms, when you don't limit yourself to two or three phrases, or today is the last time I come to you for answers. It's easier for me to turn to the Fog Stalker. There I always get a clear and complete answer. I'll repeat once again: how can I avoid the wrath of the ancient device and not fall into the slavery of Chaos? You already know my offer."

"You are quickly becoming impudent, human." I heard discontent in its voice. "Do not forget that you are merely an insect who is only here because of my will. If I will it otherwise, you will never enter here again!"

"It's funny. I threaten to never come here again, and you threaten to never let me in again. It feels like we are speaking completely different languages and do not understand each other. Good, Abyss. Since this is your decision — send me back. So that you clearly understand the seriousness of my intentions, here is your key. Goodbye!"

I pulled out the triangle and carefully placed it on the floor. I wouldn't want the object to break just because we were bickering.

The space around me began to shimmer, as if the Abyss was really sending me back, but I remained silent. Even if I were thrown ack into the main world now, I still knew a surefire way to meet the white seraph again. So, in fact, I was only risking time. The Abyss was risking much more — it could lose a stable channel for receiving essences. I suppose it was the latter that prevented the alien force from throwing me out of its world.

The surrounding space regained density, returning me back to the white seraph. Valevsky — one, Abyss — zero.

"There is another way." The white seraph's voice was filled with malice. "I can make it so that you never leave here. Ever."

"Not a huge problem for me either," I shrugged. "The echoes of Chaos sent me here. If I don't come back, expect guests. Whether you kill me or just detain me is not that important. They'll finish me off in two months anyway, unless you tell me how to avoid it. So now or later — it's all the same. I'm not sure what they'll do to you, though. Perhaps you've occupied the second orbit for a bit too long? Are you sure that you won't be removed and the same mechanoids won't be put in your place? In that case, it will be much easier to create a new force of the second orbit through One."

"The rifts will disappear and the world will be filled with the fog of Pharapho!"

"Which won't change our world at all. People used to go into the depths, but now they'll start plunging into the fog. Rift resources will disappear, but artifacts, fogspawn resources, altars, and cutting stones will appear. Mithril, for that matter, won't be so rare. Everything has its silver lining, you just need to find it. So either kill me, or leave me alone, or send me back. Or, if you've finally woken up to the voice of reason, let's negotiate. I need information, but I won't pay you for it anymore."

"The only way to avoid becoming a slave to Chaos and escape the influence of the ancients is to gain the power of the ancients."

"I already have *Author*."

"The skill is incomplete. You need the entire dictionary. Once you get it, you will become a bearer of knowledge, and the device called the sixth-generation interactive neural network will not be able to touch you. Its internal protocols will not allow it. As for Chaos, it will not be able to do anything to a being that has the complete *Author* dictionary. At least, not without diverting significant power."

"How do I get the full dictionary?" I opened my palm, and the guard's essence flew away towards the white seraph. I'd received the information and made my payment.

"You will need five sources," the Abyss answered after a pause. "Keep in mind that my information has a fifty-year lag. Of the locations available to you, three sources were in the Temple of Skron. One was hidden in the treasury of the emperors of the Kaliman and Shurghan empires, the Citadel, the Valdez and Gourfan clans, and in the storerooms of Padishah Bayazid the Second. Several more sources are located, one in each of the four caches of the first emperor. The coordinates for each of them belong to a separate board. These are all the places you can reach. The others are inaccessible to you. For example, three sources are with those you call the geniuses of the ancients. But they will not talk to you, even under the protection of Chaos. They are no longer human."

I pulled out another guard essence and sent it toward the Abyss.

"Another question. I think you'll find this topic interesting. As I said earlier, a vessel of Skron has appeared in our world. How can it be destroyed?"

As I had expected, the topic piqued the white seraph's interest. It shifted once more.

"How long is the vessel able to maintain control?"

"Right now it's fifteen minutes, but every day this time increases by a few seconds. Soon the vessel will become completely independent, and then it will declare its rights to become one of the forces of the third orbit."

"Chaos will not allow it!"

"If Skron's vessel gains power, who will stop it? Chaos has no such authority. All his powers are spent on maintaining the system in a stable state, and he cannot be distracted by fighting the vessel. I have plenty of time to be distracted. But I need information."

"In order to destroy the vessel, you need to destroy it in its active state. Not just destroy it, but erase it with a weapon of Light or Chaos of comparable strength."

"In its active state? In which the vessel exudes level 100 darkness? It will destroy me as soon as I get close enough to strike."

"It will destroy you," the seraph agreed. "However, if you adapt to this level of darkness, the darkness generated by the vessel will be safe for you."

"I need details on this adaptation. How can I speed up the process?" I pulled out the essence of the warden and several rapses. Everything disappeared into the Abyss' greedy maw.

"First, you must create a level one hundred rift. Keep in mind that there will be no living creature left within a hundred kilometers of this rift. At level eighty-five, a type of filth appears that absorbs life force in all areas accessible to it. In order to increase the rift level, you will need a special device. The problem is that it is located in a rift near the Black Mountain. A level seventy-one rift.

You will have to destroy the Riftmaster to get the device."

"And start growing a new rift," I said. "Will this require some resources? Time frame?"

"No resources required. The time frame: one hour per rift level."

"So the main issue is adapting to the dark aura. How can I do it?"

"Healing magic. Adaptation is a change in the body. Its adaptation to the surrounding conditions. However, standard treatment will not help you cope with the influence of darkness. You will die. You must find a unique support stone. The one that was given to the man known as the first emperor of the light lands."

"And currently, this stone is…where?"

The Abyss remained silent, and I had to once again dig into my inventory, pulling out several dozen simple essences.

"This is the price, including for my current question. Where is the stone?"

"Inlaid into the Pope's scepter as a symbol of purity. Your time is up, human. Take the access key. I believe we have discussed everything we have to discuss."

"Except for one thing. Creating a third force. What should I tell Chaos? What's your decision?"

"It all depends on what I get in the end. Chaos knows what I need. The question is, will it agree to it? I'm not saying no, but I can't yet say yes either."

The triangle appeared in front of me, and as soon as it was in my hands, the space floated, transforming into Hearth's main hall. The Interrogator and the Inquisitor were already sitting in their chairs, but with my appearance they stood up and in the blink of an eye were next to each other. Something like teleportation without shimmering surfaces. Or superhuman speed.

"You were in the Abyss," the Interrogator said.

"Didn't I tell you?" Communicating with the Chaos beings was tedious, but necessary. "I have the ability to communicate with this force, despite the fact that Skron banished it from our reality. The Abyss is not against the appearance of a third force of the second orbit in our world, the only question is what it will receive in turn. As I was told, you know what it needs. Then it's a matter of agreements. Have you already spoken to Pharapho?"

"Chaos has no way to communicate directly with representatives of the forces. You will have to go to the Black Mountain."

"I'll be on my way, as soon as you relieve me of the obligation to destroy the two forces and stop the Wave. I don't need *Tainted Blood.*"

"The Wave cannot be stopped otherwise. In two weeks it will reach the Kaliman Empire. Either these lands will fall under the onslaught of the Wave, or you will stop it and you will have *Tainted Blood.* There is no other option and there will be no other. You must become stronger to fight the vessel of Skron. From now on, this is your new fee for calling the Inquisitor."

I looked at the retreating thugs and diligently

suppressed my treacherous thoughts.

Maybe the sixth-generation interactive neural network was right after all and our world should be destroyed.

Chapter 9

THERE WAS A CLICK of the door lock and the owner of the office entered the room, lost in thought.

"Hello again, Father Urg." I greeted him as he entered, settling on the guest sofa by the wall. The way he jumped made me happy. He had clearly not expected to see me in his office at all. I had to hand it to him, though — he pulled himself together quite quickly.

"Max? How did you get in here?"

"I need one of the ancient tomes, Father Urg," I said, ignoring the question. "It's called the Basic Dictionary. This book is extremely important to me. Without it, I won't be able to negotiate with the Temple of Skron."

"No, Max. We agreed — first you'll carry out your part of the deal, then you'll receive your payment."

"And yet I will have to insist, Father Urg," I sighed. "I am ready to exchange it for something you need. What do you say about this mountain of artifacts?"

I dumped nearly everything I had obtained so far on the floor. Useless or barely usable devices. Sure, some of them could be used in the production of various sets, but, to be honest, they otherwise weren't particularly impressive. And you'd need a recipe and other materials, anyway. It was something I had no desire to do.

However, my generosity went unappreciated. Father Urg only glanced at the items and shook his head. He, too, knew how to understand artifacts and knew that there was nothing of value there.

"These are all trinkets, Max. They could be bought or sold anywhere. If you want the book before you get me the upgrade device, you're going to have to work for it. Here you go."

Father Urg approached his desk, pressed a few buttons, and a secret cache opened, containing several papers. The cleric handed me one of them, taking the effort to actually walk to the sofa and hand it to me. Ten names, most of which were unfamiliar to me. I had only met two people from this list in my life, and even then only in passing. I even had to look in my notebook to refresh my memory of our encounters. One of them had participated in the tournament that resulted in the appearance of the Pharapho fog, the other was introduced to me at one of the events. An industrialist involved in wood processing. His father also supplied him with materials, I remembered something like that. My brother was always complaining that the price of wood was dropping impossibly low, but there was no other way out but to sell to this man. He had a monopoly across all the southern regions of the Zarak Empire.

"What is this?"

"These are your targets. Corrupt officials, bribe takers, moralizing fanatics — that's who they are. Beasts in human skin. My personal list of enemies, if you like. Although how could I even call them enemies? They are small fry that I'm too lazy to spend effort on. However, sooner or later, the effort will have to be made. You destroyed all my fighters who were capable of ridding the world of this scum. Bring me their heads and you will receive the book. This is the only way, Max."

"You do understand that I need the book to implement your plan?"

"We should have discussed this before signing the agreement. You yourself insisted that everything be clearly spelled out. Who does what, who gets what. Do you intend to break this agreement? Please pay a decent price, and don't just offer me useless junk."

"You want to use my hands to solve your problems?" Anger began to boil in my chest.

"Ours, Max. These are our shared problems. The ten people listed here have caused more harm to the Zarak Empire than the invasion of the lithoids."

"Those are just words, Father Urg."

"Why just words? I wasn't prepared for your timely arrival, so I didn't take the files with me. They're in the treasury. Would you like to go down there again?"

"Let's go back down," I agreed. Father Urg stood up from the table, ready to leave the office, but I remained seated, actively using the *Author* skill. Twenty-five words were required to open a portal. Always the same. Another five to indicate a specific point on my map. A total of thirty words. Mentally cursing myself for not having thought of this earlier, I began to form the twenty-five-word sentence to throw into the quick access slot. This would speed my portal-forming ability up by several orders of magnitude.

"Coming?" Father Urg asked. He stopped at the door and looked back at me, not understanding why I was making no move to get up from the couch. Finally, having mastered the basic structure (I definitely need practice in finding the right words), I began adding the correct description of the treasury coordinates. Five words weren't enough — they were insufficient to accurately indicate the exact location I needed. I only calmed down after a green check mark appeared on the section of the map hanging before my eyes. The treasury required another ten words, so this now thirty-five-word sentence went into my quick access slot. That way I'd be able to peruse Father Urg's stash at my leisure. If he hadn't hidden everything in another secret niche by then...

Wait!

What was I thinking?! There was a treasury at the Citadel! I'd been there! It was on my map too! I just had to make a few changes and...There it was!

"Max?" Father Urg became concerned and even walked over to stand next to me, confused as to why I had suddenly become a statue. Instead of answering, I activated a new sentence, and a bloody portal appeared a step away from me. Now Father Urg was thoroughly horrified. The way he jumped away from the portal demonstrated not only good physical fitness, but also the fact that he knew very well who used such portals. My grandfather had somehow communicated this to him. Or there was something written about such portals somewhere. In any case, I had new questions for Father Urg, one of which I posed immediately:

"Do you have anything you want to explain, Father Urg? I have a strong feeling that you know perfectly well what this is."

"Is this your doing?" he asked. He jumped to the far side of the wall and pulled out some strange artifact that formed a shimmering protective field around him. The old man did not use magic stones, but this was not necessary for someone who got by just fine with artifacts alone.

"There was a reason I said I needed that book. It allows those with the appropriate skill to form portals. I have the skill. I also have the dictionary needed to open portals. But to complete the task,

I need more. Much more. And now we are going to the place where I plan to get one of these books."

"Where does this portal lead?" Father Urg gradually came to his senses. The protective dome disappeared, and he warily approached my creation, examining it from all sides.

"First, I need an answer. You know about these bloody looking portals firsthand. You've seen them before. When?"

"About fifteen years ago, a man came to see me and stepped through a portal just like that," Father Urg answered reluctantly. "He was looking for the caches of the first emperor and he was not very happy that I had found one. He took almost everything, leaving me with only crumbs. A book, a stone, and a few other essentially useless things. When he left, the man warned me to stop my search. Otherwise, the next red portal would be the last thing I'd see. As a lesson for what I had done, he showed me what true pain was. I had never experienced anything like that. It was monstrous. Then the man disappeared, as did his portal. Over the past fifteen years, much has been erased from my memory, but not the feelings I experienced that day.

"The man who came to you was my grandfather. The grandson of the first emperor of the light lands. He will not come again — I was forced to kill him."

"So then, you are one of the heirs?"

"One in a large pool of heirs, as it turns out. Grandfather tried his best to nurture his replacements and reject the bad material. Strange, I thought that of all people, you would know this. With your spies. As for the portal, it leads to the treasury. I am too lazy to go. It's easier this way. No need to frown so much, Father Urg. The portal does not lead to your treasury. Although we will definitely go there too."

"If it leads to a treasury, but not the Fortress', then whose?" He was taken aback. I grinned maliciously, and Father Urg's eyes widened. He understood instantly. "It cannot be!"

"Don't you want to go visit your future possessions?" I asked. "If the answer is yes, then give me your hand, Father Urg. Only two can pass through the portal."

"There must be some sort of defense system there," the old man frowned. "There must be."

"Even if there is, even if the entire Citadel goes crazy, we'll have enough time to find everything I need. A *Dictionary* of some sort. It's a priority. If you find something else you like in the process, don't hold back. In the end, if we succeed, you'll get unlimited access to the treasury."

"As will you, although everything there belongs to the Church of the Light. Can I enter the portal myself, alone?"

"Better to hold hands first. Ready?"

He extended his hand to me without hesitation. Squeezing his hand, which turned out to be surprisingly strong, I stepped into the portal. Space blurred for a moment and took shape in absolute darkness. A moment later, the mithril armor activated the Gourfan crystal on my head like an invisible diadem. Almost nothing had changed since my last visit to this place, except that the doors were closed. Without saying a word, Father Urg and I listened — no sirens, warnings or anything of the sort. If panic had arisen somewhere, it had not yet reached us.

"We'll split up. Remember, I'm looking for a book," I warned. A light crystal lit up in Father Urg's hand and the old man walked between the shelves, carefully assessing the contents. I went in the opposite direction. From what I had begun to understand about *Author* it was possible to create some special sentence of several dozen words so that the book I was looking for would jump into my hands, but there were certain problems with this. In fact, I needed not only a dictionary with new words, but also a list of the most commonly used sentences. Moreover, the latter, as it seemed to me, was of much higher priority than the dictionary itself.

Resources, gold and elixirs of all sorts, some of which had to be run through *Analyze* to understand their value. It's unlikely that the Citadel would store weak artifacts in its vault. And there were quite a few, in fact — scrolls, plates for crafting, I even found two uninitiated notebooks. After thinking about it, I decided to get my hands on one. I needed insurance in case something happened to me or Kimal Sarento. I'd give it to Eleanore to sequester away in our treasury. Incidentally, I'd need to make a treasury within the treasury, where I'd store my most valuable items.

"This is what you were looking for." Father Urg had found the book, which was no surprise. Although I could hardly call what he handed over a "book." It was some kind of plate with a glass screen. *Analyze* showed that the artifact was called the *Level Zero Dictionary*. Not a book in the usual sense — some kind of information transfer device. Closing my eyes, I remembered seeing a similar plate among the artifacts I had already encountered. I'd definitely need to go back for it.

"How does it work?"

"I haven't a clue," Father Urg answered honestly. "Everything we've gotten, we've identified using artifacts. It is impossible to activate or use the device in any way. If I'd known from the start that the artifact was so dear to you, the trade would have been completely different."

"When we started bargaining, I myself had no idea what I needed. New knowledge comes in every day. Wait a minute though, I've seen another device like this."

Taking the plate, I returned to the shelves I had already passed. Indeed, there was a similar device on one of them. But what *Analyze* revealed did not make me happy. Instead of *Dictionary*, I received a *Poetry Collection* of the ancients. I'd found something similar in one of our libraries, except on paper, so I was not particularly happy with that find. Nevertheless, this artifact also went to my storage. When I figured out how to make it work, I would return to Hearth and give it to my girls. Alia or Naira probably liked poetry. If they didn't, there is always Eleanore. She would definitely not refuse such a gift.

"Max, I don't mean to frighten you, but I think it's time for us to get out of here," Father Urg said when he heard a strange noise. Someone was banging on the door. So far, to no avail.

"I hope you saw everything you wanted to see," I said and activated the portal back to his office. With my pre-set portal sentence, it was as quick as a breeze. Father Urg brought a whole bag of objects with him and simply shrugged his shoulders at my silent question of why he needed all this. I did not object and offered him my hand. A moment later, the space blurred, and the last thing I heard was a loud click and the booming voice of one of the commanders ordering the thieves to be captured. The treasury had a defense system after all. Good to know for the future. Father Urg, from what I understood, had a similar defense system.

"How quickly does the portal disappear?" He asked.

"A few seconds."

"Could you portal somewhere and then back? We need to know whether the commander saw the red flicker or not."

It was a fair point, considering the fact that I had opened a portal to the central hall in Hearth. This time, neither the Inquisitor nor the Interrogator even twitched. A few moments later, I found myself again in the office of the head of the Church of the Zarak Empire.

"Instantly, as soon as we pass through. No residual light remains. Nor any traces. Not a bad acquisition, Max. One might even say, quite excellent. However, I would like to ask you to descend with me into the treasury on your own two feet. I don't want to cause a stir in the Fortress."

"I can wait for you here. Why would anyone know that I am in the Fortress?"

"That's also an option," he agreed. "Although I'd rather not have to travel down to the treasury at all. Ten people, Max, just ten people. Kill them, and the book will be yours."

"So it's all in the book?"

"The title speaks for itself. It's unlikely that the ancients would have put a dictionary on a useless piece of metal. The only question is — how to use it? But that will be your headache, not mine."

"So everything you took from the Citadel's treasury isn't enough for you?" I was amazed at his avarice.

"Max, listen to yourself! We only took objects that could be replicated. People who poison the air with their mere presence cannot stand to live any longer. If they are gone, Hearth will also be able to breath more freely. If I told you that some of these men are Count Vyazemsky's advisers who incited him to take certain actions, would this affect your consent? Killing these ten men will be beneficial to everyone!"

"No, Father Urg. I will not become your messenger. You have many people, you can easily solve your problems on your own. And there is no need to involve my city here. However, I will definitely remember in the future that you did not meet me halfway when I needed help. Here's your paper. Find someone more complaisant."

The portal back to Hearth opened just a few moments later. Father Urg made no move to stop me, staying true to a logic known only by him. The Skron-damned rogue and scoundrel!

I could be as indignant as I wanted, but it wouldn't help anything. Returning to my office, I pulled out the artifact with the romantic poems. Information. I urgently need information on how to activate it. The artifact did not respond to mental commands or to being transferred to the workspace. There were no buttons or icons on it. Nothing at all. Just a black panel with a mirrored screen.

"May I?" Kimal Sarento became interested in my find. After turning it over in his hands and for some reason holding it up flat against his eyeline, he began to move it along the glass, and suddenly it began to emit light.

"A touch screen," the man explained, noticing my puzzled look. "It works by touching, but you need to know what to touch. To open it, you need to move your finger in the right sequence of straight lines. A rather rare artifact. From before the other forces entered our world."

"How do you know the sequence?"

"This, my dumbfounded mentor, is as easy as pie. Look — do you see the trace? Many people have touched this object over the past thousand years, but all their prints are separate. But here, you see a clear line. Whoever used this artifact before must have had hygiene issues. Greasy fingers leave traces, and if you know that such artifacts are activated by a sequence of straight lines, there are no problems. It is worse when the entrance requires entering some kind of digital password. I have seen such artifacts in my life too. It is almost impossible to repeat them based on the traces. So, what is this? Mentor, are you serious? Tell me that you simply didn't know what this book contained? That you did not go over it first with *Analyze*?'

"I wanted to give it to the girls," I confessed, blushing.

"But this certainly wasn't the book you plied the good Father Urg for?" Kimal Sarento asked.

"Father Urg refused to provide his book until all the terms of the agreement were met."

"Which, I remind you just in case, my forgetful mentor, you yourself ordered to be drawn up. Although certain pupils of yours strongly disagreed with such an agreement, they did not dare to challenge it. For the wisdom and experience of the great Archduke Valevsky are known..."

"Enough!" I barked. "We were in the Citadel's treasury."

"What did you take?"

"I took this book. As well as this one. One that's useful," I pulled out the dictionary and put it on the table.

"Excellent, at least we will see some good from

your hopping all over the place. Come on, my time-wasting mentor, don't keep me in suspense. What else did you take from the treasury? You don't mean to tell me that you risked your head just for two ancient artifacts?"

The answer was written on my face, as Kimal Sarento rolled his eyes and sighed heavily. I decided to keep quiet about the fact that I had taken a couple more notebooks.

"And I decided to spend my best years on this man! How?! Tell me, my out-of-touch mentor, how could you not pocket anything? Wait. You said that 'we' were in the treasury? Not 'I was'?"

"Yes, Father Urg came along."

"Who, unlike one naive young man from Zarak, pulled out a whole bag of loot from the treasury, right? Great Light, mentor! You can't be so naive! Did you check — did they remove all the evidence? Did our partner leave some insignificant trifle by which the commanders could guess who was cunning enough to infiltrate their holy of holies? I hope you were watching our cunning old man's every move?"

"We split up..."

I felt I couldn't turn any redder, but I was wrong. Acting on the dictates of my soul and wanting to quickly get the artifact, I did not think about the consequences. About the fact that Father Urg could turn this little venture to his own advantage.

"What did the high priest want from you? He wanted something, right? You came, demanded the book, and he refused you, but offered you something in return. The old man doesn't do things any other way."

"He needs ten people killed."

"There it is," Kimal Sarento grinned. "The sly fox made his move again. Ten people. Probably some hardened criminals. I'm sure Father Urg even showed the files on them to prove their dirty deeds."

"He did." I said. "I wanted to open a portal to the treasury where these files were, but instead of the Fortress we ended up in the Citadel. I can't say it was an accident... But why does he need me? He has plenty of his own fighters who are capable of carrying out this task."

"That's exactly why, my slow-witted mentor. The first ten are just a taste. There's really a long list of these bastards. And I don't even need to know their names, half of the Zarak Empire could be among them, myself included. But after the first ten, there will be a second batch. The same, but you will no longer be so discerning. Sure, you'll read a couple of case files, you'll be convinced they all deserve death and you'll do whatever the old man tells you. Then there will be another list. And another. And these lists will include those who are simply inconvenient to him. Those who crossed him, looked at him funny, or didn't bow low enough. But you will no longer be able to refuse. You'll grow accustomed to it. That is how they become loyal watchdogs, fulfilling any whim of their master. The only thing you did right during today's campaign was to refuse to fulfill the whim of our temporary ally."

"Temporary?"

"Now I am one hundred percent certain of it. Once he has become pope, Father Urg will try to forget his past. He will not take revenge, he remembers gratitude, but we will not get any support from him. On the contrary, he will definitely recall a couple of our old sins. The churchmen love to do this. Can you unlock it yourself?"

The abrupt change in the conversation showed that Kimal Sarento no longer wanted to discuss Father Urg and my expedition. If representatives of the Citadel came to all, since the conniving old man left some hint in the treasury about who came to them, we would think about how to defend ourselves. For now, it was pointless. I wouldn't be able to portal back to the treasury a second time. There would most certainly be guards posted everywhere.

I tilted the book, held it up to the light and saw many prints. Over a thousand years, many people had handled this artifact, and, to my great advantage, no one had thought to wipe the book. Only brush off the dust. I saw the prints immediately, forming a sequence of lines. The screen lit up, and new messages immediately appeared in front of me:

Synchable device discovered.
Synch?

The functionality of the ancients didn't fail us

— while the book with poems was intended purely for entertainment, the dictionary could be loaded into my skill for further inspection. After reading and accepting several new notifications, I grinned to myself — my operable vocabulary had just increased significantly. But most importantly, next to the list of available words, another field appeared: *Universal Phrases.* Constructions similar to the quick access slot. Although the constructions themselves were not the most useful. How could creating a chair from available materials be useful? Or a desk? A pencil? Paper? Although you could make an argument for the paper — it was a very handy and also expensive commodity in our world. The elementary dictionary, as I understood, was good for those who had just started studying the *Author* skill. Children who were first introduced to this skill. Well, I'd have to be a child. I needed to collect four more books so that the interactive neural network would forget its threats and I could add three more volumes to my collection. Looking at Kimal Sarento, who was slowly scrolling through the list of words in the book, I began to form a new sentence.

I needed a teleport to the Temple of Skron. I figured the place where Four had interrogated me would be perfect for having a discussion with One. It was time to find out what the mechanoid that had become one of the main forces in our world really wanted, and how deep Karina Fardi had sunk her teeth in.

Chapter 10

THE ROOM WHERE I HAD ONCE MET with the servants of the Temple of Skron had changed little. The main difference from the last time was that it was empty now. The room was used for negotiations, and the mechanical creations currently had no important meetings scheduled. Although I felt some presence there in the vibrations in the floor. I hadn't felt these before. From the situation in the Citadel's treasury, I surmised that this was One's way of notifying his subjects of unauthorized entry, so I had to hurry. You never know when Karina Fardi would show up to expel the intruder from the depths of her accomplice.

Sitting down in the guest chair, I said,

"Greetings, One. No need to cause an unnecessary stir. I am Archduke Valevsky and I have come here to talk to you. Preferably without witnesses. To pique your interest, I will tell you the topic of the conversation: making you one of the great powers of our world. And yes, I have already discussed this issue with the Interrogator and the Inquisitor. They agree with my arguments and proposals. It remains to be seen whether you will agree as well."

The vibration stopped. I was right — it had been some sort of early alarm system. Considering that the entire dark pyramid comprised the body of One, its internal security system must be perfect. I was surprised that I hadn't just been squished or suffocated by toxic gas.

However, apart from the disappearance of the vibration, nothing happened for a long time. I did not hear One's thunderous voice, no notification appeared before my eyes, and no screen popped up through which the mechanoid could communicate with me. I had begun to suspect that he had sent messengers for Karina Fardi and was simply stalling for time, so just in case I rose from my chair and stood in the center of the room, ready for the door to open in any direction and for Skron's vessel to enter the room. When one of the panels moved aside, I had to make a lot of effort not to manifest a portal and flee.

One of the misty temple servants appeared in the doorway and the passage closed. It was definitely not One, as he was still the pyramid in his entirety. So it was another who had decided to take action and destroy me for the common good. I'd been the one to end Seven's life, so it was definitely not him. Or it could be a new Seven. Who knew the naming conventions of the Temple of Skron? Definitely not me.

He approached the table and sat down in the center chair, gesturing for me to take the seat opposite. It made no response to my vigilant stance. I accepted the invitation, and as soon as I was seated, he spoke.

"I am Three. One has instructed me to act as his voice before you. Everything I say henceforth are One's words, not mine. Everything you say will reach One immediately."

"Why can't I communicate with him directly?"

"One does not have access to the usual methods of communication. Is there something that bothers you?"

"The presence of an intermediary." I didn't mince my words. "I know that beings with names from Two to Seven have decided to destroy me. Seven even took direct action to end my life. How do I know that you are truly expressing the will of the dark pyramid, and not trying to play your own game, Three? Can you give me any guarantee?"

"There is no humanly comprehensible way to confirm the fact that I am speaking now. One. You must simply believe it, Archduke Valevsky. As for Seven and his antics, that will also be a topic of conversation. I know that you have removed the essence of the Seven. I want it back."

"Antics?" I was surprised. "Since when is attempted murder considered an antics? However, I did not come here to play with words and choose the best euphemism for what happened. I came here with an offer, One. I know that you want to become a third-orbital force. As does Karina Fardi. Chaos does not want to see her take that throne. She is dangerous. Unpredictable. Harsh. But Chaos cannot give you the opportunity to rise alone — seven forces in the third orbit will upset the precarious balance that has been achieved so far. But then I appeared and offered something that the two beings sitting beside my throne were quite fond of. You will be offered as a force, and not in the third, but the second orbit."

"That's impossible," One answered a bit too quickly. The news had hooked him, but he had an accurate estimation of his own power. "Skron's vessel could ascend to the second orbit, but not me."

"I know of a mechanism that could elevate you. It is known that you planned to use the mechanoids to obtain part of their power. This will not be enough to occupy the second orbit. However, there is another way. The Abyss and Pharapho."

"The path to the Abyss was lost centuries ago, when Skron expelled it from our world."

"I am aware. However, the possibility of communicating with the Abyss exists, and I have found this pathway. It does not categorically reject my idea, it is only a question of finding an agreement with Chaos. The Abyss needs something, Chaos can give it, so we must negotiate. Now I need to talk to Pharapho but before I go to him, I would like to talk to the main interested party. Are you interested in the plan I am trying to manifest? Does One want to become a second-orbital power?"

"What do you stand to gain?"

"I have many reasons to want this. Starting with the fact that I intend to get rich off this scam, due to the fact that my enemies will be destroyed."

"Are you speaking of Karina Fardi?"

"Has One grown so close to her that he wishes to protect her?"

"Karina Fardi is a vessel of Skron. I have no way to contradict her will. I don't agree with much of what this girl does, so I won't feel sorry if she ends up gone. There's no place for mad people like her in this world. However, you need to state all your reasons and demands. I won't sign up for life-long servitude."

"Do you think I have the ability to blackmail the power of the second orbit? Thank you, of course, for flattering my humble person, but no, that's not within my power. Nevertheless, I can formulate demands: I want peace. I want a normal trade flow. I want my city to become a profitable trade hub between the dark and light worlds. I want to receive new devices for my city and, more importantly, to manage them myself, without giving up control to third parties. And naturally, I want gold, resources, artifacts and other things that have accumulated in the bins of the Temple of Skron over many centuries. Having become a power of the second orbit, you will not need this, while it will be very useful for an individual and his city to get their hands on such riches. I want to have preferential rights to trade and to use the power that you receive. Nothing extraordinary or impossible. No eternal servitude. Although we have a few more points to discuss. Karina Fardi is one of them. I will need help in destroying her. No, not help — your failure to participate in her defense. This is a battle between me and her. The power of the second orbit must not interfere. This is a mandatory condition, even if the Skron vessel comes to you and demands that you take her side. You must come up with a reasonable justification for why you will not do so."

"Reasonable? What do you mean by that?"

"Whatever will make it so that Karina Fardi won't turn her full wrath on you. She may do just that. I understand the girl is quite hot tempered."

"You killed her father. She knows that your order sent him to the stake. She intends to avenge him, and only your proximity to the Interrogator protects you from her ire."

"I had to take this step in the hope that she would lose her mind and come to the Citadel for revenge. Unfortunately, reason is winning so far. Never mind, I still have many ideas on how to get her guard down. However, I really don't want the Temple of Skron to become a party in this conflict."

"Despite the fact that Seven tried to destroy you?"

"Do you have full control over all your subordinates? Something tells me that they are endowed with free will. Seven tried to play his game and lost. He is no more. As is his essence — I gave it to the Defender of Hearth. It made him stronger and more independent. If you intended to get it back, I am sorry to disappoint you."

"So Karina Fardi, and that's all? You're not interested in anything else?"

"Gold, resources, artifacts, devices. We can't forget about those. But I don't foresee that being a problem for the all-powerful being that you will become. Although, I'll have to ask for a few of these items up front. They will make my battle against Skron's vessel that much easier."

"That is what I thought. You didn't come here to offer me a place in the second orbit. You came here to wag your silver tongue and get exactly what you want!"

"You are perfectly capable of calling up the Interrogator and asking him personally about my proposal. He will confirm my every word. I will not call him — I still have to pay the price for calling the Inquisitor. Do you know what they wanted before? For me to destroy the watermen and the undergrounders. Four forces in the third orbit could create enough stability for the system to not need additional forces. Neither you nor Karina Fardi would ever get what they wanted."

"But you didn't carry out their order. Why not?"

"Because if I do that, the destruction of any of the remaining four forces will entail the destruction of the planet. I know that too. I proposed the idea of raising you to the second orbit to Chaos, got his consent, talked to the Abyss, and am going to Pharapho. Do you think I did all this just to get your device for modernizing people? And by the way, I do need that device."

"Why?" One seemed taken aback, if such a thing could even be applied to the mechanoid race.

"I'm not asking why you want to become one of the great powers of our world, am I? What drives you? The thirst for strength, power, might? What difference does it make to me? Same with the device — I have personal reasons for that. At the very beginning of our conversation, you said that I would have to believe that One is talking to me. So you'll have to believe that I want to make what I just said a reality — to make you a force of the second orbit. But for me to start working on this project, I'll need a mechanism for modernizing people from you, as well as artifacts called '*Diction-aries*.' You don't even need to give them to me — just show me that they exist. I want to hold them in my hands, make sure that you really have them, and when I've done everything I said, you'll include them in the payment for my services."

"So artifacts as well?"

"Just assure me of their existence. And before you ask, in this instance, I won't take your word for it. I need to see for myself that they are exactly what I need. You managed to activate them, right? Kimal Sarento said that it was the Temple of Skron that taught him how to work with ancient arti-facts."

"The artifacts are active, we will input the

code. However, it's not that simple, Archduke Valevsky. You're introducing a huge amount of entropy into our world. What do you need these devices for? We've studied them — there's nothing useful in them. Just words. Just sentences. In the hundreds of years I've had them, we've come no closer to understanding what they are. Do you know how to use these dictionaries?"

"I know what they are." I didn't deny the fact, and pulled out the device I had stolen from the Citadel from the artifact storage. "In order to use it, you need a special skill. Only humans can possess it."

"Demonstrate. I wish to see the result."

"Of course," I said and opened a portal to Hearth. "The sentences written in the book allow you to control the space in a certain way. For example, you can open portals. You can form objects."

Indicating the table where Three was sitting as the source material, I activated one of the standard sentences, and a crooked chair appeared next to me. Compared to the chairs I was sitting on, it looked like complete squalor, but it was not a question of beauty, but of transformation and further creation.

"And all this can be realized with the help of such books?" There was not even a hint of emotion in One's voice.

"Books plus the *Author* skill. The Abyss informed me that fifty years ago, the Temple of Skron had three Dictionaries of different levels in its arsenal. I do not demand that these books be given to me for my full and unmitigated use now. This will be the reward for what I am about to do. But I would like to ensure from the get-go that these truly are the devices I need."

"Do you always need resources to transform matter?"

"You are already fully aware of all the sentences the books contain. Look at them — first you need to indicate the source, then describe the result. The more precise the indication, the better the result."

"How does the transformation occur? I don't understand."

"I have already given the answer — the *Author* skill. Available only to people who meet certain requirements. The exact requirements are classified information. I have already revealed more than I should have. I am counting on your adequacy in keeping information secret. So, One. It seems to me that I have stayed too long as your guest. Let's return to my question once again — are you interested in this second-orbit business? Do you want to gain power? Does it make sense for me to continue working on this issue with Chaos, the Abyss and Pharapho? If so, you know my main requirements. A mechanism for upgrading people here and now, the ability to evaluate *Dictionaries* here and now, be ready to pay well for the end result in gold, resources, devices and artifacts, not interfere in our confrontation with Karina Fardi. After receiving power, you must not forget about Hearth and you must work mainly through me. I have no other requirements and, in my humble opinion, this is a pittance compared to what you will receive in the end. The power of the Abyss and Pharapho."

"I still don't understand what you'll get out of this." One wouldn't let this point go. "Everything you listed is trifles. Everything that you could have gotten without any particular difficulty anyway."

"I have stated my motives. Whether you believe me or not is your decision."

"I need time to consider your proposal. To discuss it. To weigh the pros and cons. To analyze your involvement and motives. To call the Interrogator and discuss the issue with him. Hear his version. All this cannot be done in a couple of hours, Archduke Valevsky, and you must understand this. We will meet in a couple of months."

"As you wish," I said, shrugging my shoulders. "In two months I must give Chaos the result. Either agree on your participation, or destroy the two forces. Unlike you, I do not have time. As I said — Chaos wants to establish a balance of power, using me as its hands."

"You won't be able to destroy the watermen and the undergrounders. You don't have the resources for that. Compared to the lithoids, they are on an entirely different level."

"That's why I'll have *Tainted Blood* in a week. It shouldn't do any harm to reveal that information. With it, I'll complete the mission I've been given."

"Chaos couldn't do that! It would upset the

balance!" One's reaction spoke volumes. The mechanoid knew perfectly well what *Tainted Blood* was and how it could be wielded.

"Don't go on about how this ability will kill me and all that. And yet it's true — I will have *Tainted Blood*. And against my will, from my viewpoint. But I'll have it in any case, whether you agree with my proposal or not. In the first case, you will be able to become the power of the second orbit, in the second — you will simply remain One. The Dark Pyramid of the Kerux metropolitan area. Chaos will not allow a fifth force to appear. So you don't have two months, One. Three days at most. That's exactly how much I can give you before I go in search of the watermen and the undergrounders. And if I do this, there will be no turning back."

"Are you threatening me?"

"Don't you get it? Chaos wants to make me its servant. Just as Three speaks to me on behalf of One, so now I speak, in essence, on its behalf. The Interrogator is in Hearth, First. You can send any of your servants there — no one will lay a finger on them. Why call someone if you can come yourself? Stand before the Interrogator and ask him himself how much truth there is in my words? I believe the answer will surprise you — not a single deceitful word has come out of my mouth today. Only the pure truth. Three days, One. Then my offer will become irrelevant. All the best."

With these words, I activated the bloody portal, demonstrating that any further conversation was pointless. I was not particularly satisfied with the result, but I had no right to show it. The attempt to take the Temple of Skron by force had failed, I needed to think about my further course of action. I needed to get the four *Dictionaries* at all costs. I needed to bargain with the Kalimans.

"Hold on." One stopped me the moment I was about to jump. "Let's say, Archduke Valevsky, let's just say that your proposal is interesting to me. Do we need to sign something? Somehow solidify our agreements?"

"For now, verbal consent is enough," I took a few steps away from the portal, barely containing my excitement. Had it really worked? "Then I go to the Interrogator and inform him of the agreements we've reached. I believe he will come to you himself to confirm your participation. But, as I said, in order to begin further work, I need two things."

"Are you planning to take the artifacts?"

"I'll repeat myself once again: I'll take them, but only after I fulfill my part of the deal. Right now I need them in activated form, so that I clearly understand what I'm dealing with."

"Why can't you use *Analyze* to determine what we gave you? I know that you possess the stone."

"Because this is a case where I need 100% guarantees. *Analyze* cannot give that, you know this as well as I do. Because for me, wielder of the *Author* skill, these books are important, and I must be 100% sure of their correctness."

"So you want to become stronger at my expense?"

"What difference is it to you? I'll receive the

books only after you become a second-orbital power. A power that is protected by Chaos. When I receive *Tainted Blood,* I will have no right to even look askance at you, no matter what spatial manipulation capabilities I have. Because your presence will ensure balance. Stop thinking like a simple being. You no longer have that status. The fact that, thanks to me, the light will win back part of the lands from the dark, for you specifically will be nothing more than a blip. The Abyss, for example, does not care about division into empires. Its rifts are located across all lands, except perhaps the distant lands where the undergrounders, mechanoids and watermen rule. And humans, where would we be without humans?"

"You are aware that the rifts belong to the Abyss, not Skron?" One's voice again held hints of surprise.

"Why are you always trying to catch me in a lie? I don't think I've ever given you a reason. Before Seven attacked me, we were working together quite well. The benefit was skewed toward your side, of course, but I also got a lot out of our relationship. Why are you trying to find inconsistencies in my words? Yes, I know what the Abyss is responsible for, who banished it from the world, and why people who gave themselves to Skron cannot enter the rifts without a special parameter in the development model. The white seraph told me about this."

"You really have been to the Abyss," marveled One.

"Great Light, grant me patience." I rolled my eyes, astounded that One kept testing me. "Listen, maybe you could conduct a short interrogation to be certain that I am telling the truth? To be honest, I'm already starting to regret coming up with this idea. Sure, I don't want to go to the other end of the continent to destroy the watermen and the undergrounders. I don't want to fight them. But I also don't want to see your reaction. You have three days, One. Then I'm leaving Hearth and it will be impossible to get through to me."

"Very well, Archduke Valevsky. You can consider that you have my consent in principle, I will discuss the details with the Interrogator when he comes to me. What next?"

"The mechanism and the *Dictionaries*. Everything you have. According to the Abyss, fifty years ago you had three of them, and the Gourfan and Valdez clans had one more copy each. There is a non-zero probability that during this time you could have seized the artifacts for your own use. If not, then the next step I wanted to take was to visit the clans and strongly recommend that they sell the artifacts to me. Up to and including the destruction of these clans, if we cannot come to an agreement."

"Are you so sure of yourself? Karina Fardi won't let you destroy the clans."

"As if I'm going to ask her! She can puff out her cheeks and scare everyone with Skron's aura, but she won't be able to come to Hearth. Chaos won't let her. I don't care about anything else — the Inquisitor won't let her run wild in the light lands, the dark lands don't bother me. Then I'll adapt to pure Skron, get *Tainted Blood,* and then we'll see who's stronger — the Servant of Chaos or the vessel of Skron."

"The *Dictionary* belonging to the Valdez Clan is with me. The Gourfan Clan did not report that they possessed the artifact of the ancients. The information you provided is useful — the clan will be punished. They ignored my order. I can provide you with four books immediately for review. The mechanism for modernization needs to be prepared. Right now it is a stationary device that cannot be transported. I have ideas on how to make it more compact and portable, but this will take time. Two weeks, no less. Will this time frame suit you?"

"And during this time, I can inform Chaos that you are not against the idea of entering the second orbit, and going to communicate with Pharapho?"

"Yes. In two weeks, in addition to the mechanism, you will also receive the Gourfan book. Or rather, the opportunity to analyze it. You will receive the artifact itself after everything is done."

"Agreed!" I managed to hold a pause and not scream with joy. My little chat with One had already exceeded all my expectations. Apparently, the idea of jumping into the second orbit was too tempting for even the cautious One to decide to risk it. I didn't think Karina Fardi would be happy about this news if she found out. She would probably show up to sort things out with the pyramid.

After a few minutes of silence, the wall panel moved aside and another temple servant entered. Four devices appeared on the table one after another, and the screens of all of them were activated.

"Check. Are these what you require?"

Synchable devices found.
Synch?
You have collected 20% of the *Author* skill vocabulary (5 of 25). Information sent to all interested parties.

"Oh, yes." I still couldn't help but smile contentedly. Somewhere in our world there are twenty more *Dictionaries,* and I would do everything in my power to get my hands on them. I wasn't going to limit myself to five volumes. "That's what I need. Today you've become four steps closer to the second orbit, One, and I will do everything I can to make sure your path to power is strewn with flowers."

Chapter 11

TO FIND KIMAL SARENTO, I usually had to go to the highest tower in Hearth. The former chancellor of the magic academy clearly had some special relationship with heights — something drew him there. Or, which is also an option, he liked to look down on other people, imagining them as ants scurrying under his feet. That sounded like something he would do.

But today, Kimal Sarento was not alone in the tower. Eleanore and Alia were standing next to him. Given how pregnant they both were, only a truly serious situation could have prompted them to climb so high, and looking around, I saw the reason for this behavior. There was a huge army standing outside of Hearth.

"What's this?" I was taken aback. Who would be dumb enough to attack a city protected by the creatures of Chaos? Judging by the colors and banners, the army belonged to the Zarak Empire, but I did not even think that Zurgan the First had given the order to destroy us. However, the installation of several dozen catapults left no other interpretation: they were going to storm Hearth.

"What does it look like?" Kimal Sarento answered my question with a question.

"It's General Khabensky's army," Eleanore explained, not wanting to test my patience. "He decided that the Zarak Empire has no place for the dark ones and their minions. The general has expressed a desire to personally wipe Hearth and everything that reminds him of it from the face of the planet. In a week, another army will approach the walls — the general's son's. This is in case the first one fails. Both armies of the Zarak Empire are surrounding the walls of Hearth."

"Is he out of his mind? Is this the emperor's decision?" The news was so shocking that I didn't know what to do. I was jumping around to the Temple of Skron, trying to sort out the situation with One and him becoming a second-orbital force, communicating with the Abyss, getting ready to visit Pharapho, negotiating with Chaos, preparing to shut down the Wave and receive *Tainted Blood*, and suddenly this problem appears so close to home — something I can't simply ignore! How was I supposed to react to this?

"General Khabensky only arrived this morning," Alia replied. "There is no teleport in Turb that would allow us to quickly contact His Imperial

Majesty, and sending couriers is not the smartest thing. No one can slip through something like that unnoticed. We did not want to bother you — each of us has our own tasks."

"What does the general expect? We have the Inquisitor and the Interrogator!"

"Who have already stated their position: they are not going to interfere in the affairs of humans." Eleanore was the one to respond this time. "Everything that happens is the prerogative of the Zarak Empire. If Hearth is not able to protect itself from ordinary humans, then it is not worthy of having such defenders within it. Their task is to protect the city from the encroachments of Karina Fardi, the Temple of Skron, and also to ensure the balance of power in this world, returning it to stability. As the Inquisitor noted: 'Archduke Valevsky is able to carry out our orders even without the support of the city. Hearth only limits him. If the city is so important — prove it, without our assistance."

"Not only did they come to us without permission, but they also don't intend to help," I said with undisguised anger, looking towards one of the squares where people were crowding. Despite the army at the city walls, the forces of Chaos did not stop receiving citizens, continuing to voice their position on various issues. It was easier for the dark ones — they arrived and left the city with the help of a portal, but the light ones were in for some unpleasant news. They found themselves locked in a city under construction. It was good that at least

General Khabensky's army prevented new guests from entering the gates. I wasn't sure that we had the ability to accommodate everyone.

"At the risk of sounding tactless, I'd like to remind my frowning mentor that we need to be at the walls of the Kaliman Empire in ten days," Kimal said, choosing that moment to rub salt in the wound. "And we need to solve the issue with the metamorphs. Those two level-twenty rifts aren't exactly on the way. Each of them will take additional time.

"Time that we physically don't have," I said, casting a glance back at the army standing outside Hearth's walls. "Have we tried negotiating with them?"

"Naturally," Eleanore nodded. "Max, General Khabensky is not here to negotiate. He's here to mow down everyone and everything in his path. From what I know, the first army has twenty thousand foot soldiers, about five thousand crossbowmen and about a thousand mages of various levels. The second, which will appear soon, has just as many. We are incapable of holding them back."

"Why?" Kimal Sarento said. "It all depends on how you approach the question. And who is the one to approach it."

"A thousand. Maybe even two or three. Even you wouldn't be able to take out more," Eleanore said frankly. "I know the limit of the mithril armor, Kimal. I know your magical potential. It is encouraging, but five thousand crossbowmen will reduce all your advantage to nothing. By the time you get to the striking distance, you will be turned into a hedgehog. A dead and dissatisfied hedgehog. Even if we use *Phantom,* success is still extremely unlikely. Khabensky is probably prepared and using some kind of artifact that detects invisibility. That's exactly what I would do in his place."

Kimal Sarento's lack of response suggested that he was thinking about the same thing. Fighting against a trained army alone is impossible, even if the levels of your magic stones are sky high.

"So there are no other options for settling this conflict?" I asked. Eleanore said, "Either we need to somehow come to an agreement with the Inquisitor so that he acts as a guarantor of our immunity, or with General Khabensky. Both options seem extremely unrealistic."

"Talking to Khabensky is useless," added Kimal Sarento. "He's a rather strange man, obsessed with the truth known only to him. Now he's imagined that Hearth is evil, and he'll do everything to destroy this evil. He obeys neither the emperor nor the empire. No one. Yes, it sounds strange, of course, that the empire's army doesn't obey him, but that's the reality of our strange world. The previous emperor did a lot of things, to try to please everyone. Gave out too much freedom. And he paid for it in the end. As for the soldiers themselves...They'll go through fire and water for their general. This isn't just a motley crew of scoundrels recruited from citizens who were useless during peacetime. This is the cream of the crop. Many work for years to get into the active army. They train, they learn. Because this is a real way not only to earn money, but also to provide a comfortable existence for their families."

"Where did General Khabensky get so much gold?" I asked in surprise.

"Well, he is not a poor man, but he does not spend money on the army. It is fully supported by the empire."

"At the same time, the army does not belong to her," I finally stopped understanding the essence of what was happening.

"I see you've begun to understand the world order of the Zarak Empire, my dumbfounded mentor," Kimal Sarento managed sarcasm, despite the seriousness of the situation. "Food, weapons, ammunition — all this from our beloved emperor. And he even has the right to ask General Khabensky to send his troops where the emperor needs them."

"Ask? Not order?"

"Precisely! And yes, only to direct. The emperor cannot forbid a general from attacking someone. Actually, that is why no one messes with the military. It is too dangerous in these times. I have no idea what Count Vyazemsky proposed to the general, who suddenly appeared under the walls of Hearth, but it must be something really serious. As far as I remember, we had certain agreements with the old military man. The fact that he forgot them says a lot."

"So it's not the fact that we're working with the dark ones? He just bought the army?"

"Kimal can only guess," Eleonore said. "We don't have any precise information. Khabensky doesn't want to talk to us."

"As if that ever stopped us," I looked again at the army preparing for the assault. "Where could General Khabensky be? He's somewhere here, right? With his army?"

"He..." Kimal Sarento did not have time to finish. At that moment, without waiting for the preparations to be completed, stones began flying over the wall at Hearth. General Khabensky did not want to wait — he wanted to wipe the city off the face of the planet as quickly as possible. With some detachment, I looked at the two huge boulders flying toward the city. It seemed that even time stopped, allowing me to enjoy their beautiful arc through the air. They reached the city walls, flew further, the air around them shimmered and... and suddenly both projectiles disappeared, like a small piece of snow placed under the scorching desert sun. I turned towards Eleanore for an explanation, but her expression told me that she was no less shocked than the others.

The army was undeterred. Within a few moments, several dozen stone blocks and flaming barrels of fuel were flying towards the city, followed by crossbow bolts. Several hundred archers approached within shooting distance and began testing our defenses for strength. The mages did not join — the distance was still too great and they did not risk approaching the walls yet.

The air began to shimmer again, destroying

each projectile, one by one. Same story with the crossbow bolts. The archers simply fired them over the walls, in the blind hope of hitting at least someone inside the city or setting something on fire, but nothing worked. The bolts disappeared just like the stones and barrels. The first wave was followed by a second. A third. A tenth. The defense held, easily evaporating everything they fired. At some point, the shooters concentrated their shots on the main gate. It seemed that they wanted, if not to destroy it, then at least to hit it. However, the shimmering force field prevented this, evaporating the steel.

Or had it evaporated?

Eleanore was much better than me at using the city management functionality. It didn't take more than a few minutes before she started laughing. Hearing such genuine laughter from the usually gloomy beauty was so unusual that we were distracted from the massive attack and looked quizzically in her direction.

"What a good boy," was her confusing retort.

"Everything okay?" Alia walked over Eleanore and peered into her face with concern, trying to understand the depth of the problem. It was very hard to believe that the woman who had managed to endure eight years in the rifts had suddenly snapped because the city was under siege.

"Oh, I haven't been this happy in a long time," Eleanore tried to pull herself together, although the wide smile didn't leave her face for a long time. "Open the city settings and go to the storage section. Sort by date of receipt and enjoy the result. I don't think I'm the only one who will enjoy this."

"What a clever little defender we have." Kimal Sarento was the first to follow the instructions he had received. "I suppose he's able to do this because you fed him Seven's essence, is that right, my precocious mentor? Or lucky...It depends on how you look at it."

Finally, I also found the right setting and stared at several of the lines of text:

Stone blocks (0.5x0.5x0.5): +112 pcs.
Barrels with flammable oil: +34 pcs.
Steel crossbow bolts: +452 pcs.
Vyrma crossbow bolts: +33 pcs.

"The objects didn't evaporate?" I asked in astonishment.

"Of course not!" Eleanore said as her laughter finally died down. "We've always had problems acquiring stone. Even though the mountains are close by, mining and delivery posed certain logistical issues. A lot of stone is required for construction, so there's never enough. But now, this gift! I hope Khabensky never stops and feeds us everything he brought with him in the wagons. Steel and vyrma will also come in handy — they can be smelted into something more useful. Especially the vyrma."

"Only if they don't understand that their actions are not producing results," Alia doubted. "Maybe they'll stop shooting and go on the attack?"

"And how will they manage that?" grinned Eleanore, and for some time, her eyes unfocused and she gazed into eternity. Apparently she was in the city management functionality actively communicating with the Defender. The bald mechanical hedgehog living in the treasury had really proved his mettle. Another volley of stones fell on the protective dome, the air shimmered again, evaporating the shells, and unexpectedly for everyone, thick black smoke began to pour from one of the construction sites. Alia even cried out, deciding that the army that had appeared under Hearth had managed to break through the defense, but the sharp-eyed Kimal Sarento said, with respect,

"The more I communicate with the great Countess, the more I understand that I still have something to learn. A beautiful move."

"'Countess' is a thing of the past, Kimal," she corrected him. "Just Eleanore. Or city manager. That would make me happy. Now Khabensky will have no reason to refuse the bombardment. We need the stone, so let the army replenish our supply."

"So this is your doing?" Alia said excitedly.

"Construction waste that isn't even suitable for recycling. We've been planning to burn it for a long time, but we never got around to it. Why not do it now? Besides, they've thrown so many barrels of fuel at us. It's good for us, and Khabensky will be happy that his cunning plan is successful. Let him continue to supply us with resources. We definitely can't refuse such a gift."

Eleanore was convincing, but I did not share her enthusiasm. Digging into the settings, I managed to find out something important — to maintain the dome, our defender was intensively spending our own resources. Those that I had mined in the rifts. The volume consumed was, of course, incomparable with what was falling into our warehouses, but the stable trend towards a decrease in the amount of the most valuable material was frightening. It was not critical now, but if the siege lasted several weeks, our resources would run out. The defender used dorim and burz, which were mined from rifts of the sixteenth level and higher, so sooner or later we would have to make an unpopular decision. Either abandon such extravagance, or seek out sources of these materials. And the Kaliman Empire rifts could help with the latter.

The little show clearly did us good. Seeing the smoke, General Khabensky's army seemed to pull out all the stops. Several dozen more catapults were deployed, and at one point there were thirty boulders and flaming barrels in the air, capable of turning my city into ruins. But instead of suffering from such a furious attack, we rejoiced — the sites intended for building materials were gradually replenished. The only sad thing was that the archers stopped giving us crossbow bolts. Apparently, the failure with the main gate seemed too great for them to waste the valuable resource any longer. In order to spur the enemy to continue the bombardment, Eleanore, with the help of the Defender, set fire to several more garbage heaps. Clouds of smoke began to pour out in different parts of the city, and, in my opinion, this decision was not the most far-sighted. General Khabensky decided to move on to the next phase of his plan.

All this time we were on top of the tower, watching the futile efforts of the military. The servants even brought us chairs, a table, and brought us food. Everything was going well for the city, but everyone understood that it could not go on like this for long. Sooner or later the stones and barrels of fuel would run out, and the general would have no choice but to send his men to storm. This happened two hours after the assault began, when the catapults finally fell silent for good.

The ground shook as several thousand men-at-arms advanced in unison, their huge shields raised. Crossbowmen followed a little further, ready at any moment to rain down a hail of bolts on anyone who poked their heads out from behind the wall. Or anyone who dared to engage such an army in direct combat.

"Maybe it's time to put an end to this?" I suggested. "Tell me, do you think the army will still fight without its general?"

"Are you suggesting kidnapping Khabensky?" Eleanore asked. "I'll repeat just in case, there's a high probability that your *Phantom* won't work."

"I don't need it, I'm not going to hide. The general should be in one of those huge tents. I'll open a portal, Kimal Sarento and I will go there, find the general, and then return back through the same portal. Five minutes for everything. The guards won't even have time to twitch."

"He'll have protection," Eleanore said thoughtfully. "He knows that he's up against strong opponents, and the general has never been a fool."

"Of course he'll have protection," Kimal Sarento grinned. "There are not many mages in the Zarak Empire who are capable of doing this. If General Khabensky truly believes he is infallible, then he is protected by the best."

"Count Vyazemsky and his army?" I asked.

"More like a support group, but you're right — Count Vyazemsky and several other serious figures must be standing behind General Khabensky. Otherwise, I sincerely don't understand what the old warrior is counting on."

"Count Shub too?"

"Not only that. In my opinion, it couldn't have happened without the support of our beloved Karina Fardi. She can't harm you directly, but who's stopping her from sending her mentor here? Magister Elor could very well be one of those protecting our general."

"But he's dark! Truly dark. Orthodox!"

"Light be with you, my naive mentor. Do you really think that the main reason the army showed up and is reluctant to enter into negotiations is that General Khabensky decided to cleanse the Zarak Empire of the influence of the dark ones? Forget about the fact that this world is ruled by higher ideals. Gold and mountains of resources, my honesty-seeking mentor. That's what rules the world. So behind the beautiful bright slogans that it's time to cleanse the empire of darkness, there's an excellent dark soul. I like the idea of a sortie — I want to slap the arrogant warriors on the nose, but logic tells me, my mentor who thinks himself immortal, that they'll be waiting for us there. Magister Elor, Count Vyazemsky and Count Shub will be enough not only to delay us, despite the strength, power and other attributes of mithril armor and magic stones, but also to arrange a few not the most pleasant minutes of our lives. Remember Father Urg's words: Count Vyazemsky destroyed his mithril boots while searching for a way to combat this material. Can you guarantee that they never found anything? I, for my part, cannot. Oh! They've finally arrived."

Indeed, while Kimal Sarento was enthusiastically ranting about the impossibility of a surprise attack, the first ranks of the men-at-arms reached the walls. It was this moment that our Defender decided to attack: the devices that seemed like decorative spires scattered across the entire wall came into action. There were no beams, no bolts, nothing like that. The air near the walls simply began to flicker, and a few moments later we heard the pain-filled roar being ripped from a thousand throats. There was not a single living person left within a hundred meters of the wall. The city guard acted with monstrous calm, allowing the maximum number of men-at-arms to enter the zone of his protection before unleashing some kind of aura on them that managed to break through the steel armor. Or simply paid no attention to it, since it was a product of material mechanisms, not magic. In any case, this aura somehow resonated with the human body, causing it to literally explode. Several thousand warriors, capable of reducing any other city in this world to null, were turned into mince in just a few moments. New soldiers rushed to help, to rescue if not their comrades, then at least their ammunition, but they were unable to do so — the protective aura acted immediately, destroying them as well.

"Effective," Kimal Sarento said, gulping. The others had no words to describe the shock of what had just happened. A third of the elite of the Zarak Empire army had just been destroyed. Of course, it hadn't been easy for our Defender either — he had used up half of our dorim and burz supplies. Now we could afford one more such show of force before our resources would run out.

I needed to get to the rifts as soon as possible! Preferably level twenty-five and above.

However, our city guard decided that he had not yet fully completed the task assigned to him. The main gate opened, and several dozen strange mechanisms emerged from them. They were somewhat similar to the mechanoid — the same bald hedgehogs. Only they were smaller, and each of them was dragging an impressive cart behind them. These mini-guards began to do something that caused our enemy to roar with impotent rage — they put what was left of the men-at-arms on the carts. Armor, belts, the contents of purses, weapons — everything was placed on the carts and wheeled back into Hearth. General Khabensky's soldiers tried to prevent this. The shooters put on another show, sending another volley of vyrma arrows, and I had to admit that they succeeded in taking down six of the mini guards. Their bodies were dragged back to the city along with the loot. As for the ordinary men-at-arms, they didn't simply stand idle. Having determined the distance at which the city's defenses were ineffective, they approached the edge and began to throw grappling hooks tied to a long rope toward the walls. By catching the armor, the fighters dragged it toward themselves, preventing my collectors from getting their hands on the loot. I wasn't too happy about this, as I'd liked the idea of dressing all my subjects in steel armor. And trading a complete suit of armor is much more profitable than trading just a part of it.

"I think the fun is over for today," Kimal Sarento said when we lost another collector. The Defender rightly decided that there was enough loot and returned all of his children back. "Tell me, my lazy mentor, are you going to climb down from the tower on foot or use the portal? I suppose there's nothing more for us to do in Hearth — the Defender can handle it without us. I highly recommend not getting into a pointless fight with the leaders of this madness now — they are waiting to give us a very warm welcome, and I'm afraid it would spell the end of us."

"I'm not going to portal straight to General

Khabensky," I said. There was movement in our opponents' camp as they began to set up catapults again. Apparently, the black smoke that Eleanore had created had seemed like a good sign. Since the assault had failed, they needed to throw stones and burning barrels at the city. The soldiers clearly weren't going to give up.

"However, something tells me you still plan to portal somewhere, and it's clearly not to the capital," Kimal Sarento said.

"Why not? The capital's exactly where I'm going. I turned my bloodthirsty gaze to him. "If Count Vyazemsky and Count Shub decide to come to Hearth to help General Khabensky wipe us off the face of the earth, it's time to go visit them where they live. These two bastards will rue this due. You're always asking if I am ready to face such mighty opponents. I believe the time has come to answer. Kimal Sarento, we are going to visit the estates of Counts Vyazemsky and Shub, and then Zurgan the First. We will take prisoners. Many prisoners. Eleanore, prepare a draft decree — Hearth declares war on the Zarak Empire! The time has come to return Miralda Lertan to her rightful throne."

Chapter 12

"COUNTESS, I'M AFRAID you'll have to come with us." Kimal Sarento was the quintessence of politeness. The smile never left his face for a second, even when he was destroying the servants and guards of the estate by the dozens. I must give them credit — they tried to protect their mistress to the last, but what can ordinary people do to two high-level mages who came here for more than just a glass of fine wine? During our short conversation, Count Vyazemsky managed to make a terrible mistake that would cost him: he invited me to visit his personal estate. Even Count Shub, with whom we had several contracts, held meetings in his office.

"Count Sarento, please leave my house immediately!" Count Vyazemsky's wife stood by the wall, shielding her two younger children. Georgy

Vyazemsky, the heir I had always liked, was not in the estate. He was quite possibly somewhere in the city, studying at the Guards Academy, in a restaurant with his wife, God knows where else! But stubborn logic told me that George was next to his father under the walls of Hearth. For Serlena, now Vyazemsky, stood behind the Countess and fearfully pressed her fists to her chest. There was no talk of any resistance. Those who had risked attacking us lay lifelessly on the floor. We weren't feeling sorry for anyone today.

"Unfortunately, Countess, this is impossible. Your husband attacked Hearth, my mentor's city. We gave them no fuel for such a treacherous attack, we never entered into open confrontation. All the minor misunderstandings that constantly arose between us, we managed to resolve with the help of reasonable arguments and negotiations. However, today, any sense of reason has left them. Hearth was betrayed, attacked. I regret to inform you that you and your children, and also the beautiful Serlena, who I am positive is already carrying the heir of the Vyazemsky family, will have to step through the portal and become our temporary guests."

"Don't tell me you'll take us by force if we refuse." The Countess looked at Kimal Sarento as if he were a slug. I couldn't help but feel respect for this woman. She saw perfectly well what we had done to her home — neither I nor Kimal Sarento held back. *Dark Spike*, which had begun to feel forgotten and abandoned, was finally able to have some fun. It not only destroyed its opponents, but also caused monstrous damage to the building. Since my city was pelted with stones and barrels of fuel, why should I show generosity?

"If you do not comply, we will have to take you by force," I said. Kimal Sarento's negotiations could last for days. Countess Vyazemsky was clearly well-versed in the art of spinning verbal webs, and in any other situation I would have gladly listened to her debate with my pupil. But not today.

"Archduke Valevsky," the woman said contemptuously, looking at me with an equally contemptuous gaze. "Do you really think that..."

She couldn't finish her sentence, as my fifth-level rift ousel made all members of the Vyazemsky family fall to the floor. Kimal Sarento only sighed, clearly unfond of my abrupt approach. After waiting a minute, giving the Vyazemskys the opportunity to fully enjoy the dark aura, I latched the box and addressed all those lying on the floor:

"If your behavior displeases me once more, you'll be exposed to the dark aura for two minutes. Countess, are you certain that your children can withstand such pain? Are you ready to risk their health? Their sanity? The heir to your family throne, for that matter? I don't enjoy hurting you, but my hand will not waver if I have to."

"You're a monster," whispered Serlena. She tried to get to her feet, but the trembling that shook her body prevented her from doing so.

"I don't care what you call me. I protect my

home. I'll repeat myself: from now on, you are all my prisoners. If you behave sensibly, no one will suffer. If you start getting cheeky, interfering, trying to escape, the punishment will be swift and harsh. I really hope that the initial demonstration was enough for you and I will not have to resort to such unpleasantness again. Everyone into the portal!"

With these words, I opened a bloody portal and gestured for all present to enter. By now, I had surmised that the shimmering veil would not close until the one who created it had entered the portal. No need to lead everyone by hand.

"Everything will be fine," the Countess managed to cheer up the children and, taking them by the hands, went to the portal. Although the look she gave me could have killed me on the spot.

"Not so fast," I stopped Countess Vyazemsky. "The children go first. They will be met on the other side. You, Countess, will have to stay here for a few more minutes."

"I will not leave my children!" she said, nearly screaming.

"They will be fine. They will not be harmed," assured Kimal Sarento. "In fact, Countess, your presence is not necessary. We have reliable information that the Vyazemsky family treasury is located in this building. We will find it in any case, it is a matter of time, but if you help us save time and tell us where to go, this will help save the lives of your servants. Everyone we meet along the way, to my great regret, will have to be killed."

"So you are not only murderers, but also thieves?" There was enough poison in the Countess's voice to fill several barrels. After all, upbringing and heredity give people a lot of confidence — despite her unenviable position, Countess Vyazemsky behaved as if she were in charge of the situation.

"Serlena is right, you are a monster!" For the first time, Countess Vyazemsky's voice was filled with fear. The contempt and poison were still there, but something new had been added. Something that hadn't been there before.

"Is that a no? Well, it's your choice."

"Stop! I'll tell you."

Soon Countess Vyazemsky and her children went to Hearth, where Eleanore received them as dear guests, not prisoners, but the proximity to the Interrogator and the Inquisitor, who looked askance at the new arrivals, knocked all the arrogance out of the high-born aristocrats. I closed the portal to the main hall and jumped into the hole in the floor that Kimal Sarento had cut. The Vyazemsky treasury was on the second basement level and we weren't about to walk around looking for stairs. A direct route was easier.

Kimal Sarento followed me after a short pause — he lit the fuse leading to four barrels of flammable mixture that we had dragged to the Vyazemsky estate as a gift. We had to leave our mark after all they had done to us. When we went down to the second underground floor, we heard such an explosion from above that the entire building shook.

Formally, we had cut off our own escape route, but no one was planning to run out the main gate.

The Vyazemsky treasury was surprisingly small. I'd asked them to build something along the lines of the Citadel treasury in Hearth, so I sincerely believed that all the great families of any empire had a similar place to store their valuables. Both in size and in content. However, the Vyazemsky family was a disappointment. When we tore out the steel doors, we hoped to see a huge hall filled with gold, artifacts and resources, but we found ourselves in a somewhat large, but unimpressive room. I might even downgrade it to a midsized room. Sure, the shelves here were full to bursting with gold bars, coins, precious stones, artifacts, elixirs, jewelry, even a few figurines. But, if I assessed the contents without unnecessary emotion, there was not even a tenth of what I managed to see in the Citadel or Fortress. The cleric's treasuries were an order of magnitude greater than what Count Vyazemsky had managed to accumulate. Either that or the Countess had led us on a false trail to a specially designated treasury, while the real one, huge and filled with the most valuable items, was located somewhere else.

"We won't be able to carry all of this, my insatiable mentor. Everything will fit in the backpack, of course, but we'll be rooted to the spot. We have to give up something." Kimal Sarento glanced around the room and immediately summed up what he saw.

"Who says we have to carry it all ourselves?" I

asked as I formed a portal. Grabbing the nearest box of gold, I threw it into the shimmering shroud. The loot disappeared, and new gold appeared on the castle's balance sheet. The portal led to the treasury, where our Defender immediately accepted the gifts and distributed them to the right places.

"That's also an option," agreed Kimal Sarento and dragged a huge rack with all its contents to the portal. The boxes began to disappear into the portal one by one, and when my pupil had completely cleared the rack, he disassembled it and sent it in after the valuables. I nodded in agreement — additional storage space was always useful. My treasury was large, of course, but there had been certain problems acquiring racks. Count Shub had promised to deliver some, but for some reason the delivery had been delayed.

Unfortunately, among all the standard verbal constructions that I received from the five books, there was nothing useful for automating this process. No levitation, no telekinesis, no assistants to help me drag all this back to Hearth. I even considered running to the city and taking a dozen servants back with me, but abandoned the idea. The Vyazemskys didn't have the biggest treasury. I'd spend more time looking for assistants than I would simply doing the job myself.

It took thirty minutes in total. We raided the entire place and burned it to the ground. The clouds of smoke gradually filling the surrounding area told us that a fiery inferno had broken out above us. It really was a pity — the last time I had visited the Vyazemsky estate, I had seen many beautiful objects. But I had no other choice — everyone must remember what happened to those who attack Hearth.

"Let's go," I said, forming a portal to a location not far from Count Shub's office. This sly rogue, who had all the industrialists under his control, was supposed to be the second target of our march to the capital. Of course, we should have visited Shub's main estate to take another batch of hostages, but Kimal Sarento recommended visiting his main office first. Because contracts, letters, receipts and other waste paper were valued in our world much more than any human lives. If it came down to it, you could always find more people, but paper documents, once lost, were gone forever. They were unique items.

We didn't stand on ceremony with the guards. Everyone who stood in our way died. Those who tried to catch up with us died. In fact, everyone who caught our eye died. The door to Count Shub's office flew off its hinges, blown off by *Dark Spike.* We stepped inside and stood there for a moment.

"Ahem," Kimal Sarento coughed meaningfully, suggesting that I take the initiative in the conversation. For standing behind Count Shub's desk was Count Shub himself, surrounded by several assistants. The mages surrounded themselves with protective spheres, used artifacts with the intention of selling their lives for a higher price, but, as it turned out, this was not necessary. Count Shub did not join General Khabensky. He was nowhere near Hearth, at least not personally. Sure, there was a high degree of probability that he supported the attack, perhaps even was a sponsor, but he did not come to my city personally. Which automatically saved his life.

"It seems we were mistaken, my tongue-tied pupil," I said calmly, as if discussing the weather. "Count Shub did not succumb to the general hysteria and join the madmen. Gentlemen, I offer my sincere apologies for disturbing you. We are leaving."

"Archduke Valevsky, what is the meaning of all this?" Count Shub flared up.

I looked at Shub, then at Kimal Sarento. "Pupil, please explain the reason for our abrupt appearance here."

"This morning, General Khabensky's army attacked Hearth. He is supported by Count Vyazemsky. His family was just sent to Hearth as hostages, and the estate, if you will look out the window, is burning so brightly, you can see it from here. The general would not have come to Hearth without the support of high-level mages, leading us to assume that Count Vyazemsky was not the only one participating in this crazy endeavor. So, we are walking around the city and visiting everyone who might be supporting the crazy general. Whatever one may say, Count Shub has always been famous for his strength. It would be foolish of me not to show up on your doorstep right after visiting Count Vyazemsky."

"They made me an offer," Count Shub said, deactivating his shield, and even sat down at his desk as if nothing out of the ordinary had happened. "But I had to abandon the idea. Cooperating with Hearth is profitable for me. Sure, now Count Vyazemsky and the Emperor have strengthened their ties, essentially prohibiting any trade with the autonomous city, but this is only temporary. I don't think he will be able to refuse the Shurgans or Kalimans free passage to Hearth. I will still get what I want — even if not directly, then through the mediation of other empires.

"But you didn't think to warn us?" Kimal Sarento chuckled.

"What for? I know that the Inquisitor and Interrogator sit on their thrones in Hearth. If something goes wrong, they will intervene, even if Count Vyazemsky swears the opposite. You are aware that he sent his own man to meet with the Inquisitor, to ask him about how he might respond in the event of an attack on the city by those who do not agree that the light empires have a portal leading to the dark ones? Those against whom we have fought for a thousand years are now flooding our lands, eating our bread, drinking our water, and we must accept this fact without the right to dispute? Count Vyazemsky's man was convincing and managed to get the Inquisitor to declare non-intervention if the city is attacked by ordinary humans. Which, as I understand it, is what is happening now. However, I am interested in another issue. You came to my office, killed my people, destroyed my building. I would like to receive compensation for your outrage. As I understand it, you have some kind of remote communication capability. You were somehow informed about the attack on the city, right? I also need remote communication. I believe this will be worthy compensation for your mistake."

"I have another proposal, Count," I responded in the face of his monstrous impudence. "I can give you two hours to leave Turb with your family. Any later and it will become extremely difficult for you to do so. Since my city has been attacked by a regular army, I have no other solution but to declare war on the Zarak Empire. With all the ensuing circumstances. Two hours, Count. Then we will go to the palace and destroy everyone who stands between us and the Emperor. Zurgan the First made a mistake by leaving the imperial army entirely to General Khabensky's disposal. The emperor will call upon everyone currently in the capital to defend it, including you, Count. If we meet in the palace before we find the emperor and transport him to Hearth, there will be no discussion. We will simply destroy you. But you cannot simply prove yourself a traitor either. Those who entrusted you with such a high-ranking position wouldn't understand. However, if you are not in the city, no suspicions or dirty speculations will arise against you. You just went to visit, say, Al-Khorezm. You have long wanted to see the capital of the Shurghan Empire. This is truly worthy compensation for the mistake we made. We grant you life."

"Are you getting a little too ambitious, Archduke?" Count Shub grinned, becoming a dangerous beast.

"Only as ambitious as I can handle. Two hours, Count, that's all I can give you. Then we go to the palace. Either you'll be safe by then, or you'll be called to defend the city. It's up to you to decide. The time for pretty words, florid phrases, and downcast eyes is over. The time to be strong has come."

With these words, I activated a portal to Hearth. Judging by Count Shub's long face, he had not expected this.

"Count," Kimal Sarento nodded and was the first to disappear into the portal. I looked around, as if choosing what to take with me, and then followed behind him. A show of force would not hurt in this situation. Whether I like it or not, Count Shub was a useful figure in the empire. I was even glad that he was not involved in the attack on Hearth. Such people should be treasured. Keep an eye on them, don't trust them, be ready to destroy them at any moment, just in case, but treasure them nonetheless.

"Have we already found accommodations for our guests?" I asked Eleanore. She was already sitting in her office. There was no point in hanging around on the tower all the time while the city was under attack. The Defender would handle it himself.

"In our best guest rooms," she replied.

"Prepare Countess Vyazemsky for her departure. She is leaving Hearth."

"Leaving?" Eleanore frowned. Even Kimal Sarento, who followed me like a silent shadow, peered at me with interest.

"Why did you suddenly decide to throw away such an asset, my wise mentor? The more such guests we have, the less agility the attackers will demonstrate."

"Countess Vyazemsky will leave Hearth and join her husband," I answered definitively. "However, tell her that she can move freely. She will be able to return to Hearth whenever she wishes. But only she alone. I cannot even imagine a situation in which a mother would not return to her children, who are in danger. Eleanore, make sure that the Defender does not destroy her."

"Trying to get on Count Vyazemsky's nerves isn't a bad idea," said Kimal Sarento. "But I don't think he's the main decision maker here. General Khabensky won't listen to him."

"I think it's time to play another card. It's not about the general and his decisions. The point is that they will find out about Hearth. Eleanore, make sure that Countess Vyazemsky meets and talks with Miralda Lertan before the campaign. How is she, by the way?"

"She's slowly coming to her senses, but she's still quite weak. She eats practically nothing. She's showing an unprecedented interest in the construction process. She's even trying to help. She's also interested in the portal and the minotaurs. It seems she's even made friends with one of the guards. In general, she's behaving as a twenty-year-old girl should behave upon finding herself in an unfamiliar city."

"Countess Vyazemsky must understand that the legitimate ruler of the Zarak Empire stands before her. Even if Miralda is not yet ready to claim her power. In a year, she will turn twenty-one and declare her rights to the throne. We must make sure that Countess Vyazemsky goes to her husband with precisely this information. General Khabensky's entourage must know who they are fighting against. Let's see how the soldiers react to the fact that they are about to destroy the legitimate heir to the throne."

"They created a hell-raiser, and now it's coming to bite them in the ass," Kimal Sarento sighed. "Very well, I will handle this matter personally. I will first speak to the princess, describe the situation to her, then prepare the countess and bring them together. Are you certain that this is the course of action you wish to take, my revolutionary mentor?"

"Absolutely. Zurgan the First wanted to capture us in Turb. The standing imperial army is attacking my city. I have no choice but to rid this world of such a short-sighted emperor. I don't see the slightest chance of reaching an agreement with him. Miralda owes me her life and will owe me her return to the palace. It will be easier to talk to her."

"Without the support of the nobility, this kind of trick won't work. They will not accept her."

"They accepted Zurgan, didn't they? They will accept her too."

"Let me remind you just in case, my forgetful mentor, that Zurgan had the support of six dukes. We don't have that. The regions won't recognize the new empress. Not even the regions — Turb won't recognize her."

"They will recognize her," Eleanore said, taking my side. "Count Nikitin, aka the Duke of Turb, dreams of overthrowing the usurper. The fact that he agreed to your terms, Kimal, means nothing. As soon as Nikitin learns that the princess is alive and that we support her in her quest to get rid of the tyrant, he will join us. As will an entire army of other aristocrats who are dissatisfied with the current state of affairs. All that remains to be done is to remove Zurgan from the throne. As long as he is entrenched in the palace, Miralda's position is insignificant."

"He won't be sitting comfortably on that throne for long," I said. "Why are you still here, my slow-witted pupil? Don't you have anything better to do?"

Kimal Sarento just grinned and left. After some time, the central gates of Hearth opened, and, holding a white flag in her hands, Countess Vyazemsky headed towards General Khabensky's army. The woman really didn't want to leave her children. She even got down on her knees and begged, forgetting all her pride. But we were adamant: the Countess must speak to her husband and tell him what had happened. If she wished, she would be permitted to return afterward, but only alone. Kimal Sarento fulfilled my request perfectly.

"Two hours have passed, my generous mentor," Kimal Sarento reminded me as we observed a strange stirring in the enemy camp. People were running every which way, checking things, as if preparing for another assault. But I was sure that until the second army approached Hearth, there would be no new attack.

"Let's start with his office," I agreed, forming another portal. For a few moments, the space floated to form an office with a huge map of the Zarak Empire. But the emperor was not here. Instead, there were about a dozen armored guards in the office, ready for battle. The pikes moved in our direction, but a blow from *Chain Lightning* sent the poor guys off to meet the Light. The steel frets withstood the barrage of magic, but were unable to protect their owners.

"I suspect you've made a mistake about Count Shub, my trusting mentor. He's clearly not going to run away from his problems. And yes, I'll bet half my estate that Zurgan the First is no longer in the palace. We'll have to run after this sly scoundrel. Nobility doesn't always play into your hands, my magnanimous mentor. Sometimes you must take a little off the top. Alright then, let's see how well our local militia has been able to prepare for our next encounter in the two hours you so generously gave them."

Taking a deep breath, Kimal Sarento shouted,

"Greet the envoys of Empress Miralda Lertan! The true heir to the throne of the Zarak Empire! Lay down your arms, and your lives will be spared! Death to the usurper and all who support him! The Zarak Empire will regain its true greatness!"

Chapter 13

"I HAVE THE SUSPICION that the imperial guards are completely apathetic to our presence," Kimal Sarento said in astonishment, mowing down another group of guards. Despite all their steel, protective amulets and artifacts, all four men went to meet the Light. I didn't try attacking — it had been experimentally proven that neither my *Dark Spike* nor Kimal's *Lightning Strike* could break through their defenses. The Emperor spared nothing for his personal guard, turning them into monsters capable of resisting any *human* magic. Emphasis on *human*, as level fifty *Chain Lightning* was clearly outside the realm of human abilities. It shredded any defense system like paper. Even fatal damage blocking amulets were useless — his attack inflicted multiple kinds of damage, incinerating everything in its path. Kimal Sarento walked through the palace, leaving a smoking trail of remains behind him. He was terrifying.

Of course, I could have activated the dark aura and advanced on my own with no issue, but there was a caveat. First of all, neither the guards nor the servants were to blame for their ruler being such a bastard. They were just doing their job. If I activated the aura, everyone who fell within its radius would die. While a level five ousel wouldn't pierce through steel armor, the level fifteen would kill everyone, including Kimal Sarento. Not immediately, of course, but it would kill him eventually, as mithril armor didn't protect against darkness. He would experience everything ordinary humans did and will become the same Kimal Sarento who encountered the metamorph — the one I had to save from the brink of death. I could give him all of my rings to reduce the damage and hope that they would suffice, but it was a moot point. *Chain Lightning* was perfectly suited for the situation, so why complicate things? Simplicity was the key to success.

And wherever there's a "first of all," a "second of all" comes after. Yes, there was another factor, aside from my general reluctance to kill. It concerned the future ruler of the Zarak Empire. The more I ruminated on this plan, the more I realized that it would essentially just be trading one headache for another. Zurgan the First or Miralda Lertan — it would make no difference to how my city was governed. Sure, Miralda must now feel some semblance of gratitude towards me and my people, perhaps even friendliness, but all this would quickly pass as soon as she ascended the throne. If I killed all the current inhabitants of the palace, there would be no one to stop the girl. Sooner or later, she would still send an army to Hearth. Why? Because my city represented the most undesirable sort of freedom, precisely the kind that most monarchs cannot afford. Because it might start giving the heads of the regions ideas about seizing some of their own freedom. There would be a massacre across the Zarak Empire, and Hearth would be the tinderbox. Simply by existing. So any emperor worth their salt should understand that while an autonomous city existed, there could be no talk of any absolute power. The absence of an absolute ruler meant the presence of free thought. If even I grasped this concept, surely everyone else understood it too. I didn't consider myself a political genius by any means. So, we needed to make sure that no one in the Zarak Empire even cast an eye toward Hearth. Another option would be to gain not just autonomy, but independence — although this was nothing but a pipe dream. No one would recognize a fourth empire consisting of only one city. Neither the light nor the dark. Everyone would try to take us down a notch. The only option was to make sure that the emperor stayed too busy to waste his precious time on us. He needs to be occupied. But what could Miralda be occupied with? Sweets and treats? That was a Skron-damned political game I wasn't willing to play. There was no one to even consult with. I wouldn't voice my concerns to Kimal Sarento. He was a good companion, but blindly following his advice would be a huge mistake.

Alright, these were all problems for future me. First, we needed to figure out why the palace guards weren't paying us enough attention. They were making an attempt to stop us, but they weren't particularly enthusiastic about it. It was as if something was distracting them, somehow taking up more brain space than the two deadly mages who came to the palace to destroy the emperor.

"That's right, they're breaking into the throne room!" Kimal Sarento continued to be surprised when we finally reached the central place of the imperial palace. A field of smoking bodies stretched behind us — we weren't chasing anyone, but we couldn't leave those alive who might compromise the integrity of our mithril armor with a coordinated crossbow strike. Restoring the armor was too tedious and expensive a process.

I had no desire to respond to his words. I'd realized a while ago that he was talking to himself more than anyone in particular. As wielder of *Golden Dome of Protection*, I was the first to approach the entrance of the hall and stopped, surveying the room. There were only three passages leading to the throne room — two regular ones and one secret one. We, incidentally, were moving through the secret one, intended for the emperor and his entourage. Actually, it was for this reason that there were so few guards along the path —

only a few dozen. The majority were trying to break through the two main entrances, which, surprisingly, turned out to be barricaded. They were blockaded with chairs, tables, and even a few cabinets that had been dragged in. Guards tried to break through these barricades from the corridors, but several dozen crossbowmen held the defenses quite confidently, constantly firing back and hiding behind piled-up furniture. Like the guards, the archers were clad in steel armor, so no non-magical human mechanisms worked on them. The barricade was also on the side of the secret passage, but Kimal Sarento managed to destroy not only those who besieged it, but also the defenders. Two *Dark Spikes* were enough for me to scatter the wooden fragments in different directions and completely clear my path.

"So, you weren't lying after all. You really did come to the palace," came the voice I least expected to hear. From what I knew, the owner of this voice should currently be accompanying His Imperial Majesty, fleeing our wrath. No crossbow bolts flew in my direction, so Kimal Sarento boldly followed behind and grinned, assessing the situation. In addition to the three barricades in the throne room, there was another next to the throne. And the throne was far from empty — on it sat Zurgan the First, bound and tied. The Emperor of the Zarak Empire had been captured and, judging by the symbols on the armor of the people around him, not by his own guards.

When the Emperor noticed me, his eyes, already huge, widened even more. The huge mass of a man even tried to twitch several times to throw off the shackles and escape, but was unable to. Next to the shackled Zurgan the First, I finally saw him. Count Shub was sitting next to the throne and cradling what was left of his right hand. Judging by his appearance, he had suffered greatly — his crumpled and in places shredded armor indicated that he had resorted to brute force to get into the throne room, and that even this was barely enough. The men standing around him were just as bedraggled. Some of them even stood woozily over huge pools of blood. Nevertheless, they didn't abandon their master, continuing to serve dutifully without ever asking why one of the main shareholders of the Zarak Empire had decided to capture his emperor.

But we were not Count Shub's men. While I was busy pouring dozens of *Heals* into the wounded, Kimal Sarento began asking questions:

"Please tell me, my good man — how did we end up here? If my memory serves me right, we agreed on something completely different. You should be getting on your horses going now, hurrying towards Al-Khorezm."

"Run away and let you seize power on your own?" Count Shub rose to his feet and clenched and unclenched the fist on his new hand several times, as if getting used to its presence. "Count Sarento, you don't think I could just let that happen, do you? Sooner or later I was going to stage a coup anyway — Zurgan the First's politics are completely unsuitable for me or my business. Production is suffering, trade is suffering, auction houses are suffering. Everyone is suffering, but not His Imperial Majesty, who is eager to grab as much as possible for himself. I warned you not to step into my territory. I promised to support you if you stopped pressuring me. But no — power has completely overshadowed the mind of our beloved emperor. When you burst into my office, we were just discussing the attack on the palace. So your appearance was extremely unexpected for me and — I won't deny it — I'm happy to see you here. Having strength such as yours on my side is always useful. But after what you said, it became clear that I wouldn't be able to pull off my plan any longer. Sure, we had to improvise and there were unnecessary casualties, but please note, that it was I who captured the Emperor, Count Shub. Not Archduke Valevsky or Count Sarento. And I will also be the one to direct the future of the Zarak Empire."

"If you have the power to do it," I couldn't help but retort.

"And who is going to stop me? I have power behind me — not personal power, but financial power. I have serious people standing behind me. I am able to pique the dukes' interest and prevent them from avenging the previous emperor. I know how to negotiate with General Khabensky and what to offer him. Even the high priest will support me if necessary. I have all this, but what do you have, Archduke? And moreover, I do have personal power. I have strange magic that I do not understand. I have a pupil whose power scares me so much it makes my knees shake. But there are only two of you. This will not keep the empire from falling apart. Even if you manage to stave off internal conflict, how will you protect it from the Shurgans or the Kalimans? They will swear their eternal friendship to your face, but then they will lead all their troops here as soon as they sense weakness. Or the dark ones. Do not forget that the Wall is no more. The beasts have practically captured the northern region, left without defenders after the invasion of the lithoids, but our beloved emperor does not care about this. He only cares that you two can't be captured and destroyed. The order for General Khabensky to march on Hearth was given by Zurgan the First. This was not the general's personal whim."

"The empire will not recognize either of us," Kimal Sarento said calmly. "One usurper was enough for people to understand one thing: only the true heir is capable of ruling the empire. The one who has been prepared for this from childhood. We are upstarts, Count Shub. You, me, my frowning mentor. They will not acknowledge us."

"Yes, I've heard that the young princess is staying in Hearth, I've heard. But exchanging Zurgan for Miralda would be exchanging one broken stick for another. You sit there in Hearth and do not see what the empire has become in just three months under his rule. It rests on the word of honor and the will of those who care about it. The leader must be someone who can not only govern, but also make balanced decisions based on the interests of the entire empire, and not its individual representatives. A person like me is quite suitable for this role. But you are right, Archduke, the public will not accept me. Just as they will not accept you."

"So the current princess isn't here?" Kimal Sarento looked around just in case. "I bet she's not even in the palace anymore."

"Princess Marisa is heading to one of our family estates with my family," Count Shub confirmed. "Albeit not of her own free will. I'll work on the girl, explain everything to her, raise her to have a good temperament, and she'll become a great wife."

The bound emperor struggled against his bonds, trying to break free. He clearly did not like the news that his daughter was destined to be betrothed to Count Shub. Zurgan even tried to mumble something, but the gag prevented him from speaking clearly. Besides, who would listen to the emperor now? Clearly not us. However, Kimal Sarento could not resist making a remark,

"The idea of taking Princess Marisa as a wife is amusing, and perhaps even the right choice, but how will you get your current wife on board? I always liked Sharmila. She has an unusual charm. Some special feature that makes her stand out from other women. Did you really decide to give up your life partner of over twenty years for the sake of the throne?"

"It's been three days since our divorce. If you

had gotten out a little more often, you wouldn't have missed this news. You're right, Count Sarento, sometimes it's worth sacrificing something for the throne. Sharmila herself suggested this option. The only effective one among all the others. She will remain my wife. Maybe not on paper, but in essence."

"However, you and Marisa will need an heir. Is Sharmila prepared for you to have to sleep with the princess?"

"Are you really so concerned about who I will sleep with and how my wife feels about the matter?" Count Shub asked. "Maybe it would be more prudent to discuss our next steps. Zurgan the First is my prisoner. After my wedding, the emperor will abdicate power in favor of his daughter, which will save his life. My people are now approaching the palace. Sooner or later, they will take control of everything here, but, I admit, it will be much easier to do this with you. Help destroy the defenders of the old emperor, and I will not forget you. Hearth will remain an autonomous city, will receive additional preferences, will become…"

"I'm not happy about this," I said, cutting Count Shub off. As if on command, everyone near the throne aimed their crossbows at us. Even Count Shub himself. No one cared that just a few minutes ago they were suffering and practically dying from their wounds.

"Is there something specific that you are unhappy with, my mysterious mentor, or is it Count Shub's proposal as a whole?" Kimal Sarento asked, in a tone as if nothing unusual was happening. So what, almost twenty loaded crossbows are looking at you practically point-blank. Was this the first time?

"I like the proposal, although I'm not fond of some of the details, my slow-witted pupil," I replied, turning away from Count Shub. I couldn't show fear in front of the crossbowmen. I could definitely withstand the first volley, and there wouldn't be a second. Because the box with the fifteenth-level ousel was already in my hands.

"Perhaps I should clarify my thoughts," I continued. "Count Shub is right. Replacing Zurgan with Miralda is not an option. Neither of them is suited to govern an empire. They do not have the business acumen of our mutual friend, my frowning pupil. However, I also have no right to allow Count Shub to lead the empire on his own. As our practice working together with the respected count shows, many things are sometimes decided not by agreements, but by some momentary desires. He wants to work with Hearth, he strikes up a deal. If he decides this has become unprofitable, even despite all of our existing agreements and signed papers, he will cease working with us. Let's be honest, at one time we depended on Count Shub. On his auctions, on his merchants, industrialists. We depended on many things, and it was very painful when we were deprived of all of this. If we put Count Shub on the throne now, would it happen..."

"Put me on the throne?! What do you mean by

that? I took it myself!" Judging by the shade of maroon he turned, my words had clearly upset the man. However, I continued as if nothing had happened,

"Will the same happen as before? We are friends now, but in three or four months, another army will suddenly surround Hearth. As if the piles of corpses from General Khabensky's army weren't enough, we would then have to bury Count Shub's people on top of that. This particular point is what irks me the most. Giving all power into the hands of one person when it is unclear where his loyalties lie is an extremely stupid decision, don't you think, my completely clueless pupil?"

"I fully support it, but I have to agree that we will not find a more suitable candidate for the role of emperor," Kimal Sarento also used words that put us in control of the situation, which made sense. What were crossbows against the man who won the imperial tournament? Count Shub's grimace said that he understood this as well as anyone. In any case, he had not yet given the order to destroy us.

"I have no objections to his candidacy, but I do not want to give him all the power. I am not sure that he will be able to handle it. Power must be divided."

"Divide power in the empire?" Kimal Sarento frowned. For a while he looked at me, trying to understand the logic of the decision, then understanding flashed in his eyes. He smiled and asked,

"Miralda Lertan? But you know perfectly well

that she is not capable of governing.”

“Neither is Marisa Shor. But Count Shub somehow solved the issue with her? Why not solve the issue with Miralda too? At the same time, we’ll be placing her in reliable hands, so she won’t get in the way.”

“The empire will not tolerate two rulers! It has never been and will never be!” Count Shub was clearly not in a great mood, because he allowed himself to show emotion. It wasn’t a good look for the future emperor.

“Let’s say you’re correct,” Kimal Sarento said, ignoring Count Shub’s outburst. “Where will we find a worthy candidate for Miralda? You understand that we won't find any strong ones now, and our esteemed count will devour the weak ones alive?”

“So, we need to find those whom the respected Count won't devour. I have one candidate — perhaps unwilling, but I think we have a mutual friend who would be the perfect choice.”

“Count Vyazemsky?” Kimal Sarento guessed on the first try, but immediately clarified: “Senior or junior?”

“The younger one has done nothing to us, so the elder one. This man can become an excellent counterweight to Count Shub. The counts will have to negotiate with each other to decide something in the empire. Two opinions, sometimes radically opposed, will lead the Zarak Empire to greatness.”

“Or they will plunge it into an even deeper

hole," Count Shub said. "How do you imagine governance under a diarchy?"

The answer came from Kimal Sarento. After all, he was much more experienced in such matters than I was.

"It's simple. There are the two princesses — they will act as the figureheads. Sit on the throne, smile at ceremonial receptions, meet ambassadors from other empires. In order for a decree to appear in the empire, it must have the signatures of two princesses. Although why princesses? Empresses. If one signature is missing, the decree is illegitimate. But, in addition to two young maidens, there are two mastodons thirsting for power. You will have to agree on all issues related to the empire. Who, what, when, where, why and how much — only with the presence of two of your signatures will the draft decree go further."

"Aren't you afraid that Count Vyazemsky and I will become fast friends and turn against you?"

"As if that would affect anything," Kimal Sarento grinned. "My friend, our ambitions don't extend beyond Hearth. It's enough that the city will be ours. But we won't give up what's ours. Will you turn against us? Become friends, no one is stopping you. But if the army of a new general suddenly appears at the city walls, because we still have to destroy Khabensky's, we will return to the palace. You don't think that you will gain immortality or immunity by becoming the empress's husband, do you? Our plump friend over there thought so too. The Zarak Empire doesn't touch us, we don't touch you. It's simple. My mentor, wise beyond his years, is right — you cannot be left with sole power over the empire. You are too unpredictable."

"Count Vyazemsky will never agree to this," Count Shub answered after a pause. "He will not divorce his wife."

"We can check in with him right now," I suggested. "Are you ready to make the trip to Hearth? Your people can handle things here without you. Especially since we will take the acting emperor with us. While he is in the palace, the guards will fight to the last. These are your future people, Count. You should start taking them into consideration more. You take Zurgan, Pupil. I'm afraid I lack the strength to hoist such a large frame."

A portal to Hearth appeared next to the throne, and the fighters who were ready to finish us off with crossbows recoiled from it as if from Skron himself. The monstrous and incomprehensible magic frightened people much more than some young man and former chancellor of the magic academy. Kimal Sarento calmly approached Zurgan and lifted him onto his shoulders. No one said a word when he disappeared into the shimmering veil, taking the prisoner with him.

"After you," I gestured to Count Shub to go first. "There's no point in taking any assistants — they won't be of any use in Hearth. We are a peaceful city, Count. But if you push us into a corner, we will bite. There's no point in testing the limits of what is acceptable. You are in no danger now, and I promise to return you to the palace at your first request. And don't forget — the men standing against you now will be your men once you are emperor. You should inform them that the emperor has been captured and is in Kostrishche. It's time to stop unnecessary bloodshed."

Count Shub needed a few minutes to give his subordinates instructions, and soon the shimmering veil behind me evaporated. We entered Hearth.

"Eleanore, invite Countess Vyazemsky to my office," I said through my remote connection. "I'm afraid she'll have to play the role of messenger once again. Invite Miralda as well. The girl should also be present at the negotiations. The Zarak Empire is long due for a good shake-up. And that's just what we have in store."

Chapter 14

"YOU'RE A MONSTER, Valevsky!"

"Can I take that as a 'yes?'" I ignored the remark. The meeting, originally intended as an intimate gathering of "close friends," turned into a full-scale congress of all the important figures in the Zarak Empire. While the blushing Count Vyazemsky was thinking about what to answer, I looked around the crowd once more. The Inquisitor and the Interrogator acted as guarantors of security. The creatures of Chaos had finally come out of the shadows, deciding to take a direct part in the fate of humans. For which they really deserved enormous gratitude. Which, of course, I would never show. There was no point in giving Count Vyazemsky any illusory hope that his insane attack on the city could bear fruit.

The interests of Hearth were represented by

me, Kimal Sarento, Eleonore, Alia, and even Naira. The Interrogator personally dragged my official wife from the Bartolomeo Clan, without even thinking of explaining the reasons behind this decision. The girl had not changed in the few weeks that we had been apart. She was pale as chalk, but it was not every day that the strongest creature of this world came knocking at your door.

The Zarak Empire was represented by a more impressive delegation. Zurgan the First, from whom all fetters had been removed, Count Shub, Count Vyazemsky with his wife, Georgy Vyazemsky and Serlena, General Khabensky, Princesses Miralda and Marisa, as well as five courtiers unfamiliar to me, who I was instructed to portal to the palace. Which, although this was no longer relevant, happened completely under the control of Count Shub. Once we started the conversation, it became clear that the courtiers were lawyers who knew all the intricacies of the Zarak Empire's legislation by heart. They were the most difficult to handle — for every word I said, they would chime in with five of their own. Moreover, they were so literate that it was quite difficult to simply ignore them. If it were not for my clear understanding of what I wanted to achieve, they would definitely have skewed the situation in favor of the current government.

But this was still not a full list of participants. Father Urg, the head of the Church of the Light of the Zarak Empire, was also present and maintained a neutral stance. Judging by his dumbfounded face, it wasn't every day that the Inquisitor pulled him out of the bathhouse and, after giving him just a few minutes to pack, dragged him off to an autonomous city besieged by a huge army. Nevertheless, Father Urg pulled himself together, and after quickly getting up to speed, he even put on an aura of understanding and wisdom, occasionally inserting his remarks in particularly difficult discussions. Magister Elor, as it turned out, was not in General Khabensky's army — Kimal Sarento had been mistaken, deciding that Karina Fardi was the reason behind the army's sudden appearance outside the gates. But if he had been there, I was certain that the Interrogator would have dragged him along, too. Just to give the meeting additional status.

"No, Skron tear you limb from limb! I will not get a divorce on your whim!" Count Vyazemsky could hardly control himself. What I had proposed to him went beyond all possible bounds of decency.

"It's a pity, you would have made a good husband to the empress. But..."

"I'm not finished, Valevsky!" This time Count Vyazemsky gave in to his emotions and slammed his fist on the table, leaving a deep dent. The wood didn't crack, but it did dent.

"You refused, Count." I wasn't going to wait humbly by. "Or did I misunderstand you when you said 'I will not get a divorce?' Is there any room for ambiguity here?"

"I will not become this brat's husband. I don't

want you sticking minors in my bed, Valevsky. It is low even for you. Miralda will marry George."

"Father!" George, who had turned white, was indignant, but the elder Vyazemsky could not be persuaded. One look was enough for the young man to shut up and sit back down, lowering his head. The Vyazemskys understood perfectly well what duty was and what they must do when the interests of the family conflicted with personal preferences.

"I agree," said Miralda Lertan, continuing to look straight ahead. Initially, the princess, like almost everyone else gathered, was categorically against my proposal, but after two hours of heated debate, she was forced to agree that sharing the power between two people was the only way to keep the empire from falling apart. Of course, she did not even want to touch the senior Count Vyazemsky, but Miralda managed to hide her desires behind a screen of indifference. Now, when the old Count was replaced by the young and handsome George, the screen fell.

"High Priest, I ask you to dissolve my son's marriage to Serlena Przhedetsky. What will it take?" Count Vyazemsky continued, for some reason not taking his eyes off me. Why did everyone want to burn a hole through me?

"Conduct the ceremony in the Fortress," answered Father Urg. "However, I must warn you — both parties must want this. If either spouse is against the dissolution, the Light will not allow it."

"When can we do it?"

"Today, if Archduke Valevsky delivers us all to the Fortress," Father Urg said, also turning his gaze toward me. But no one could penetrate the armor of my imperturbability. Otherwise, the look Serlena shot me would have incinerated me on the spot.

"The decision will be mutual," assured the elder Count Vyazemsky, leaving no hope for his son nor daughter-in-law that their marriage would be preserved. "The family and its interests are above personal affairs. Anything else?"

"That will be all," Father Urg said, and there was a quiet sob. Serlena covered her face with her hands and quietly mourned her unenviable fate. The girl realized that she had been used as a bargaining chip and, as soon as she proved too useless, thrown to the side like rubbish. Granted, it couldn't have been a pleasant experience, but no one would show her pity. Life went on, and there was no room for the sorrows of one individual.

"Gentlemen, allow me to intervene — this diarchy is not enshrined in law!" One of the court lawyers said indignantly. From what I'd surmised, he was also the master of ceremonies and keeper of the seals. Basically, an important old man who had served the previous emperor.

"You have two weeks to draft and agree on all the necessary legal norms," Count Shub allowed no room for doubt in his own mind that he would become the future husband of the empress, so such small details didn't bother him. "This is a technical issue that there is no point in working out within the framework of this meeting. Princess Marisa, do you agree to become my son's wife?"

"Son?" Confusion went around the room. Count Shub grinned.

"Since our esteemed partner throws his son into a cage with tigers, why shouldn't I do the same? Yes, Herbert is only sixteen, he still has a year until he will enter the magic academy, but age is a disadvantage that goes away with time. Besides, he is a much nicer person than me. Count Vyazemsky is right — there's no reason to bring minors into this, unless there really is no other way out. But I have found another way out, and I ask you — which suits you better? Me, or my son Herbert?"

"H-Herbert," the princess stuttered. She looked up at her father and he returned her gaze. Marisa's consent was a guarantee that Zurgan Shor would remain alive. Moreover, it had been decided, despite my objections, that the new residence of the still-acting emperor would be in Hearth. This was the only place his bodily safety could be guaranteed.

"In that case, Zurgan the First must carry out the abdication procedure," Count Shub concluded. "By that time, all the necessary laws, rules and instructions must be developed, and both weddings must have occurred. Becoming the husband of an empress who has not yet reached twenty-one years of age is much more difficult than marrying a princess who has already turned eighteen. I believe two or three weeks will be enough time for all this. Anything else?"

"Of course there is," Count Vyazemsky said, preparing to fight for his own future. "In addition to the wedding and abdication, there is one more point to discuss. The appointment of two main advisers with the right to veto the decisions of the empresses."

"I assume you had yourself in mind?" Count Shub said. Receiving an affirmative nod, he laughed: "Really, Count, we're already beginning to understand each other! I fully support my partner. The status of advisers must be defined and approved at the level of...I don't even know, the church? High Priest, what do you say? Will you agree to take patronage over our empire and become the guarantor of its prosperity?"

"The Church of the Light will humbly accept this difficult role," Father Urg readily agreed. "Of course, we will discuss separately how much it will cost the two advisers and the future empresses. Any guarantee must have a solid backing."

Judging by Father Urg's smile, he wasn't going to let this chance slip through his fingers. The Zarak Empire would pay dearly for two powerful advisors.

"There is one last issue left to decide," I said, remembering my own needs as soon as the discussion fell silent. "Hearth. The status of my city, our security and involvement in the economic life of the Zarak Empire. We do not interfere in politics. That is your field, but we will not allow you to limit our trade. You do not touch us, we do not touch you. Hearth will retain its autonomy, portals to the dark ones, and no one — this is imperative — will send people to attack us. Moreover, if such attempts are discovered, both empresses and their advisers must do everything to punish the guilty parties. Am I right, Count Vyazemsky?"

Vyazemsky Sr. knew how to take a punch. He didn't deign to answer me, but from the way he exhaled, I knew he wouldn't forget this blow and would try to make me pay later.

"The details will be settled between the lawyers," Count Shub concluded. "I believe it makes sense to sign a memorandum of intent, what do you say? Even though there are respected people present, that is precisely why this agreement is necessary. The Zarak Empire must begin to live by the rules. Sir Master of Ceremonies, you kept the minutes of our meeting, right? How much time will it take you to formalize them for approval?"

"Two hours," the old man said, looking through his papers.

"Excellent news," Count Shub nearly rubbed his hands together in the satisfaction of everything going according to plan. "Archduke, you will have to work again. In order for the protocol to be fully valid, my son's signature must be on it. Please bring it here. While the documents are being prepared, I suggest we take a walk around Hearth. I think no one should leave the city until we sign the agreement. Madam Eleanore, I believe you owe me a tour. I would like to see with my own eyes the city that was able to so easily wave off General

Khabensky's army."

The general, who had been silent all this time, grimaced. He clearly hated being in Hearth, but the Inquisitor's demand left no other choice. Either his personal presence at the meeting or death. Death did not frighten the old general, but the Inquisitor managed to convey the idea that it wouldn't stop with him, and that his family would be involved. They would all suffer. He had to accept the invitation and listen quietly as they decided that from now on the army would be subordinate to two empresses. And any movement must be agreed upon with their will. Or the will of Counts Shub and Vyazemsky, to get down to the root of it. The general silently accepted this fact and only the withering glances that he constantly threw in my direction showed that the old warrior categorically disagreed with the current state of affairs. But he would not dispute them. His military training would not allow it.

Eleanore acted as tour guide, showing the guests around the city. Almost all the iconic places were located near the center, so the square, the statues and the hotels under construction were just a short walk away. The dark construction teams worked tirelessly. The Temple of Skron provided us with the best builders, using not only physical strength but also magic in their work. The speed with which the walls were erected amazed even me. As for cladding and interior decoration, we used the best marble money could buy. I didn't even want to think about how much all of it would cost me, but, although it was far from finished, the results were already dazzling. The design of the entire city resembled the dark bishop's estate that I had managed to destroy. The palace of the emperor of the Zarak Empire didn't even begin to approach Hearth's beauty. Perhaps the palace of the now-dead Padishah Bayazid the Third would have come close, and even he would have stepped aside, nervously fiddling with his handkerchief at the sight of the city.

"Why did you invite me here?" Naira asked in a whisper, seizing the moment during the excursion. Sixteen-year-old Herbert was already with us — after I had visited Shub's estate for Princess Marisa, it was not difficult to portal there. In fact, now all members of the secret grand deal of the Zarak Empire were in one place. Even the future wife of Count Shub. Or ex. I didn't even know what to call her now — after the decision was made to unite Herbert and Marisa, Count Shub decided to remarry his ex-wife. It was all very mixed up.

"The Interrogator's decision," I answered my official wife, after which, glancing at her, I answered honestly: "I, personally, am glad to see you. It was a pity you left Hearth in the first place."

"Would you like me to return?" Naira asked, surprised.

"Strange question. Of course I would."

"But what about Alia? I don't wish to share a bed with her. I understand perfectly well the reasons behind our marriage and why it is necessary, I am ready to bear this burden with honor, but I do not want to live in the same house as the woman sharing my husband's bed. Leaving the bedroom every night or sleeping alone, knowing that you are somewhere in another room with her, is not a fate I wish upon myself."

"..."

I didn't even know how to respond. Naira was right — Alia used to spend all her nights in my bed. But that was before her belly started to swell. Now I had to sleep alone. Although I was rarely even home lately. If I was sleeping with anyone, it was Kimal Sarento. At least we didn't share a bed.

"I would be very glad if you came back," I said after a pause. Alia was somewhere ahead, walking alongside Eleanore. My two ladies, although I considered Eleanore mine more by inertia than by right, worked together perfectly, managing the city, removing that weight from my shoulders. I myself had no idea how, and hated doing it.

"From what I understand, you'll soon be leaving again for a long time. I'll be left alone for several months. You are the only one in Hearth who casts a fond eye on me. Even Alia sees me as dark, not human. Perhaps I can settle in Hearth as soon as you return?"

Naira looked dazzling. Every time I glanced over at her, something in my chest squeezed. I wanted to hug my wife, kiss her, rip off all the unnecessary clothes and immerse myself in a sweet world of pleasure. My gaze involuntarily slid towards the indifferent Serlena. Compared to the girl whom I had long considered the crown jewel of creation, Naira looked like the Light itself, descended from heaven. They were different in every way. Starting with appearance, and ending with the way the girls behaved in society. Naira, who grew up in the leading clan, was similar in stature to Eleanore, which was head-turning. And that made my knees go weak.

"Stay. Even if I'm not here during the day, I'll teleport to Hearth in the evenings. Now I have that ability."

"You will teleport to me?" Naira asked.

"To you. Only to you."

I wanted to tell her that Alia was busy now and would be busy for the next six months, preparing for the birth and the period immediately after, but I decided to keep my mouth shut, so as not to aggravate the situation. First, I needed to sort out Karina Fardi and push One into the second orbit, and then I'd think about what to do with Naira and Aliya. But I had no desire to sleep alone. Especially when I had such a dazzling wife.

"Thank you," Naira mouthed and blushed, making her even more enchanting. Then she suddenly asked: "Max, you're close with Kimal Sarento. Tell me, did he say anything about his plans for my sister?"

"Adeline?" I asked. "What about her?"

"As far as I know, their marriage was as purely political as ours was. Count Sarento went along with Magister Elor's wishes and took Adeline as his wife. For a while, they worked together quite closely, Adeline carried out special assignments for the Count, and even began to consider herself, if not a wife, then a pupil of the great manipulator, but after Magister Elor became Karina Fardi's mentor, the relationship between Count Sarento and my sister came to naught. She settled at home, he travels with you and doesn't even think about contacting his wife. My sister is a strong person, she understands, but she would also like some sense of certainty. Do you know if the marriage between her and Kimal Sarento is still valid? Or can it be broken off due to the changed circumstances? Did Count Sarento say anything about this? I don't think he still intends to fulfill the promises he made to Magister Elor."

"I have no idea," I answered honestly. "We never brought it up. Just like he never asked what I was going to do with you."

"And what do you plan to do with me?"

"Cherish, love and adore you," I replied, and was surprised to realize that there was quite a bit of truth to these words. I really wanted to keep Naira, despite where she came from. Dark, light — what difference did it make if I loved her?

"But I would still like to help my sister. She doesn't show it, but the current uncertainty of her situation weighs heavy on her."

"Why is she changing her mind all of a sudden? Is my pupil not good enough for her? If not now, then in a couple of months he will definitely remember her."

"Max, enough time has passed that he should have already. But, as I said, once the pressure from Magister Elor disappeared, the need for my sister went along with it. Besides…"

"Don't tell me she's found someone else!" I almost exclaimed in surprise. Had Sarento really brought such scandal into his own estate? I couldn't imagine him as a cuckold. After all, he was a distinguished gentleman and a prominent figure, who I certainly would have problems getting out of my head if I were her.

"Adeline is faithful to Count Sarento, if that's what you mean," Naira quickly assured me, blushing deeply. "But…please don't tell anyone about this. I found out by accident. Adeline didn't tell me. Do you remember the time I used her perfume to please you? Then, when I was rummaging around in her room, I found some interesting letters. I never thought that someone would write to my sister. She always seemed so detached from any relationships that sometimes it seemed as if Gerard Moises of the Gourfan clan had burned not only a brand on her face, but on her heart as well. I was astonished to find such a set of carefully preserved letters. As for what they contained…Max, do you know a man named Alejandro Gorbunov?"

"A Baron from the Western Region," I answered automatically. "Actually, that's when I met Adeline. She stayed with him because he was wounded and…Oh, come on! Don't tell me he wrote to her? He hates the dark ones with all his heart, especially after his father turned out to be a bloodhound for some dark clan."

"I only saw the letters he sent her, but from

what he wrote, my sister was replying. And her letters must have contained some explicit material. For some reason, Alejandro had a hook on her soul, but then Kimal Sarento appeared, and she hid her feelings deeply. And now that it has become clear that Count Sarento does not feel anything for my sister and the need for their marriage has disappeared, a reasonable question arises: what does he plan to do with their relationship?"

"I can't make any promises, but I will try to clarify this with him. Although I have no idea how I'll bring that conversation up. Knowing him, he will either laugh it off or not even answer. We need to approach it at the right moment."

"I'm not forcing you or anything. I'm just worried about my sister. But thank you for listening anyway," Naira snuggled up to me, and we spent the rest of the tour listening to Eleanore's enchanting voice, telling the guests of Hearth what would be located where. Several times, we heard a hoarse exclamation from General Khabensky. The old man was interested in the city's defense system, but the wise manager carefully watched her tongue and did not give in to his provocations. She even cracked a joke, making the general go red in the face.

After the walk, there was a gala dinner, where the guests reluctantly praised Hearth for its beauty and pragmatic design. Everything was arranged as any decent city should be. Starting from the buildings, ending with the sewerage system and the lighting system. The question of protection was raised again, and again Eleanore floridly avoided the answer, while managing not to offend anyone. No one asked me — apparently, my facial expression put them off of it.

"Gentlemen, everything is ready," the master of ceremonies appeared in the hall at the end of the dinner. "We have prepared copies of the protocol, I ask everyone to read them, make their amendments, and after they are agreed upon, we will begin signing."

Surprisingly, there were few amendments to be made, and they all concerned the distribution of responsibilities between the empresses and the chief advisers. Neither Count Shub nor Count Vyazemsky were going to give up even a fraction of their power. In essence, the Zarak Empire would have not two decision-makers, but four. And they would all have to somehow come to an agreement with each other. I no longer doubted that I would have to compromise with the princesses, and not bend them to my will. It was not even Father Urg who acted as the guarantor of their inviolability, but the Inquisitor himself. The Force of Chaos had apparently become completely fed up with my continued presence in Hearth. Instead of running as fast as I could towards the Kaliman Empire, I was busy handling the small details. So the Inquisitor decided to take part in order to send me on my way as soon as possible. *Tainted Blood* wouldn't obtain itself.

"The princesses' wedding will take place in two weeks," the old master of ceremonies carefully placed the signed letter of intent in the folder. "It will be a closed event, without invitations to nobility or representatives of other empires. His Imperial Majesty will spend all this time in Hearth, officially on a leave of absence. The order to this effect will be issued today, retroactively. The empire will be governed according to protocol during the monarch's vacation. The abdication of the throne will take place immediately after the wedding. The venue where all these events will take place is the palace in Turb. We will begin preparations today. Does anyone have any comments?"

There were none. Soon the sound of horns informed us that General Khabensky's army was retreating from the city walls. I'd won the battle for Hearth. The top brass of the Zarak Empire would have no time for us over the next few years. Let them squabble in their capital, we were doing well enough on our own. Now, all that was left was to win the battle for the planet. This, I thought, would be more difficult. Because there were only seven days left until the Wave hit the Kaliman Empire.

Chapter 15

"YOUR PLAN SOUNDS so simple — run two thousand kilometers in a week and immediately meet the Wave chest first, right?" Kimal Sarento looked at me like I was a child. It was an unpleasant feeling, but I saw no way out. I had no way to open a teleport to a place where I had not yet been. Horses weren't an option — they would die long before I reached my goal. The conclusion was simple: I needed to run. Because no one but me could handle a marathon like that.

But something in my pupil's tone caught my attention. "Instead of being sarcastic, you could suggest a practical option, " I muttered discontentedly.

"We can use the transport hub. The Kalimans must have one somewhere," Naira suggested, which grabbed everyone's attention. From now on, my wife sat by my side, and Alia quietly stepped aside. I didn't object — let her give birth to my child, then we'll deal with her still-active desire to join the Church of the Light. Father Urg promised to set Mother Alia up to stay with me, but I still had to live to see that happen.

"We should," Eleanore agreed. "But the dark ones won't let Max within a kilometer of there. After he destroyed two road junctions, the transport system in the light lands suffered greatly. The Temple of Skron won't take that step."

"The Temple of Skron just might," I disagreed. "They also have a vested interest in me enacting the next point of our plan as quickly as possible. But my conscience won't allow me to let this transport hub remain open and operational. I'll have to spend time destroying it. Then sort out the problems with the Temple of Skron. No, it's easier for me to run two thousand kilometers on foot. I have seven days. That's more than enough for such madness."

"Do you even have any idea what state you'll be in when you arrive at the Wall?" Alia couldn't help but ask, outraged by my calm.

"I'll try not to push myself too hard," I promised, although no one believed me. Me, not pushing myself to the Max? The world had never heard such nonsense.

"Fine, you don't want the transport hub, we'll use converts." Naira wouldn't give up so easily. "The Temple of Skron will send two supreme converts to the Kaliman Empire. They will reach the

Wall in two or three days, after which they will open a portal for you. Firstly, you won't need to destroy the transport hub, since you will not know where it is. Secondly, you won't need to run two thousand kilometers."

"Does anyone else here have any brains among you?" Kimal Sarento said, looking at the girl with respect. "Gentlemen, it's time for you to stop thinking from the perspective of the light. I expect it from Alia and my hero-loving mentor. But you, Eleanore? Why didn't you think about the fact that we have such a useful resource as converts?"

"I don't work with those beasts," Eleanore spat with vitriol. "If even one of them comes near Hearth, they will be destroyed. The Defender has been given very specific instructions on the matter."

"You need to be more flexible, my dear. Broaden your perspective, do not let your personal feelings rule your decisions. Otherwise, your opponents will take advantage of this. If not now, then decades from now. Don't forget, you are to give birth to an heir of the Valevksy line—"

"We agreed that my son would not have the right to inherit," Eleanore abruptly cut him off.

"Who, if not you, should know that you could always change your mind? Today he has no right, tomorrow he might. He could be used as a means to put pressure on you. As soon as your son leaves Hearth, a convert may suddenly leap out of the shadows. What if our wise Eleanore instantly loses her mind, and, unable to keep her complexes in check, she rushes to her son to protect him from the terrible creatures? Your opponents are waiting for such an opportunity, dear Countess. The sooner you understand that your own personal qualms about converts are harmful to Hearth, the better it will be for all of us. Hearth needs you working at your full capacity. Think about it. As for you, my mentor who had seemingly lost his mind, I am disappointed. The solution was so obvious that I'm surprised that you did not find it yourself. Of course, your readiness to run two thousand kilometers in a week is so valorous, even I would like to see it, but sometimes you need to know your limits. And act as logic dictates, not as your first whim tells you to do. I hope everyone has drawn the right conclusions from what happened and in the future will turn on your brain when it is required of you. Naira, my congratulations, in our little swamp, which has become cold and stagnant, you turned out to be the only person accustomed to thinking more broadly. Of course, your background plays a role in this, but still, you have definitely earned a bonus for your piggy bank."

"Maybe that's enough? We still need to come to an agreement with the Temple of Skron, and not listen to your sarcasm," I couldn't stand it. Kimal Sarento always managed to find words that made you want to burn with shame. After all, he had been honing his craft for the past fourteen decades. Sometimes he was an insufferable bastard.

"There is no need to come to an agreement with anyone. In two days, a portal will be opened twenty kilometers from the Kaliman Wall. Three converts will move to a predetermined point along three different routes to reach their goal with a higher probability. Exactly at noon, they must open a portal to Hearth. I had to take care of this while we were solving the problem with the Zarak Empire. If it weren't for Adeline, who kindly allocated three converts from the Bartolomeo Clan, you, my dumbfounded mentor, would have had to work ten times harder. Where are you all going? We're not finished yet. Eleanore, don't you think you're forgetting something?"

Everyone looked quizzically at Kimal Sarento. After he had solved the issue for which the meeting had convened with a single sentence, it seemed stupid to waste time on any more meaningless talk. However, knowing my student, he wouldn't hold us here without good reason. There was still some important, unresolved issue we hadn't considered. But even after several minutes of intensive brainstorming, we still came to no conclusion. No one understood where Kimal Sarento was going with this. He could only sigh.

"Alright, I'll start from the beginning, since you can't seem to see the obvious. After we signed the memorandum of intent and planned to put two princesses on the throne, it would be right, at least on our part, to stop causing mischief in the Zarak Empire. Eleanore, my dear, stop the saboteurs and return them to Hearth. Let them train hard and prepare for future campaigns. I hope no one doubts that we will need them in the future. If anyone thinks that the chief advisers of the future empresses will forget about their shameful defeat, then I have sad news for them. Neither Count Vyazemsky nor Count Shub will ever forgive us for what we did to save Hearth. Instead of crawling to them on our knees, we essentially brought the entire Zarak Empire to its knees. Not right away, but in about five years, the advisers will definitely turn their gaze towards our city. By this time, we should have a highly effective rapid response team capable of solving problems of any scale."

"Are you saying that sooner or later we'll have to eliminate both advisers?" Eleanore didn't hesitate to ask directly.

"Elimination, intimidation, kidnapping, setup. There are many options, but the result is the same — our city will be secure. Sending my immensely zealous and over-ambitious mentor all around the world will not work. We will involve him only in solving especially important tasks. Everything else should be provided by a specially trained group. Or does our city manager have any objections?"

"Not a single one. We do need to train a group like this. And I have an additional proposal — Hearth needs its own squad of rift conquerors. Kimal is right, not everything should be on Max's shoulders. We need to have additional means of closing rifts. I don't want to portend doom, but today Max is here, tomorrow he may no longer be. I can't rely on the goodwill of providence. If Max dies, and this will happen sooner or later, we must be certain that our world will not collapse with him. That there will still be people here who are capable of closing high-level rifts. My child will have a dark mirror, like the heir of the first emperor. The children of Alia and Naira will have similar abilities. These are already three potential high-level conquerors, but they need to be prepared, trained, adapted. Are you going to send them to study in the Fortress? The Temple of Skron? I don't want that. So, our own people should do the training. We need to create these people."

Judging by the silence that followed, even Kimal Sarento hadn't thought of such a thing. However, he was the first to appreciate the proposal,

"Despite the fact that your words are slightly frightening, considering the fact that neither I nor my esteemed mentor are stunned by these words, as we are not planning to die within the next fifty years at least, I am nevertheless forced to admit that your proposal is not unwarranted. If Hearth wants to remain independent in the future, it needs a leader who can extract mithril and high-level resources from the rifts. I fully support the decision to create our own group of rift conquerors. Eleanore, you have lived in this environment for eight years, you know better than anyone here who we need on our team. You are the one to deal with this issue. As well as all the others, actually. Now it is really time we go our separate ways."

Two days of freedom. You would think it would be all I could ever dream of, given the past few months, but they turned out to be chock full of mundane, everyday activities associated with work for the common good of our little community. Hearth demanded too much attention. It seemed that Eleanore took all the major concerns on herself, but between sorting out all the paperwork that had accumulated during this time, meeting with merchants, taking part in the ceremonial laying of the first stone at a dozen hotel construction sites at once, using *Heal* on thousands of sufferers who came to Hearth to restore their limbs, all my free time disappeared. Yes, there was a hospital in our city that offered everyone who wanted it, for fabulous money, and of course, full healing. It was sad that I was the only one who had good healing magic, but Kimal Sarento promised to solve this issue. All I needed to sustain a stable cash flow was the support stone *Reflection Blocker.* Kimal Sarento was already negotiating with the Bartolomeo Clan and rumor had it they were approaching a solution that would please both of us. Yes, it would be expensive, but it would be worth it — Hearth would become a pilgrimage place not only for those eager to receive the Inquisitor's or the Investigator's judgment, but also for those who wanted to regain their health. The latter, in my humble opinion, were several orders of magnitude more numerous. Overall, I had my work cut out for me, and I had to promise Eleanore that I would portal to Hearth once every two or three days to fulfill my duties at the hospital. The only thing that made me happy at that time was communicating with Naira. She remained in Hearth, as I had requested, and made my nights a lot brighter. Naira was a passionate, insatiable and tremendously arousing woman, keeping me engaged even when it seemed all my limbs were about to fall off.

The portal appeared, as always, unexpectedly. Honestly, I had forgotten all about it, in all this chaos. The servants brought food and water, which were safely hidden in the immaterial backpack. Of course, it weighed me down a little, but remembering my previous journeys, I wasn't going unprepared this time. Sure, now I could return to Hearth at any time, but who knows what could happen. What if a particularly well-cooked chicken leg puts the Wave beast in a constructive mood and it decides to sit down at the negotiation table with us? Crazier things have happened in our world.

Space rippled for a few moments to form a small undergrowth. Somewhere on the horizon, mountains towered, but it was difficult to see them through the trees. Looking around, I saw all three converts sent by Kimal Sarento. One of them formed a portal, and the other two were lying on the ground, crossbow bolts in their backs turning them into grotesque porcupines. The number of crossbow bolts protruding from their bodies was frightening. It was unlikely that the converts would be capable of doing such a thing to themselves. I took a step away from the portal to assess the situation better when a menacing cry rang out,

"Dark Ones, you are surrounded! Surrender, and your lives will be spared! You will stand before the judgment of the Stronghold. One wrong move, and we will destroy you!"

As the voice spoke, several crossbow bolts pierced the portal arch, completely destroying it. Kimal Sarento, who had come out after me, turned around sharply and extended his hand, ready to release his deadly *Chain Lightning*, but there was no one in sight. No one came out from behind the trees, no one was rushing towards us with a sword at the ready, so it was unclear who to attack. There was only a voice and bolts, two of which pierced Kimal Sarento's back. Of course, they did no harm — his mithril armor handled the attack beautifully, but the message it sent was that they would not be exchanging any ceremonious words with us. One false move and we were toast. Although, even if steel bolts were ineffective against conventional "dark" humans, if I were in the attackers' place, I would stop all attempts to negotiate and rain steel down on our opponents. If not from the tenth, then from the hundredth bolt, the creatures' defenses would be broken and they would die. I was glad that the commander leading the attack against us did not share my thinking.

"I am Archduke Valevsky, head of the autonomous city of Hearth of the Zarak Empire. I have arrived here at the personal request of Emir Hadji! And I intend to destroy the rifts that gave birth to the metamorphs!"

"Quiet, dark one! You will not defame the good name of Emir Hadji! The Kaliman Empire will never work with the dark ones! Sooner or later the

Light will gain strength, and the dark ones will know our full wrath!"

"I suspect that negotiations are futile," said Kimal Sarento, standing next to me, within *Golden Dome of Protection*'s range. "I must admit, I haven't been this nervous in a long time. I don't see where to attack. If the first strike misses the target, the lightning won't branch off. You, my pumped-up mentor, will have to use the dark aura. Most likely, level fifteen."

"Opening our conversation with the Kalimans with an act of aggression isn't the best move, don't you think?" Despite the fact that Kimal Sarento's reasoning was clear and logical, I didn't want to give in to him.

"Are you suggesting we surrender?" said Kimal Sarento. "They already know we're mages. We'll be leaving here with steel hoops around our hands and necks."

"We're prepared to surrender!" I shouted, shaking my head. Steel hoops didn't intimidate either of us. We both had vyrma blades that would easily render them useless hunks of metal. The Kalimans wouldn't be able to pierce through mithril in mere seconds (they were unlikely to pit a hundred crossbowmen against us at once. Or would they?), so there would always be time to react. On top of that, I had my dark aura, with which I could transform all living things within a hundred-meter radius into poor, wretched creatures writhing on the ground. We were not risking anything at all, so I didn't want to show aggression towards the Kalimans, who were honestly just doing their job. I want to establish a mutually beneficial and cooperative relationship with this empire, and christening this relationship with the death of several dozen warriors would likely not work in our favor.

"Don't move, you're under fire!" the voice shouted. "A man will come out to you now to put on magic-blocking hoops. If you move or hurt him, it will be the last thing you do! Hands at your sides, dark ones!"

"I hope you know what you're doing," Kimal Sarento said, obeying the order. "In any case, you must remember that we still have to reach the Wall in five days."

"I don't think it will take long," I checked the map. "We are not far from Olro, the capital of the Kaliman Empire. We will probably be taken there for questioning. Besides, they won't treat someone who calls himself the Archduke of another empire so rudely, will they? That could lead to problems..."

How naive I could be sometimes. It drove me nuts.

We were not simply tied up, we were wrapped head to toe in a chrysalis of ropes and chains. Only our heads remained unencumbered. Our arms were tightly tied to our bodies, as were our legs. Steel hoops were put on our necks, legs, hands and even our belts, intended to block magic. The Kalimans even tried to pull off our clothes, but they did not succeed — the mithril armor that mimicked a field suit cannot be pulled off without the owner's consent. This greatly angered the Kalimans — they even wanted to shoot us. Kimal Sarento was silent the whole time, allowing me to get my own kicks in communicating with the swarthy men, but when we were roughly thrown to the bottom of the cart, he could stand it no longer and gave me a piece of his mind through our remote communication link. He couldn't use magic — the Kalimans turned out to be unusually wise mage hunters, effectively incapacitating us. Moreover, using the vyrma didn't help — even if I engaged the blade, I wouldn't be able to turn my wrist to cut through the chains.

There were many of them — I counted fifty fighters. They didn't talk to us, didn't answer questions, didn't explain anything. Only once, when I got on everyone's nerves with the demand to contact Emir Hadji, they warned me that they would cut out my tongue if I didn't shut up. Anger began to boil within me, but I still managed to calm myself down, convincing myself that these ordinary soldiers were not to blame for doing their job. I had to shut my eyes and wait.

We arrived at our destination when the sun had already disappeared behind the horizon and darkness blanketed the world. The surrounding area was not visible from the bottom of the carriage, so it was impossible to appreciate the beauty of Olro. However, the whisperings I heard indicated an unhealthy excitement surrounding our cart. Too many rude shouts and unpleasant words, the general gist of which was that the dark ones must be burned post haste.

Then something completely beyond the bounds of reason — thick sacks were thrown over our heads and we made the rest of the way in complete darkness. I couldn't even see the torch light. The cart stopped, and we were thrown to the ground rather roughly. Considering that we were tied hand and foot, only the mithril armor saved us from injuries. Soon the muggy stuffiness that hung around the Kaliman Empire even at night was replaced by a cool breeze. But it was not any coolness that I would have liked — judging by the smell, we were being dragged into some kind of sewer. It stank so much that we even had to activate the mithril armor to create a full hermetic seal from the smell. When the bags were finally pulled off, it turned out that we had been dragged into a small chamber created from steel rods. An ideal place to protect society from violent mages. All this time, Kimal Sarento was having fun, communicating remotely with Eleanore. I was included in the conversation only as a listener. I managed to learn so much about myself during this time that I was even glad that I succumbed to humanity and allowed us to be captured. Eleanore, having learned that I could hear, did not mince words. She understood that the Kalimans would not be able to do anything to us, but the very fact that the Archduke of the Zarak Empire was tied up like a lowly criminal and thrown into some stinking cell infuriated her. The highest aristocracy should not allow themselves to be treated like this.

"I am Archduke Valevsky!" I continued to shout, although it seemed to me that no one was listening. "I came here to carry out the Inquisitor's order!"

"It's no use, my mentor, who continues to have faith in the good of humanity. I wonder if this faith will ever leave you. The Kalimans don't give a damn what you say. To them, you're just a dark human who stepped out of a portal. I'm sure that in the morning, the Stronghold's inquisition will come knocking and we'll learn first-hand all the delights of communication with servants of the Light. The same torturous interrogation the Evil Engineer handed out in Turb will be exacted upon us tomorrow. Are you prepared to face that?"

I didn't have time to answer — I heard foot-steps and a man approached our cage. Craning my neck, I saw a red robe — one of the Stronghold's investigators had come. This man's face was hidden by a hood, but the color of his skin gave him away as a Kaliman. And he also exuded undis-guised hatred. The kind that true warriors of the Light had, those who had fought in the front lines against the darkness.

"Tomorrow you will die. The pyres are already being prepared. We have witnessed no public burnings of dark humans in Orlo in a long time. The cleansing fire will take all your darkness. You will appear pure and immaculate to the Light. The way a person should be born. I am here to help you prepare for your final journey. Do you want to tell me something, dark ones? Repent for some sin?"

"So you won't even send us to the Dark Inquisition?" Kimal Sarento chuckled, and only now did I realize that my pupil was not at all afraid of the situation. Personally, my nerves were already starting to give way. When you don't have control of the situation, you start to feel very uneasy. But the former chancellor of the magic academy didn't feel this, as if he had some kind of backup plan. Could it be that all this time he was egging me on not to vent his anger, but for the sake of learning? So that next time I would make balanced and reasonable decisions right away, without giving in to my own feelings?

"Why should we send anyone who stepped out of a portal to the dark inquisition?" He asked, surprised. "Your guilt is proven by your very appearance. We have been watching the converts from the moment they left the transport hub. We did not destroy it on purpose, so that people like you would fall into our nets. Three different paths that led to one point are not a bad move, dark ones. But the Light is great. The Light sees everything. All your futile attempts to break into our empire will be stopped and eliminated. Darkness will never rule where the Light reigns!"

"I am Count Sarento from the city of Hearth in the Zarak Empire. We have come to the Kaliman Empire on the personal orders of the Inquisitor, who resides in our city. I hope the Stronghold knows that the Inquisitor has changed his place of residence from Al-Khorezm to Hearth? The converts were sent by the Interrogator, who is also in our city. We are fulfilling the order of the great powers and have come here to stop the Wave that will crash against your Wall in five days. Needless to say, if something happens to us, will the Stronghold not cease to exist? It will. The Inquisitor will stop at nothing to avenge his messengers. Is the Church of the Light of the Kaliman Empire prepared for such a turn of events? Do you think I'm bluffing? You can send messengers to Hearth to confirm our words with the Inquisitor. Don't want to go to Hearth? Send people to the Pope. The head of the Church of the Light will explain to you exactly who Archduke Valevsky and Count Sarento are. Our people already know that we have been captured. Through them, the information will reach the Inquisitor. If tomorrow they send us to the stake, the Stronghold will not be able to get away with claiming two or three fanatics were allegedly involved in our tragic demise. Everyone will be punished, including the High Priest. And also, we need a meeting with Emir Hadji. Archduke Valevsky was called to the Kaliman Empire to destroy two rifts with metamorphs and return the lands to the bosom of the empire, but now I'm not sure if it's worth the trouble, it this is how we're going to be treated. We've been telling you all day who we are and why we came to Olro, but they don't listen to us. And, in violation of all the rules of the Church of the Light, they don't even send controllers of darkness to us to make sure that there are no dark ones among us. For this, the Stronghold will also be punished, but not as severely as for our burning. Now you can go, nameless father. We have already said everything we wanted."

The red-robed man left, and Kimal Sarento stretched out on the floor and sighed blissfully, addressing me over the remote connection.

"Don't say anything out loud — we'll be overheard. Now, my blind mentor, we can bargain with the Kaliman Empire on our terms. Personally, I didn't really like how we had to cave in during our first meeting with Emir Hadji. Then we had to agree to almost all of the Kaliman's demands, because Hearth still wasn't a serious player. But now we have power behind us, and I plan to take full advantage of the situation. I really hope that Emir Hadji will be wary and not show his face right away. Everything that's happening now is nothing more than a game called, 'Bring down the trade price with Hearth.' They'll keep us here for a week so that we'll be even more accommodating. Then, of course, they'll apologize, find someone to blame, but in order to let us out, they'll demand that we sign some enslaving agreements. That's in the spirit of the Kalimans, which is why I've never liked dealing with them. But now, as the Wave that will sweep away the Wall is moving closer, the Kaliman Empire will pay dearly for the fact that we'll be lying here, tied up for five days."

"Blind — you used me?!" I practically cried out.

"If I had made you privy to my plans, you

would never have been so convincing. You played your role perfectly. Those cries that we were here to save them…Even I believed it at some point. Sooner or later, my still naive mentor, you must understand that the only word you can trust in this world is your own. Everyone else will use your weakness to gain benefit for themselves. Similar to how I just did, knowing how you treat other people's lives. You must become tough. Sometimes cruel. No matter, we still have plenty of time. I will knock this nonsense out of you and turn you into a worthy heir to the first emperor. This world will fall at your feet."

"You must be confusing me with someone else. I don't need the world to fall at my feet."

"Of course you don't. That is why you personally placed two princesses on the throne of the Zarak Empire, and are also going to spawn second-orbital power on your own. You. Yourself. You do not have to rule the world, my mentor, who does not yet realize his true power. It's much nicer to watch others rule the world, and once they misstep, to make decisions about how the guilty parties should be removed. That is where true power lies. And I am immensely happy to have become part of the team of the future owner of this world. Not the ruler: the owner. I hope you do not need to explain the difference? Now rest and don't even try to wriggle out of those ropes. For the next five days, we must suffer. And the more we suffer, the more the Kaliman Empire will pay — and they will definitely pay. Or my name isn't Kimal Sarento!"

Chapter 16

"EAT UP, DARK SCUM!" The warden shoved the iron plates, which slid in our direction. Half the contents spilled along the way, but I didn't mourn the loss. What the Kalimans fed us wouldn't be fit for pig slop in any self-respecting village. I paid no heed to the food, continuing to study the dirty ceiling instead. According to my timer, the Wave would hit the Wall in two hours, completely demolishing it, and a swarm of dangerous creatures would rush into the Kaliman Empire. But I didn't care anymore. In those five days we spent in prison, I had thoroughly revised my attitude on many things. Amazingly, sometimes a steel cage was an excellent catalyst for personal development. I finally realized that the Kaliman were not friends of Hearth. Partners, a source of money, resources, anything, but definitely not friends.

We had been untied the morning after our capture and even brought a bucket so we could relieve ourselves. Several dozen crossbowmen crowded around the cage, constantly keeping us in their sights. We were forbidden to approach the steel bars. We were forbidden to speak loudly. Even standing was unacceptable. Only sitting or lying on the bare floor. There were no beds in the cage. Every day a churchman in a red robe came, asking if we had any last words, but we didn't have anything new to share with him. All we did was warn them of the Wave. We didn't even ask after a meeting with Emir Hadji anymore — there was no point in that either. If Kimal Sarento was to be trusted — and after what he'd done to me, I very much doubted that this man should be trusted at all, but still — if his words were to be trusted, then there was little separation between the Church of the Light and state in the Kaliman Empire. These were not two independent institutions, but one united whole. In fact, since there were so few dark humans in this area and the methods for combating them were quite effective, the dark inquisition had full access to all humans throughout the empire, and if they began to suspect someone, the full power of the cleansing mechanism would be pointed in their direction. Both the church's and the empire's. So there was no doubt that Emir Hadji was well aware of our arrival, as well as where we were. But he did not even lift a finger to free us, instead leaving us to languish, enjoying all the delights of what passed for hospitality in the

Kaliman Empire.

"Dark ones, do you wish to unburden your soul?" the cleric approached the cage again. The only difference from previous visits was that this time the cleric's robe was white. The Stronghold's security service was tired of talking to us, or the servants of the Light had decided to bring in the big guns.

"We have nothing more to say, Nameless Brother," I replied. As much as I wanted to be angry at Kimal Sarento, I had to play his scenario out. Otherwise, everything that had occurred in the last few days would be rendered pointless. I'd definitely take it out on him later, and he'd learn to regret the moment when he decided to use me blindly, but now the implementation of his plan was still beneficial to Hearth, so I had to play along.

"You have no more threats about the Wave that will sweep away the Wall?" The churchman was surprised.

"What's the point? We've failed the Inquisitor's task — it will be impossible for me to reach your section of the Wall in time. Now I must answer to a higher being or the Light itself if you burn me. From now on, the Wave is entirely your concern. As are the rifts. Hearth breaks all agreements with the Kaliman Empire. You are free to do whatever you want with your soon-to-be hole in the ground. I find keeping an Archduke under such conditions completely unacceptable."

"Make no mistake, young man. You are not an

Archduke. You are dark. And you deserve no other treatment."

"The Kaliman Empire is free to call me whatever it pleases," I acted strictly according to Kimal Sarento's instructions. "However, I also have free will. The Stronghold prevented me from fulfilling the Inquisitor's order, so from now until I meet with the higher power, I am taking up a vow of silence. I believe that I should be punished for the fact that my words could not convince anyone that I came here to help. If the Inquisitor spares my life, I will have a lesson for the future. Pupil from now on you are my voice. I will remain silent."

I sat down and took out the remains of the food that they had given us in Hearth. When we returned home, I would have to personally thank the servants who had prepared it. Eleanore had already promised to write them a reward, but I wanted to meet them in person. Good should be repaid with good. My parents taught me this, and I wasn't about to betray this principle. As for our food, the guards tried to confiscate it several times, but they couldn't access our personal immaterial inventory. Kimal Sarento and I managed to eat the food before the guards ran into the cage, so we were by no means starving. After three days, the guards gave up on their tyranny and allowed us to enjoy a good meal without causing a commotion.

"A vow of silence?" the cleric was taken aback, clearly not prepared for such a turn of events. According to the Kaliman plan (according to Kimal Sarento), by now we were supposed to have finally broken and become compliant slaves, eager to sign any documents. This plan clearly did not envisage that I would take a vow of silence and renounce all my obligations to the Kaliman Empire before that. Let them take their agreements and close rifts wherever they want. The fact that they'd kept me in this cage for five days would cost them dearly.

I didn't reply, but Kimal Sarento finally took the reins.

"That is correct, Nameless Brother. My justice-seeking mentor deeply grieves the fact that the Kalimans did not give him the opportunity to carry out the Inquisitor's task. The Archduke is well aware of the punishment he will suffer, and the vow of silence is an attempt to somehow preserve his life. Everyone knows that the Inquisitor is merciless when it comes to unfulfilled tasks."

"We sent messengers to Al-Khorzem to confirm your words," he said apologetically, but I didn't care. Soon the white robe left without getting any words out of me, while I was deep in conversation with Naira via remote connection. In fact, this was the only way I survived five days in the cage, by speaking to the girl almost constantly. My wife turned out to be an amazing woman. I didn't know how I couldn't have seen it before! Well-read, interesting, with her own opinion on almost any issue and, what won me over most, accustomed to working with the principle that Kimal Sarento had been hammering into me since the first day of his apprenticeship: always verify the words of others. Always. Even if it seems that the person who told you could not be lying. Check and double-check. Despite Kimal Sarento's efforts, I, unfortunately, still was terrible at this. I was used to taking people at face value and I couldn't do anything about it. I had not been raised from childhood for the fate I faced now. It was time to rid myself of my inner provincial baron.

When the timer blinked for the last time and disappeared, I experienced indescribable feelings. My heart was beating wildly and wouldn't stop. The Chaos creature rushed into the Kaliman Empire, and I had practically no idea of how I would fight it. One thing was clear: any non-physical method was not suitable. Magic in all its diversity did not work against a creature of this level. Neither magic stones, nor the darkness of rifts. Ideally, the creature should be brought to a huge detachment of crossbowmen who would fill it full of steel bolts, but there was even a significant flaw in this plan: the Chaos beast could easily turn out to be a thick-skinned bastard with a hide no crossbow bolt could pierce. The only weapon I had against this monster was my *Author* sentences. I was slowly beginning to understand the syntax. I could even create a table, which was not originally in the list of templates. But I couldn't fight a monster with a table. I needed a serious weapon, but the type of spatial manipulation offered by the skill was completely unhelpful on this front. I didn't find anything interesting or useful in the templates, and all my attempts to create a simple spear had the same issue of the source material requirement. I didn't have anything in my inventory that I could sacrifice for testing purposes. Kimal Sarento forbade me from destroying the steel cage — the Kaliman must think they are in control of the situation. Essentially, all my research was purely theoretical and unconfirmed in practice. Therefore, all hope was on Kimal Sarento and his level fifty *Chain Lightning.* I suspect it was even a bit over level fifty.

"Archduke Valevsky, finally, I have been able to reach you!" Twelve hours later, we heard a voice filled with unprecedented cheer say. Emir Hadji himself descended into the cold stone box where our steel cage was located. The plump, swarthy man radiated joy, as if he had finally managed to accomplish the impossible: breaking through all the obstacles of the Stronghold to get to us. If I had not been prepared in advance, I might easily fall for such a ploy. The emotions that Emir Hadji radiated felt sincere. Such a person could easily be trusted.

As if by magic, the guards surrounding us vanished, as if they had never been there. The warden who disgustedly threw the slop they called 'food' at us every day ran up to the cage and opened the doors.

"Gentlemen, I beg your pardon for the misunderstanding," Emir Hadji continued to play his role and entered our cage. "It is all just a terrible miscommunication. You appeared from a convert's portal and the servants of the Stronghold simply had no other option but to recognize you as dark.

You don't know what I did to get through, the Stronghold is unshakable. If you're considered dark, naturally you were treated the same way. I had never been involved in dealings with the dark before, so I had no idea what conditions they were kept in. Everything concerning you was veiled in secret, and I only found out about it completely by accident a few hours ago. I immediately dropped everything and concerned myself only with getting our dear guests out of the dungeon. I went all the way to the High Priest himself! Finally, I am here, and your suffering is over. Only a few formalities remain, and we will be able to leave this place that is so unbecoming of your status. I even have all the paperwork with me already."

One of Emir Hadji's servants ran into the cage and handed his master a thin red folder. I looked at him indifferently, not moving a finger to accept the papers he held out toward me. I was not here.

Kimal Sarento came to my aid. "Archduke Valevsky has sworn a vow of silence, Respected Emir Hadji. Until our meeting with the Inquisitor, he will neither speak, nor write, nor read any sort of documents. My long-suffering and defeated mentor is ready to accept death, and so all worldly desires no longer hold any meaning to him. If the criterion for our release lies in Archduke Valevksky signing some sort of papers, I'm sorry to disappoint you. We will remain in this cage for some time. Precisely until the Inquisitor personally appears in Olro."

"What papers, Count Sarento?" Emir Hadji

slipped the papers back into the folder so quickly that all we could do was marvel at his deftness — something completely unexpected for someone with such a heavy-set frame. "Of course, you will leave this terrible place. We have already sorted everything out, all the guilty have been punished, and I assure you, this will not happen again. Sometimes, plans require a bit of flexibility, don't you think?"

"I fully support you, Esteemed Emir. Flexibility is the basis of survival in our complicated world. That is why we were compelled to eat this wonderful food for five days to avoid dying of hunger. Would you like to share a meal with us? I just happen to have some of our freshest delicacies left."

Kimal Sarento offered the same plate that the warden threw in our direction every day. Emir Hadji's mask of feigned friendliness and cheer cracked. Our prison already smelled disgusting, but the food gave off such an unpleasant sour odor of spoiled food that only those with strong stomachs could resist gagging. Emir Hadji was not among them — a look of sincere disgust appeared on his face. Kimal Sarento only grinned and continued to forge full speed ahead,

"Really, esteemed emir, you were just speaking on the need for flexibility. Believe me, it is only at first glance that the food we were fed for five days looks disgusting. In reality, it is even worse. But we had to be flexible. In order to survive and stand trial before the Inquisitor, my silent mentor had to stomach it."

"Has the Count Sarento decided to abandon all tact?" smiled Emir Hadji, returning to his usual friendliness of a merchant. The friendly mask went up again. "Why would you tell such an outright lie? Yes, you were given food unfit for even dark humans, but we knew for a fact that you had some incomprehensible and immaterial travel bags with your own food. Only the Light knows what else you might be carrying. Weapons? Valuables? I managed to convince the Stronghold not to conduct a full-fledged search. The food that was given to you is more a tribute to tradition than a real attempt to feed you slop."

"I think there is no point in our continued conversation," Kimal Sarento said, a grin creeping across his face. "At first, the esteemed Emir Hadji said that he had learned of our unenviable situation literally a few hours ago, but then it turned out that it was he who recommended that the Stronghold not conduct a full-fledged search and that he was aware of everything that was happening to us in our lovely little cage. You ignored all the messages of my magnanimous mentor, who was simply and honestly trying to seek justice in the Kaliman Empire. You were aware of who sent us, but decided to play your own game in order to slip us a few additional conditions. You deliberately condemned Archduke Valevsky to death, knowing full well how severe the punishment for failure to carry out the Inquisitor's orders can be. And after that, the esteemed Emir Hadji says that I am acting without tact? Frankly, I am a little disappointed. Could such a childish provocation concerning food really have achieved the goal of catching the wise Emir Hadji in a lie? We are ready to appear before the court of the Stronghold, the Kaliman Empire, even the pope himself. In any case, this court would be more humane than the Inquisitor's decision. We really have nothing more to talk about, Respected Emir. Our fate has already been decided."

"Twelve hours ago, one of the sections of the Wall was attacked by dark beasts," said Emir Hadji. The smile had vanished from his face. Before us stood the stoic ruler of an enormous empire. "Three hours later, the Wall was destroyed. Not breached — destroyed. The creatures rushed us. According to our generals, the Wave could reach the capital in two days."

"We warned the Kalimans about exactly this five days ago. Archduke Valevsky was sent to prevent the Wall from being destroyed. However, instead of helping us, you decided to hide us in this cage. But even from here, we tried every day to appeal to the voice of reason, to tell you what was coming. Now it has arrived, and it is not our fault you are caught off-guard."

"You intended to stop the Wave, just the two of you?"

"Thus was the Inquisitor's order. Who are we to dispute it?"

"So you can stop the Wave?"

"After the Wall has been breached?" Kimal Sarento feigned surprise. "Haven't the valiant armies of the Kaliman Empire finished the job already?"

"That's not what I was asking!" Emir Hadji said harshly, but Sarento couldn't be broken that easily:

"Neither was I. By some ridiculous coincidence, the esteemed Emir Hadji forgets that before him stand not two peasants who have crawled out of the forest and flinch at every hasty movement, but the Archduke of the only autonomous city in the light world and his pupil, a count by birth. We will easily accept death if such is the will of the Light, but we will not allow anyone, not even the pope himself, to tarnish our honor with rudeness. Five days ago, we were ready to act in defense of the Kaliman Empire. But you stopped us, and now the Wave is your responsibility. How many have you lost already?"

Judging by how taken aback the emir was, he had not expected such a question. Remarkably, he was in no hurry to reply.

"My dear Emir Hadji, let's be frank with one another. At least once in our lives. They say total openness is such an extraordinary phenomenon that sometimes it leads to extraordinary results. You want to use us to destroy the Wave. Despite how you have treated us. I won't hide it — we can help. Even now, when the Wall has fallen. But in order to understand the threat level, we must know precisely how many losses you have faced. Do we need to seek out the Inquisitor right now, or can we stop the Wave on our own?"

"Three hundred defenders of the Wall, a five-thousand-strong army, and two thousand combat servants of the Light," the emir answered reluctantly. "We took your words seriously, but the enemy was too strong. It almost didn't notice there was a barrier. People died instantaneously."

"Can I see the documents you prepared for us?" Kimal Sarento nodded at the emir's assistant, who had long since left the cage and was looming at the entrance.

"No," Emir Hadji answered too sharply, which only confirmed my suspicions that the conditions proposed were not at all in Hearth's favor.

"That's a shame. In that case, we'll have to use mine." The cunning man who was somehow my pupil pulled out a practically identical folder from his immaterial inventory, except this one was blue, and handed it to Emir Hadji.

"These are our demands. If the Kaliman Empire wishes to use the services of Archduke Valevsky, who will still have to stand trial by the Inquisitor, they will have to pay a hefty price. I need the emperor's signature on this document. We will not bargain. Either you accept our demands unconditionally, or we remain in this cage protected from external attack and wait for the Wave to reach your capital."

"Have you lost your mind?!" the emir exclaimed in shock when he read the documents. I wondered what astonishing thing Kimal Sarento could have written to warrant such a reaction, but I remained silent, staring indifferently at the ceiling. The ongoing conversation did not concern me. Although the very fact that Kimal Sarento had prepared for this expedition so thoroughly that he had even jotted down a list of demands in advance, commanded respect. Of course, Kimal Sarento still infuriated and angered me by using me without my consent, but it was impossible not to acknowledge his effectiveness and usefulness for Hearth. For the sake of the city, I could tolerate worse.

"I will repeat: this is a mandatory list. If we don't get anything, we'll turn to the Inquisitor for justice. If you want to stop the Wave, sign this document. You have no other option."

"Don't you think your ambitions are a bit lofty?" Emir Hadji asked, irate. "Don't forget where you are. It would be easy for us to close the cage and forget about your existence. How long can you hold out here?"

"I'm actually quite glad you brought up our particular predicament in this interesting little prison, Esteemed Emir. We have an additional demand: we need the perpetrator. Not the warden who fed us slop, not a handful of servants of the Light who are supposedly responsible for our captivity, but the real perpetrator. The high-born. The one who made the decision to put us in this Light-forsaken cage and keep us here for five days. That is a long time, esteemed emir. An impermissibly large amount. You have to pay for everything, including your mistakes. As far as I know, you have a daughter. Now, if my memory serves me right, she's seventeen years old. Even if the emperor signs these documents, we won't budge until you swear that your daughter will become Archduke Valevsky's concubine. Not his wife. My magnanimous mentor already has a spouse, and polygamy is not practiced in the Zarak Empire. A concubine, emir Hadji. Without the right to inherit. If you thought we were kind and sympathetic people, you were deeply mistaken. We are vengeful, and we will hit you where it hurts the most. The next time you decide to bend Hearth to your will, you'll think twice. Your daughter is the main condition for my mentor to stop the Wave. You can go now, we will not detain you any longer. The sooner you sign the documents, the fewer Kalimans will be destroyed by the invading creatures. And remember, the agreement to destroy the rifts is no longer valid. You will have to pay much more for them than you originally offered."

Emir Hadji left silently. Several dozen crossbowmen took his place. Without even turning in our direction, the Emir gave an order that would forever determine the fate of the Kaliman Empire:

"Kill them!"

Chapter 17

"THAT'S IMPOSSIBLE," Emir Hadji said in shock, when a squad of fifteen crossbowmen were lying motionless on the floor. I didn't even have to switch on my dark aura — *Golden Dome of Protection* was enough, reflecting all the bolts back at my opponents. They were simply not prepared for such a turn of events and went to meet the Light, undoubtedly to ask what in Skron's name was happening in the cellars of the Stronghold.

It would be reasonable to ask how I managed to activate my shield with so many steel hoops hanging on me? After all, these were the most effective magic blockers our world had to offer! The answer was simple. Even in the magic academy, I had noticed a certain peculiarity about myself - my mind began to cloud not before using magic, but later, literally three or four seconds later. Moreover, *Heal*, enhanced by the *Block Reflection* support stone, successfully dealt with the consequences of using steel hoops. You could roll me into a steel barrel, I would still retain the ability to resort to magic without harm to my own health. Which, by the way, could not be said for Kimal Sarento. He had to use the vyrma blades to cut the hoops off of himself.

When the terrible order sounded out, I activated the protective dome and came close to the bars of the cage, bringing one of the edges of the dome out. It did everything for me — a coordinated shot from fifteen crossbows could not penetrate my level thirty shield, and the support stones *Damage Reflection* and *Steel Resistance* demonstrated to the archers that all the world's ills could not be solved with steel.

"Hasn't the respected Emir Hadji realized yet who he's dealing with?' Kimal Sarento stood next to me. "I would think that one of the four emirs of the Kaliman Empire, and the greatest one to boot, would understand people better. Has the respected emir not even asked himself why both the Inquisitor and the Interrogator settled in Hearth, and Archduke Valevsky was sent alone to stop the Wave, which your army couldn't handle?"

Kimal Sarento leaned over and picked up his folder, which Emir Hadji had thrown aside like a piece of trash. Hiding it in his immaterial backpack, my pupil immediately pulled out a new one, only this time it was red.

"I assumed that the Kaliman Empire would try

to pull something like this off. Well, everyone must pay for their actions. These are our new demands, Esteemed Emir Hadji. Now they are significantly higher than those you so zealously refuted. Your daughter must still become the concubine of my silent mentor, but now the youngest son of the great Sultan of the Kaliman Empire, Emperor Boro, will have to go to Hearth for ten years of training. We will make a real fighter out of him. You are free to do as you wish. You can agree with our demands, you can reject them. Hearth will come out on top in any case. We will return here in exactly two days. If the papers signed by Emperor Boro, his son and your daughter are not waiting for us here, we will leave again. And then the Wave will turn the Kaliman Empire into a desert, once and for all. It will do what two rifts could not. Two days, Emir Hadji. You have only two days."

His eyes nearly popped out of their sockets when I activated the portal with a wave of my hand. The bloody shimmering veil that appeared in a split second without the voluntary sacrifice of a convert could have scared anyone. Including one of the four great emirs of the Kaliman Empire. The information that Archduke Valevsky had magic in his arsenal that was not subject to steel cages, as well as the hoops with which I was still hung like a buffoon in multi-colored ribbons, had not yet reached the Kalimans. That was their problem. I, for my part, was doing everything I could to help them.

However, my mood was worse than ever. When I returned to Hearth, I stared at my throne for a long time, as if I couldn't understand why it was so empty. Both forces of Chaos were currently meeting with people, enacting their own twisted sense of justice, so the main hall of the palace was empty.

"How long do you intend to suffer, my unfortunate mentor?" Kimal Sarento was clearly in a good mood. "You have two days of freedom."

"Have you thought about how many innocent Kalimans the Wave will destroy?" I asked him directly.

"Many," he replied shamelessly. "If you need more precise data, I can give you that too: way too many. According to my estimates, in two days the Kaliman Empire could lose a tenth of its population. But these are the sacrifices we must make to achieve our goal. You did everything you could. You sat in a cage for five days, every day trying to bring the fools who imagined themselves to be the center of the world to their senses, but it did not help. Any healer who does not possess magic will tell you: in order to save the entire being, it is necessary to cut off the rotting flesh. And, as scary as it may sound, along with the rotting flesh, they cut off a part of the still-living tissue. Because otherwise the infection will spread further. That is the situation here, my mentor, who loves people too much. If you did not notice, he gave the order to kill you. Not to scare you, not to leave you in a cage for another week — to kill you!"

"That's how Emir Hadji should have responded, and not sacrificed a thousand simple peasants!" I almost screamed, but held back. Emotions were not my best advisor at the moment.

"First, look at the map, my overly sensitive mentor, and then go into hysterics," Kimal Sarento always knew how to justify his actions. "We did not commit any mass genocide. All the main settlements of the Kalimans are located behind the capital, relative to the Wall. On each side where the Wave penetrated, there are desert lands — both rifts with metamorphs are there. Some even think that a portion of the Wave might rush into the depths of the desert to meet the deadly creature head-on. The only large city that stands before the Wave is the capital itself."

"You said that ten percent of the population of the Kaliman Empire would die."

"That's right. The residents of the capital plus the army and the combat servants of the Light. Not the nicest guys — in fact, without their existence the Kalimans will become much more accommodating. But if our friends come to their senses and accept our demands, no one will die. In two days we will arrive in Olro and meet with Emir Hadji again. I am sure he will not hide any information from Sultan Boro. This would only make more problems for him, and our esteemed emir certainly loves his life. His well-fed frame speaks for itself. So you can rest and...Where are you going?!"

Kimal Sarento's exclamation was entirely justified — a portal had popped up next to me. I wasn't going to explain anything to the man who was so brazenly using me in his dirty plans. Even if logic dictated that these plans were useful.

"I'll be back soon."

"As you say, my mysterious mentor. As long as you don't cause trouble. The Kalimans must suffer. If you stop the Wave before it becomes visible from the walls of Olro, our extended stay in the cage will have been for naught."

"I'm not going after the Kalimans," I reassured Kimal Sarento and, before he could utter his next grandiose phrase, disappeared into the portal. Five days of idleness and constant communication with Naira finally determined my further plan of action. If I wanted a quiet life, I needed to get rid of Karina Fardi. Only then would it be possible to safely travel through the dark lands and destroy high-level rifts. So it was time to act.

The portal led me to one of the deserted rooms of the Citadel. Once upon a time, my first, seemingly frank conversation with Kimal Sarento took place here. It was only later that I realized that the then chancellor of the magical academy of the Zarak Empire wasn't being transparent at all, but rather playing one of his long games. The portal disappeared and the room plunged into darkness. For a while, I listened, ready to jump back to Hearth, but it proved unnecessary. No one had noticed my arrival. The first step of my plan had been accomplished.

I carefully cracked the door, letting in a sliver of light. There was no one in the corridor. I activated the magic stone *Phantom,* reinforced by several useful support stones, and the space in front of me blurred. One of the main requirements of the concealment stone was that it required you to be in shadow. The shadows themselves seemed to glow suggestively, urging you to step into them as soon as possible. A five-second countdown timer appeared in well-lit areas. If you did not step back into shadow during this time, the ability would be deactivated, and a new timer would appear: three hours until the next use of *Phantom.* The stone knew how to punish for improper use. I'd found this out the hard way, but if you switched it off yourself before the timer did, the ability would remain available. There was always a way to cheat the system.

The path of illuminated shadows led me to another corridor, from there to the street, and soon I was sneaking up on the main building of the Citadel. Today was the first time I had used *Phantom* in a long while, so I was encountering some issues for the first time. For example, the servants of the Light scurrying around the Citadel were constantly about to crash into me. The brothers in various robes did not notice me and, wanting to overtake their slower comrades, accelerated suddenly and made sharp movements, forcing me to demonstrate my acrobatic skill, sometimes even balancing entirely on the big toe of one foot. It was easier to avoid people in open spaces, but as I approached my main target, certain doubts began to arise about the pragmatism of my plan. There were guards at the entrance to the main building of the Citadel. Moreover, the doors were closed. I had to scan the perimeter of the building, looking for other places of entry, but there were none. The pope's residence had absolutely no windows. The solid walls rose up several dozen meters, and another group of guards was located above. After what Karina Fardi had done in the Citadel, they had begun to take their own security much more seriously. Such incompetent spies as I would not penetrate their defenses so easily.

Nevertheless, I got lucky. I returned to the main entrance and began to think about how to neutralize the guards when a large multi-colored delegation approached the building, with representatives from all shades of frock. I even chuckled in surprise, noticing the Pope himself among the crowd. He was walking in the center, surrounded by the attention of his closest henchmen. Eyes filled with Light slid over the place where I managed to hide, and a sense of danger arose. As if the head of the church somehow incomprehensibly saw me. Which would be quite a feat — my *Phantom* was pumped up to level twenty. In our world, there are not many creatures or devices that could detect a person hidden by such a magical stone. And it was unlikely that I was noticed — the pope continued to calmly speak to the cardinals and other heads of the church.

The main doors opened, and the entire delegation slowly moved inside. Considering that none of the simple servants of the Light were in a hurry or trying to overtake such respected people, it was quite easy to adjust to their pace while hugging the walls. In addition, the shadows that people cast were my saving grace. The timer didn't pop up even once. Soon the group began to thin out — first the simple clergy left, then the heads of some services, followed by the cardinals, and I went up to the fourth floor of the main building accompanied by the pope, the commander and several guards.

"Thank you for your service, you may leave for today," the pope said to the guards as soon as we reached his office. Or the spot that must serve as his office. Recently, I had spent a whole week living in the Citadel as I hunted down dark ones, but I had never been on this floor. And to be honest, I'd never set foot inside this building. So I had no idea what this was — an office or the personal living quarters of the head of the church.

The doors to the room opened, and before anyone realized what was happening, I slipped inside fast as lightning. It was dangerous to be near the commander — some kind of inner light emanated from him, making the shadows unsafe. Even now, when I passed by, a timer appeared, and the warrior of the Light twitched as if he'd sensed something. He began to turn his head from side to side, trying to find even the slightest hint of movement. The slightest scent. The slightest trace. But there was nothing. Over the course of my adventures, I'd finished off more than a dozen high-ranking invisible figures, so I now had the best support stones our world had to offer.

"Your Holiness, something's not right. I sense danger. Allow us to stand guard outside your office," said the commander, clearly dissatisfied with his uselessness. But the fact that he did not hide his fears from the head of the church inspired respect. Many in his place would have decided to remain silent about their groundless suspicions.

"No need. No one and nothing threatens me in this place. You can rest."

The pope's voice, as always, seemed serene, pleasant, and somehow enveloping. For a moment, a treacherous feeling of betrayal arose in my chest. I wanted to quickly get out of this place, go up to the first servant of the Light I came across and dump all of my problems onto him, but I managed to swallow the impulse. These were not my true feelings. My true desires. I came here with a very specific goal and I had no right to retreat. My life depended on it. Instead, I looked around. The office. There were no beds, in any case, but there was a huge table covered with various papers.

"Yes, Your Holiness," the commander bowed and closed the door behind the pope. The head of the Church of the Light slowly ambled behind the table like the ancient man he was and took his seat in a luxurious armchair, somewhat reminiscent of my throne. He sorted through the papers for a while, after which he suddenly said,

"How long are you planning to stand there, Archduke Valevsky? I suppose the matter that brought you to my office is quite serious, since this is how you show up. Sit down. Pour yourself some wine. I highly recommend it. I can guarantee that it is no worse than the miraculous elixir produced according to the secret recipe in the Sarento estate. By the way, I am surprised that you showed up here without your pupil. He has the reputation of being a much more skilled wordsmith than yourself."

"Good day, Your Holiness." I deactivated *Phantom* and accepted the invitation, sitting down on the guest chair. I was right after all — the pope's Light-filled eyes had spotted me, despite all my high-level magic stones.

"What has brought you here?" he asked, gesturing for me to pour the wine myself.

"Your scepter," I answered honestly. What was the point of beating around the bush? "Or rather, the magic stone inlaid into the top as a symbol of purity. I need it, Your Holiness."

The pope looked at me for a long time without blinking, then stood up and walked over to the wall. There was a safe there, and inside was the item I needed. The head of the Church of the Light stared at the symbol of his power as if seeing it for the first time and finally found what I was talking about — an inlaid octagon. Not the stone itself — a voluminous "box" where the real stone was hidden. If you didn't know about the contents, you would never guess that there was something inside. The stone was firmly wedged inside.

"You do realize the huge number of questions you have just generated, Archduke Valevsky?"

"From what this stone is for to how I learned about it?" I asked with a smile, and was greeted with a smile in return. "There is no secret in this, your Holiness. True, many things may seem very unusual to you, but they are what they are. You know about the great powers and the three orbits in which they reside, correct?"

The pope nodded, demonstrating that he was, in fact, aware.

"Excellent. In that case, my story won't take long. It all started when Karina Fardi and the Temple of Skron decided to occupy the vacant spots in the third power orbit..."

I didn't see any harm in letting the pope in on the current affairs of the world. At the same time, he would also know that I wasn't just running from one empire to the next, but carrying out specific assignments and saving the world from a global catastrophe.

"So you are a messenger of the Abyss?" The pope said thoughtfully when I finished my fascinating story.

"More like a messenger of the ancients, but without their desire to destroy the world. In fact, I like to think that I am my own messenger. I am in support of preserving the balance in our world to finally put an end to the endless cycle of madness."

"However, you yourself generate this very madness with enviable regularity."

"Madness? Hearth is the only city in this world where the light and the dark can exist side by side without regard for others. Where nothing threatens them. Where they can fully realize themselves. How is this madness?"

"Is that why you decided to flee the Kaliman Empire, leaving it to be torn apart by the Wave?"

The pope's question caught me off guard. I didn't even know how to respond, so he continued,

"The church has its own ways of transmitting information over long distances, young Archduke. Your abilities are not unique to you."

"Then you should have known that I was kept in a cage for five days."

"From which you could have escaped at any moment you wished. But you decided to play your pupil's game. A game of chicken, to see who would go further. Congratulations — you've gone farther than anyone else has ever gone. This unusual Wave is truly a threat to be reckoned with. Which the Kalimans are powerless to stop. But instead of standing up for innocent people, you decided to give them over to be torn apart by the beasts in order to get a little more profit for your city. You say you want to fight madness? Aren't you the one who breeds it, more than anyone else in this world?"

"No, Your Holiness, that won't work with me. Yes, I was in the cage of my own free will, but I've been warning the Kalimans for five days about what would happen. I tried to convince them to let us go and give us a chance to fight back the Wave. To protect their empire. It's not my fault that they didn't listen to me. It's not my fault that the Wave proved too tough for the Kalimans. It's not my fault that Emir Hadji ordered me to be killed. Oh! You don't know that yet? Yes, just a couple of hours ago, before we jumped back to Hearth, Emir Hadji ordered the crossbowmen to kill me and my pupil. He didn't like our demands. There is no madness in my actions, Your Holiness. But I won't let others take what's mine. If someone has decided that they have the right to communicate with me from a position of strength, they must demonstrate this strength. The situation is currently such that the Kalimans are not only unable to prove it, but are also unable to protect their lands. You know as well as I do where the demolished Wall is located in relation to the capital. The Wave will not be able to cause significant damage until it reaches the capital."

"No significant damage? I wonder at what point this young man, who was once concerned for every doomed soldier sacrificed for protection symbols, became a cynic who places no value on human life and has decided that he has the right to decide who lives and who dies."

"It happened the moment I went from being a doomed soldier to the ruler of an autonomous city, Your Holiness. When I was alone, I could risk my life to save others--everyone I could. But now I have a city behind me. People who trust me with their lives. Swore allegiance. I am not responsible for the people of the Kaliman Empire. I have no such right. Sultan Boro, Emir Haji, and even your High Priest have that right. Everything that happens in the Kaliman Empire, with the people living there, is the result of their actions. Good or bad, it makes no difference. They decided that it was best for them, and the people who trusted them are responsible for the decision of their rulers. It is not for me to judge or save them."

"Nevertheless, you still want to stop the madness that reigns in the world. Why? What good does it do you if One ascends to the second orbit?"

"Because Karina Fardi in the third orbit is dangerous for my city. I do not protect the whole world, Your Holiness. That is too much for me. I protect my city. Skron's vessel promised to destroy all the light touches once she received power and authority. Hearth is light, so I cannot just step aside and see what happens. I need to protect my people. And to do so, I need this stone. With its help, I can destroy Karina."

"Well, young Archduke, I appreciate your openness. It's amazing that you don't try to dodge, hide information, or portray yourself as a victim or a hero. The Citadel closely monitors what's happening in the Light lands. When I say 'closely,' I mean that it thoroughly and meticulously studies everything that has any value for us. Starting from your venture into our treasury with a full list of everything that was missing, ending with your extremely amusing agreement with the High Priest of the Zarak Empire. Using the mechanism for modernizing people to compromise me and the cardinals in the eyes of the Inquisitor is quite an interesting move, I must admit. I always appreciated Father Urg's unconventional approach to solving problems. But I have a question: why do you want to be involved in this? Why does the young Archduke of an autonomous city want to change the government in the Church of the Light and put on the throne a person whom the Light will never accept as one of its own? I hope you will answer this question with all your inherent openness and honesty. For, and I will not mince words — your life depends on it, young Hunter of Darkness."

Chapter 18

"ISN'T THE ANSWER obvious?" I asked in surprise, refraining from glancing around. I had a feeling that we weren't alone in the office, but I couldn't prove it. In any case, the box with a level fifteen ousel appeared in my hand. That would be enough to cool the ardor of any zealous invisible man, if he somehow managed to hide in the room. The mithril armor, of course, helped me see all the people who used *Phantom*, but the Church of the Light had already proven more than once that it was full of unpleasant surprises. You had to be prepared for anything.

"I'd still like to hear it," the pope remarked calmly.

"Alright, I can say it out loud. I have a lot of serious questions for the Citadel, Your Holiness. You permitted the circumstances that led to a whole cabal of dark ones to settle within your walls, one of which forced me to employ the Inquisitor's services. I'm sure you already know what he demanded as payment? The Inquisitor wanted me to destroy two third-orbital forces in order to restore balance. The wave that has now rolled over the Kaliman Empire is the Inquisitor's creation. It is led by a being carrying a special ability that he wants to pass on to me. Despite the fact that the Inquisitor now lives in Hearth, I do not separate him from the Church of the Light. Therefore, when Father Urg rolled out his demands, I had to agree with them. Whether it's you or him makes no difference to me. The Church of the Light is already compromised, so it does not matter who sits on the white throne. In fact, I'd prefer him — I know exactly how to talk to him. You, no."

"Well then. I asked for the truth and I got it. I can't say that I liked it, but I understand that I deserved nothing else. This is a list of everything that was taken from our treasury."

He pulled several sheets of paper out of the drawer and placed them on the table in front of him. Apparently, I was supposed to take them, read them, and moan and groan for a while about how I was going to return all this, but I wasn't going to do that. After rummaging through my immaterial backpack, I pulled out two ancient tomes. They were useless to me now — I had already downloaded everything I needed.

"This is all I took out of the treasury. If you want the rest, contact Father Urg, whom you like so much. It was his grubby little paws that cleared out half your shelves. He took everything he could lift."

"He was in the treasury with you?" His genuine surprise suggested that he hadn't been aware of this.

"I suggest we return to the scepter, Your Holiness. I need the stone. I'm afraid it's something I simply must obtain, otherwise no one will stop Karina Fardi."

"And who will stop you, young Archduke? Once you gain power, who will limit you?"

The pope knew how to ask the tough questions. But I had an answer to this, too:

"Chaos. After I stop the Wave, I will gain an ability that will make me a weak-willed servant of the higher entities. For now, I still have the opportunity to argue with them and not instantly rush to carry out their orders, but this freedom will be taken from me. Any deviation from the desires of the Inquisitor or anything done of my own volition will lead to my death."

"And you're willing to make this sacrifice?" For the first time, the pope seemed at a loss for words.

"I can go back a few minutes and remind you once again that I got into this situation at the moment when the former head of the Citadel's supply decided to destroy me. When I had to call the Inquisitor to stop him. Now I simply have no choice, Your Holiness. I have an order and time to fulfill it. If I do not get the stone now, I will get it later, and I'll leave a trail of corpses behind me. As the

Inquisitor's envoy, I will be physically unable to exchange niceties with anyone preventing me from fulfilling his will. I will return to the Citadel and leave a mountain of bodies in my wake. I know this better than anyone, so I decided to come here before I lost my free will."

"By sneaking in like a criminal."

"Are you trying to tell me that if I just showed up at the Citadel, out in the open, and demanded an audience with you, you would grant me one instantly? It would take at least two days. I'm sorry, but I don't have that much time. In two days, the Wave will reach the capital of the Kaliman Empire. I don't need any unnecessary casualties."

"I do not understand your motives, young Archduke. You are speaking too calmly for a man who is about to lose his free will in two days."

"You have bad spies, Your Holiness. I've been shouting and crying about it, and I'm out of steam. Now I'm in the acceptance stage and trying to make sure that even after my disappearance, Hearth remains strong and independent. I'm sure that sooner or later the Inquisitor will give me a task that will be impossible to handle. So for now I'm running around like a chicken with its head cut off, trying to be everywhere at once."

"So your priority is the city? The one that is governed by everyone but you?"

"It is," I said. "I don't need to micromanage every construction worker in order to feel like the rightful master of Hearth."

"Are you so confident in your city manager?"

The pope had set out to plant a seed of doubt in me. "Do you know why her family was stripped of their privileges and struck from the registry of families in the Zarak Empire?"

"I don't care who Eleanore was nine years ago. She is now the governess of Hearth and the mother of my child. That is enough to trust her. Your Holiness, please stop turning me against my people and just give me the stone. I have too much to do to waste time on useless arguments.

"Very well, young Archduke, your people are your problem. After all, who better, if not a high-level *Analyzer*, to detect betrayal? There remains one last issue to be resolved: the High Priest of the Zarak Empire. Why do you insist on calling him by name?"

"I don't think that's a question I'd like to answer. It's personal."

"That's answer enough," he laughed. "So, deep down, you know that this man is not worthy of even occupying my current position, yet you stubbornly try to help him take my place. Why? Wasn't Bishop Zwat, one of the nine heads of the Church of the Light of the Zarak Empire, allied with the dark ones? After all, it was in the battle with this traitor that you received a limit on the number of rifts you could destroy per year. Why didn't the Fortress' betrayal irk you, but as soon as it came to the Citadel, you immediately got up in arms? Or do you think that Bishop Zwat was the only accomplice of the dark ones? Did the High Priest really allow you to check all the servants of the Fortress, as the Citadel did?"

"Perhaps it's time to stop beating around the bush, Your Holiness. I can see that you have some idea that you are persistently trying to lead me to. As you yourself pointed out, I am not Kimal Sarento. He is the one who is adept at grasping at vague hints and building coherent, logical constructions from them. I'm still not at his level, so let's be clear and specific. What do you want?"

"Has the Temple of Skron already given you the modernizing device?"

"I'll have it in about a week and a half. It takes time — the modernizer is currently immobile."

"So the High Priest will come to the Citadel in person," the pope smiled sadly. "I thought that he would catch the cardinals one by one outside the Citadel and send them to the device with your help. But I didn't even consider that the device could be dragged to the Citadel and used here. You said that Father Urg made his demands, which you had to agree to. What are we talking about?"

"A book of the ancients," I said, nodding at the device I had thrown on the table. "Father Urg is in possession of a certain artifact I require. In order to obtain it, I agreed to get him the modernization mechanism. He will do everything else himself, without my help."

"Let's say that I get you this book," the pope suggested. "What will you do with the Temple of Skron's device? Will you still give it to your High Priest?"

"It's not mine," I answered after a pause. The

pope's question puzzled me greatly. "If I get the book, then the modernization device will remain in the Temple of Skron. Father Urg will not receive it."

"So you're not bound by any other agreements with this man? What about the fact that he's considered the adoptive father of Mother Alia, your would-be wife? As far as I know, Father Urg promised to talk to her, encourage her to stay by your side and not return to the Church of the Light after the birth of your child."

"I'm not sure what answer you expected from me. Alia will remain in Hearth. It has already been decided."

"Even if you receive an order from the Inquisitor?" He had hit a sore spot. Now, while I had not yet received *Tainted Blood,* I could still talk back to the powers of Chaos. As soon as I stopped the Wave, and I would have to do this no matter what, there was a chance that the ability would put me in a position of eternal servitude. Of course, I had slightly embellished the consequences of receiving the ability, but I had to accept the fact that soon, I wouldn't be able to destroy any orders from the Inquisitor or Interrogator. They had already forbidden me from taking Alia as a wife, who knows what the creatures of Chaos would come up with in the future?

"I propose we cooperate, young Archduke. Father Urg is well-suited for his position. He holds the Zarak Empire with an iron fist, and now that the main competitors are gone, he will continue to do so for the next twenty years, despite the elections. There are simply no other alternatives. Father Urg is too far from the Light — I would not like to see him at the head of the church. Bring the modernization device to the Citadel, and you will receive the book of the ancients that you so desire. Moreover, Mother Alia will remain with you. I will talk to the girl personally. If necessary, I will defrock her and excommunicate her. You need her, young Archduke. She makes you more human."

"So you are suggesting that I betray Father Urg?"

"Do you have warm feelings for him? Are you bound by something more than your current agreement? I don't think so. The High Priest will keep his position, I have no desire to remove him."

"Why does the Citadel need the modernization device?"

"Not all dark ones are loyal to Skron. Some of them, like your former mentor, the Evil Engineer, deserve a second chance. But without modernization, we are unable to rid them of Skron's influence. Anticipating your question, the development crystals that turn dark ones into gray ones are in fact a very unreliable means. Crystals are fallible. Today a person is gray, tomorrow he is dark again, and we cannot change this. Modernization eliminates this defect. The dark one will remain dark, but out from under Skron's control."

"If it were that simple, then the Temple of Skron would have modernized all the dark ones long ago in order to escape from external influence."

"Skron is lenient about his children hiding behind development crystals, but he cannot abide them completely and unconditionally leaving his sphere of control. The dark ones use modernization in a different manner, unrelated to their attitude toward Skron. Changing appearance, upgrading abilities, restoration, take your pick. The Citadel wants to have a mechanism that will allow those who want to escape from the dark guardianship and get a chance at a new life."

"A life like the Evil Engineer's?" I couldn't resist a little sarcasm.

"Even a life such as his is better than death," answered the Pope. "And do not forget, young Archduke, it was this dark one who taught you to survive. To fight. To stand up and fight where others would have given up long ago. But it seems to me that we have strayed from the topic. If the ancient tome you require is delivered to you within a week, are you ready to cooperate with the Citadel, and not with Father Urg?"

"You didn't even ask what book I need."

"It's unlikely that you snuck into our treasury just for a volume of ancient poetry," the pope smiled. "The world doesn't need global upheavals now, young Archduke. Father Urg will remain the High Priest of the Zarak Empire and will continue to make his global plans to take my place. He is serving his purpose, so he will live."

"What purpose is he serving?" I frowned at this news.

"It is impossible to carry out a coup alone. You need assistants. Traitors. Those who are unhappy with the current state of affairs and are ready to change it. When evil is known, it ceases to be evil. It becomes a useful tool in the fight against dissenters."

"The book, Alia, and the resource conversion mechanisms," I said, weighing the pros and cons. "Hearth needs the Citadel's express approval to produce all kinds of elixirs. Accordingly, we need the equipment delivered, and subsequently, for it to be maintained."

"Anything else?" the pope asked coldly. Elixir equipment had always been the cornerstone of any negotiations with the Church of the Light. I had already tried to obtain the rights to create elixirs, but last time I was refused. Well, I wasn't too proud to demand a second time. Looking at the head of the church, I nodded,

"Yes, there is one more condition. My path forward is simple — close the Wave, obtain the new ability and pass through the level seventy-one rift. That being said, I will need to create a level one hundred rift. The highest available. Using the rift, I will adapt to the darkness of Skron, and I'll have a chance to actually come out victorious in my upcoming battle with Karina Fardi. Destroy the Skron vessel in its active phase. The cons: there will be nothing left alive in a hundred-kilometer radius. Maybe more — it's better to plan on a hundred twenty, a hundred thirty kilometers. And when I say nothing will be left alive, I mean even the insects will die. It will be even scarier than the desert. If you really claim that the Citadel now works with Hearth, I need a rift that I can increase to level one hundred."

"And destroy a huge swatch of land in the process. Why don't you want to do it in the dark lands?"

"Karina Fardi. She is working closely with the Temple of Skron. As soon as I start growing the rift, I'll attract their attention. Until I pass a hundred, I can't meet Karina. If I step into the dark lands without her permission, she will kill me. So I can only make a rift in the light lands."

"Kaliman Empire, the rift to the right of the capital," he said, making his decision in a split second. "I will issue a special decree granting you full powers. Anything else?"

"Everything else, I can handle on my own."

"How do your portals work?"

"A skill of the ancients, called *Author*. It can only be obtained in special locations, of which there are three left on the planet. Only the heir of the first emperor can receive it. Kimal Sarento was not given the skill. Neither was Meram."

The pope nodded and looked at the scepter he had been twirling in his hands all this time. As if having decided something, the head of the church tore off the gem box with a sharp movement, and a magic stone shrouded in a red aura fell onto the table. After twirling it in his hands, he rolled the octagon toward me.

"All necessary decrees will be issued within 24

hours. Hearth will receive the right to a device for processing resources from the rifts. You will receive the book in a week. It will be delivered to your city. You will deliver the modernization device to the Citadel as soon as you receive it. I hope our cooperation will be productive, Archduke Valevsky. Everyone can go free. I see no reason to destroy our mutual partner."

Several wall panels moved aside, and three commanders appeared at once. The fiery swords in each of their hands indicated that they were ready to rush into the attack at the first signal from the pope, but this was not necessary. I involuntarily shuddered, trying to recall if the pope had ever given the order to set up an ambush in his office. But I came up blank. The whole way, the pope walked majestically with his head held high, occasionally nodding at questions.

"Not bad," I said. "I'm not sure it would have worked, but it's not bad."

"If you mean the mithril armor, then rest assured it would have worked," the pope said, refusing to let me have the last word. "Don't forget who founded the Church of the Light. Your distant ancestor. The first emperor understood perfectly well that sooner or later the secret of mithril armor would become public property. He protected his creation by giving us the means to fight against those who wear full mithril sets.

This is how he indicated that he was not at all deceived by my appearance. I did not check whether this was really so, or whether His Holiness was simply bluffing, passing off wishful thinking as reality. Despite the fact that three commanders stood against me, their only chance was to attack before I could react. Otherwise, the level twenty-five ousel would quickly show them the flaw in this plan. Although...what did I know about the influence of darkness on the commanders of the Light? As far as I remember, I have not yet had the chance to check this in person, and one such commander at one time guaranteed that he would be able to descend to the eighteenth level of the infected rift. Maybe the Light in their eyes somehow protected them?

"I'm glad there was no need to lead the discussion in that direction. I'm waiting for the book and your decrees, Your Holiness. After that, the device will be yours." I squeezed the stone I'd received in my hands and activated the portal to Hearth. Meeting the pope always meant trouble, even if he didn't have the power of the Inquisitor behind him, so I couldn't wait to get home.

Kimal Sarento was found shamelessly sleeping on my throne. The Inquisitor and the Interrogator had not yet returned from their fruitful work, which brought Hearth a good profit, so no one had disturbed his slumber. I didn't either. Since Kimal Sarento seemed to feel so comfortable on the throne, let him sit there a while.

"Naira, I'm back," I said over my remote intercom.

"Excellent. The portal will open in two hours. I'm in my room. Will you stop by?"

"Is that a hint?" A predacious grin shot across my face.

"A hint? You haven't removed your armor in six days! No, my husband, no hints. Let's just drink some wine."

"If we're just having wine, let's do it in my office," I sighed sadly. Naira was right — after six days in a hermetically sealed suit of armor, any intimacy would have to wait until after I'd bathed thoroughly. I should have instructed the servants to draw a bath, but instead I buried myself in papers. Eleanore's signature alone wasn't always sufficient. I didn't want to go to the hospital. There were already loads of people there eager to hand over their savings for a chance to regrow limbs or rid themselves of terrible diseases, but I simply didn't have the strength right now to interact with strangers or see their emotions. My meeting with the pope had been enough for me.

"Finally!" I said as the door to the office opened. "Do I deserve at least a kiss?"

"Look before you leap, my beloved mentor." In the doorway stood not Naira, but Kimal Sarento. I even made a face. I wasn't in the mood to see anyone, particularly him.

"I was visiting the Pope. I received a gift from him," I showed the exclusive gem. "His Holiness is well aware of my agreement with Father Urg and has offered me a better price."

"That's their forte," Kimal Sarento grinned. "What did we agree on?"

"We'll be friends with Father Urg. He will remain in his position. They will give us devices for creating elixirs. Nothing that is worth your attention."

"The pope promised machinery?" Kimal Sarento was taken aback. "What did you promise him? To surrender Hearth?"

"Max, the portal has opened!" Naira burst into the office. "But for some reason, it's two hours early!"

"What are those kids up to?" Kimal Sarento could barely maintain his cool demeanor. He was evidently uncomfortable with being out of the know, and besides, he was furious that someone was doing something in the city without his knowledge.

"What else could they be up to, my over-excited student? Playing in the sandbox, making sandcastles, and measuring their spades. Everything that good little boys and girls should do. Naira, do you know why they opened the portal early?"

"The situation changed and they could no longer wait. They're not exactly in the most peaceful area."

"Let's go," I almost ran to the portal arch. Kimal Sarento followed behind and dove into the portal before I could step in. All I could do was growl with anger. This cunning fox was always doing things his way! The shimmering veil accepted me without question, and as soon as space stopped floating, I found myself in the shadow of a huge mountain. It towered over the world, soaring upward almost vertically. So this was the Black Mountain. Pharapho's habitat was oppressive, and I felt like a grain of sand before it. There was fog everywhere — it reached my chest, hiding myriads of Pharapho's children. *Golden Dome of Protection* began to sparkle, showing that the fish were wasting no time and had begun to feed. Kimal Sarento stood not far from me and treated the surrounding fog to a taste of his lightning, releasing not only *Chain Lightning* but even the lower-level *Lightning Strike.* Essentially, he did everything he could to destroy as many creatures in the surrounding area as possible.

"Come on!" I shouted, activating the teleport back to Hearth. I didn't have to ask the man twice, and literally a couple of seconds later we were back in the main hall of my palace. Not much had happened, except that now I had a small point on my map that I could portal to near the level seventy-one rift. Even if the converts sent by Naira did not reach the entrance directly, I would not have to cross half the continent in order to get to Black Mountain.

Kimal Sarento clearly wanted to tell me something, but I stopped him with a gesture and, sitting right on the floor, took out ten essences. I didn't have time for a showdown. The portal to the Abyss didn't open — apparently, I had formulated something incorrectly. I really should have arranged a meeting with the interactive neural network to complete my *Author* training, but I would only do so once the pope took the book from Father Urg and gave it to me. Looking up at the silent Kimal Sarento, I activated the triangle, and the world once again floated, turning into the habitat of the white seraph.

"Welcome, human! You've become a frequent visitor. Have you managed to convince Pharapho of your maniacal plan to create a new second-orbital force?"

"Not yet. I'm here for another reason. I have a stone that will help me adapt to the darkness. Soon I will receive a device for creating rifts. You said that if the hole in the ground reaches the maximum level, everything within a hundred kilometers will die. Including, as I understand it, the one who came to destroy this rift. My question is simple: how do I come out of this alive?"

Chapter 19

THE DUNGEONS OF THE STRONGHOLD had not changed much in the past two days since we'd been let out. The same stench, dampness, dimness and steel bars. Even the two dozen crossbowmen were quite familiar — they had stayed with us for all five days, regularly changing guard according to schedule. The biggest difference was that the cage now held a table, four chairs, and the heavy body of Emir Hadji. The dark-complexioned Kaliman was busily sorting through papers, pretending that the cage was his personal office. On the table there was a red folder that my pupil had left. I had recently been given the requirements to read, and, I must admit, in the first moments my eyes almost popped out of their sockets. Kimal Sarento had practically demanded complete vassalage from the Kalimans. No joke — ten percent of all profit the Kaliman Empire extracted, produced or bought over the next five years would be transferred to Hearth in kind or in gold. Moreover, the Inquisitor himself, who would receive reports from the Kalimans once a month, must monitor the fulfillment of these conditions. And I suppose there's no need to mention what would happen if the voice of Chaos sensed a lie or some kind of forgery. So I sincerely had no idea what Kimal Sarento was doing. If I were the Kalimans, I would never agree to such conditions. Although...they were in an unenviable position. My journey via cart had opened up a long path of places to which I could now portal on my map. We had visited one literally a few minutes prior to observe the havoc being wreaked near the capital. People crazed with fear fled to Olro in vain hope of salvation and huge clouds of dust were already rising on the horizon. The Wave was approaching the Kaliman capital and there was nothing anyone could do about it. The fear and horror written on the faces of the wall guards was reflected in the faces of the citizens fleeing the protection of the city walls.

The portal behind me shut and without saying a word, Kimal Sarento and I sat down on the chairs. Footsteps were heard, and one of the servants practically ran into the cage, laying out wine glasses on the table and the wine itself in a special cooling bucket. The servant took a few steps back and froze, ready to fulfill any of our wishes. If we were not in the depths of the catacombs, one might assume that he was a waiter in a nice restaurant.

In fact, if I really used my imagination, I could picture this as a particular sort of restaurant with a specific clientele and "authentic, rustic" smell.

"Gentlemen, I am glad that you did not delay and arrived exactly at the appointed time," the smile on Emir Hadji's face demonstrated openness and readiness for negotiations. Not a hint that two days ago he ordered us to be killed. Hypocritical bastard. "How did your meeting with the Inquisitor go?"

"The vow of silence has been extended," Kimal Sarento sighed sadly. "It took a meeting with the pope for my silent mentor to save his life, but fortunately, it is being solved. The Inquisitor sent my mentor on his next mission, giving him only a few days to resolve all his affairs. Now we have come here to determine whether the Kaliman Empire is ready to participate in these affairs, but as I see, the conditions of our participation have not been met. I do not see here the two young ones whose presence we agreed upon. I do not see any signed documents. I am afraid, gentlemen, that we are wasting our time. Although, I must admit, the wine is a nice touch. Let's get down to business, Emir Hadji. We were just at the Wall. We saw the dust approaching the capital. The wave will be here in a few hours, if not sooner. Are you prepared?"

"You know perfectly well that we are not," another voice rang out. A shadow near the cage took shape, turning into a man in a golden robe. The High Priest of the Kaliman Empire had deigned to grace us with his presence. He somewhat resembled Father Nor — a strong, distinctive face, a rather ascetic build, tall — but there was one fundamental difference. This man's eyes were filled with Light. The kind that Father Urg could only dream of. A true minister of the church. He stepped into the cage.

"Your Eminence, what an unexpected meeting," Kimal Sarento stood up and made a graceful bow. I had to repeat his movements so as not to look like a complete rube.

"Yesterday I had a long and very productive conversation with the pope, Count Sarento. His Holiness told me many interesting things." Despite the fact that the High Priest was talking to Kimal Sarento, he looked at me. Evidently he was trying to break through my defenses and break my spirit. But compared to Father Nor, all other people looked like ordinary kittens mewling next to a true tiger. I had no issues standing tall before him. For just a moment, dissatisfaction flashed across his face at the lack of results his appearance had produced, but he quickly pulled himself together and took the last free chair.

"Permit me to ask what interesting things these were?" Kimal Sarento was the epitome of politeness.

"The Inquisitor has not released Archduke Valevsky from the duty of destroying the Wave," the High Bishop stated, as if he had caught us red-handed.

"We never said that we had been released from the duty of destroying the Wave," Kimal Sarento said, arching his eyebrows in surprise. "We only said that we were given a few days to get our affairs in order. Because it's time to move on to the next task. If you recall our conversation with the respected Emir Hadji, before he ordered us to be killed, we said that from now on the Wave is the concern of the Kaliman Empire. Because this very Wave has already passed the Wall and is moving towards the capital. We were ordered to stop it on the other side of the Wall, but were detained. So yes, we will still fight these beasts, in any case, but there's an important point to clarify: where and when we will do it. The more creatures the Kalimanians destroy through their own heroic deeds, the easier it will be for us to finish them off. We can sit back and watch for three days, let the Wave stretch out, and then, when there is not a single living creature left, we will go and destroy the leader. We won't even have to deal with the small fry — they'll be busy devouring the Kalimans."

"The pope warned that the warmth of Hearth's name does not extend to its treatment of humanity."

"After they kept us in this cage for five days, fed us slop, ignored our warnings, and then decided to kill us?" Kimal Sarento's face showed genuine bewilderment. "Your Eminence, what humanity can be found here? It seems the word has been banned in the Kaliman Empire."

"There is no need to twist the facts, Count Sarento," the High Priest snapped harshly. For perhaps the first time during our entire meeting, he looked intently at my pupil and, of course, I could be mistaken, but Kimal Sarento seemed embarrassed. However, all his fourteen decades of life experience had not been in vain — he managed to control his emotions and even plaster on his usual discouraging smile:

"Of course not, Your Eminence. You know, can we agree to set aside the unnecessary niceties for now? Honestly, it's boring. We both understand that with every passing minute, the Wave is getting closer to the walls of Olro. The longer we flex our verbal prowess here, the more good Kalimans will die. Moreover, if the Wave reaches the capital, we will no longer be able to protect it. Running all around the city trying to catch beasts is a terrible plan. Now, while the advance detachments of the creatures are only now approaching the capital, the city can still be saved. Is that what you want? If so, then our conditions have not changed since last time. If not, we are leaving. Yes, we will mourn the senseless death of so many people. Maybe we will even worry and grieve. But we will not retreat from Hearth. You shouldn't have locked us in this stinking hole and tried to kill us. Retribution is like that, you know. It always comes back to bite you."

"The Kaliman Empire offers you the life of Emir Hadji," the High Priest said suddenly to the bewilderment of everyone else in the room. "It was his idea to lock you up here and kill you so as not to leave any traces. He is the one who should answer for it."

"If Emir Hadji were a simple craftsman, the

head of a city or even a province, we might consider such a proposal. Those who have done wrong should be held accountable, we fully agree with you on that. The only problem is that the esteemed emir is one of the four leaders of the Kaliman Empire and, dare I say it, the most influential of the four. The third person in charge, if you'd like, after the emperor and, of course, the High Priest. People of this caliber cannot and do not have anything personal. They are the Kaliman Empire. Otherwise, what is the point of an empire? No, your eminence, everything must be paid for in proportion to the offense. We do not plan to be parasites on the back of the Kalimans forever. Five years is enough time for you to ruminate on your decision to lock the archduke of an autonomous city, who was simply carrying out the orders of the greater powers, in your basements. And again I want to remind you that while we sit here chatting, the Wave is getting closer to Olro."

The High Priest was silent for a moment, looking from me to Kimal Sarento and back again, and then said,

"The Kaliman Empire is ready to give ten percent of all profits to Hearth for five years, if the capital remains intact. The papers will be signed by the emperor within an hour, and for now you have the word of the high priest. The Wave must be stopped before it reaches the capital."

"Not so fast, Your Eminence." Kimal Sarento was not backing down. "There was one more condition, and as I see it is not being met."

"What does Hearth want with two innocent teenagers? The Kaliman Empire is paying in full for the mistakes of its leadership."

Judging by the displeasure that flashed across the High Priest's face, he was categorically opposed to the topic.

"The Emperor's youngest son is now fifteen. He will undergo training as a high-level rift conqueror with subsequent enrollment in the Zarak Empire Magic Academy. Believe me, as its former long-time chancellor, there is no better academy in the entire bright world. We invite the prince to Hearth as a student and are ready to provide not only unique teachers, which have no analogues in any other empire, but also with level twenty-five magic stones. After graduating from the Zarak Empire Magic Academy, the prince will be enrolled in a squad of rift conquerors and will destroy rifts from the tenth to the twentieth level for five years. At the age of twenty-five, the prince will be free to return home without any restrictions or conditions on our part."

"Ten years of training to become a rift conqueror?" It was the high priest's turn to be taken aback.

"Education, magic stones, training with the best mentors," Kimal Sarento confirmed. "Moreover, the prince will join the governing council of Hearth and will also oversee all relations with the Kaliman Empire. The only condition is that he will have no assistants from your empire by his side. He will have to cope with all trials and tribulations on his own."

"What do you need this for?" the high priest finally lost his composure.

"Our motives remain our own. The prince will be returned in ten years, but the daughter of Emir Haji will never be returned. She will remain the concubine of my silent mentor for the rest of her life."

"This is unacceptable!" Emir Hadji barked. The strongest emir of the Kaliman Empire looked quite intimidating. But it was impossible to deflate Kimal Sarento with any sort of threat.

"This is a mandatory condition, without which we will not leave the walls of the city. I repeat, Your Eminence, it is easier for us to let the Wave run rampant in the capital than to stop it on its approach. Moreover, it will become more difficult to stop the creatures with each passing minute. I believe that in five to ten minutes it will become completely impossible."

"The Archduke will have the concubine he so desires. You have the word of the Church of the Light," the High Priest, backed into the corner, answered after a pause. Emir Hadji gritted his teeth, but said nothing. Just one look said that I had made another enemy in this world. Strong, dangerous and devoid of any moral principles. The emir would do anything to get his daughter back. At some point, I even began to doubt that I needed this concubine, but Kimal Sarento had laid everything out on the shelves that morning, explaining why we needed both teenagers. Proper upbringing, unification against the backdrop of distance from home, friendship turning into deeper feelings and, as a final chord, putting into their heads the thought that they were only able to become a couple thanks to Hearth. In ten years, the leadership in the Kaliman Empire could suddenly change and a new sultan and his wife would ascend the throne. A couple who would be indebted to Hearth. For this, one could tolerate the schemes and machinations of Emir Haji. Of which there would, no doubt, be many.

"In any case, if you'll permit me, I'll stay here and draft all of the agreements and my silent mentor will go to carry out the mission assigned to him. No one is opposed, right?"

There were no objections, and soon a portal appeared by my side. It led to the exact location I had been just a couple of minutes prior — the main gates, where the city residents, maddened by fear, were trying to shove their way out of the capital. Of all the places available to me, this was the closest to the rolling Wave.

The horizon was already darkening. The creatures were rushing towards the capital in a huge front. I had some doubts that I would be able to stop all the monsters, so Kimal Sarento stayed in the capital. If anything happened, he would back me up. I didn't need him in the battle, he would only get in the way. Several *Dashe*s took me far from the walls, where I turned up the maximum available range of the auras — one hundred meters. Some silhouettes began to flicker ahead. The creatures were rushing towards the city as fast as they could toward the fresh meat. I didn't want to risk losing the level fifteen ousel to the beasts, so I instead pulled out the more accessible level twenty-five ousel. When I ventured into the level seventy-one rift, I'd definitely take a few extra steel boxes with me to capture an even higher-level creature.

Unlatching the box and switching on the dark mirror, I rushed toward the approaching Wave. According to the logic that Kimal Sarento had been actively drilling into me for the entire five days I had been in the cage, as soon as the Wave creatures sensed me, they would immediately forget about everything else and would do everything just to reach my mortal form. Of course, there were certain doubts about the effect the dark aura would have on the Wave monsters, but I didn't really have a choice. I had to take risks.

A few more *Dashes* took me close enough to get a look at the individuals. Usually, Waves were composed entirely of kronas, as they were easiest to grow and prepare for future battle. But the Chaos Wave was special. Instead of kronas, some beasts that somewhat resembled humans were at the forefront. The anthropomorphic creatures had two arms, two legs, one head and even a human-shaped torso, but the overall effect was terrifying. To begin with, these creatures ran like animals on four limbs. Each one had been stretched out to grotesque proportions — four to five times longer than the body. As if someone had taken a human and stretched them out on a rack like rubber. The head was also elongated — a huge zucchini, on which a toothy mouth was located. At least this was similar to the riftbeasts I was familiar with. I didn't notice any eyes, but I was able to determine that if it stood on its hind legs and stretched its arms to the sky, it would easily reach the third floor of any building. And this is despite the fact that, as I said, the monster's body was of completely human proportion. They wore no clothing and their bodies were covered in small scales. In general, repulsive freaks. Where did Chaos find them? And, saddest of all, *Analyze* turned out to be useless. No one had encountered such creatures before, no one knew their strengths or weaknesses.

I was noticed. The long limbs allowed the creatures to move very quickly, and as soon as the first one sensed me (not saw me — sensed me, I still couldn't find any eyes), it immediately rushed towards me, ignoring all the dark auras. The level twenty-five ousel, its aura stretched thin across a hundred meters, psychically squeaked in grief — the creatures of the Abyss had no effect on Chaos beasts. The long-legged creature covered a hundred meters in a few seconds and, joyfully clicking its mouth, jumped on me with all four paws, like some kind of spider. The ends of the limbs glittered like metal, and an instant before the blow came the realization that mithril armor would not help against the creatures of Chaos. Because you cannot protect yourself from a zero-orbital creature with second-orbital armor.

From there on out I acted on pure instinct, forgetting all logic. I needed protection, and, not finding anything better, I fell to my knees, grabbed a handful of earth and formed a table. The same one I had designed in the cage while enjoying the hospitality of the Kalimans. The object appeared at the same time as the blow. Something crunched, and the space shook from a thunderous roar that managed to deafen me even through my mithril armor. Raising my head, I saw the monster jump away from me. It was rolling on the ground and screaming in pain — all four of its limbs had been crushed and viscous white liquid was flowing out of them. Stretching my hand towards the creature, I fired a vyrma crossbow bolt, wanting to test one of my theories. The result was exactly what I predicted: the bolt bounced off the monster without causing it any harm. The spawn of Chaos could not be killed by the resources it brought with it into this world.

I raised my head and looked at the crafted table that was still hanging above me. A deep dent had appeared on it, and cracks had appeared all over the tabletop. It worked. Not as perfectly as I would have liked, but it still worked! Apparently, the source was too flimsy, and the creature was able to destroy the final structure. If I could get to the stones, it would be easier. A bloodthirsty grin appeared on my face. The creature I had dealt with had significantly overtaken its comrades, as if it wanted to be the first to enjoy the warm meat. The main Wave was only now approaching the radius of the still active and useless dark aura, so I had time. Grinning, I latched the box and stuck the ousel back into my immaterial backpack, after which I lowered a hand to the ground so that *Author* knew exactly what kind of material I would be using as my source, and extended the other towards the deadly creatures rushing towards me. Since these monsters were unaffected by magic, darkness, mithril armor, or even vyrma, I'd have to use the gifts of the ancients.

A table on the right, a table on the left, a table above and a table behind, just in case. In theory, I should have used some flat structure, but I didn't want to waste time looking for them among the list of prototypes available to me. I had to use what was at hand. Besides, it was my personal invention, not a hint from the ancients. But it was impossible to fight the creatures with shields, so another structure appeared in front of me. The one that I had been designing with such care for five whole days in the steel cage of the Kalimans: a meter-long flying spear. Until now, I hadn't had the opportunity to check how effective the magic of the ancients was. Did it have the same hundred-meter maximum range, or was it unlimited, like an inherent part of this world? Taking aim at the first creature, which was literally ten meters away from me and was about to leap onto me and shred me with its paws, I sent the spear flying. The tip hit the monster's hide and there was a bright flash, as if several hundred lanterns had been lit at once, after which a deafening roar was heard, even louder than the one emitted by the creature with shattered limbs. The flash quickly disappeared, the tables that surrounded me shook from the blows of other creatures and screams of pain were heard again, but I did not take my eyes off of the carnage — the screaming creature was decaying right before my eyes, as if the inflicted wound had set it on fire and was actively consuming it. The roar choked in an instant, and not even ashes remained. The spawn of an alien world had been expelled from ours without a trace. The spear was undamaged — it froze in midair as soon as it had completed its mission. Only the tip was slightly dulled, but this was a trifle compared to what appeared before my eyes:

You have destroyed the spawn of Chaos.
Item Obtained: Magic Stone Experience Crystal.

Despite the fact that my shield was being actively destroyed, I still found a second to look at the description of the item I had received. And as soon as I did, my spear went into action again, crashing into another creature. All thoughts of somehow skirting around the Wave to reach the leader disappeared. The item description compelled me to declare open season on them all.

Magic Stone Experience Crystal. *Description: You gain experience for each Chaos spawn* *you kill or any other representative of other worlds that have come to the planet. The experience crystal can be used to increase the level of magic stones in accordance with the required experience table (table details). Item features: experience crystals allow you to upgrade magic stones above the default max value.*

The spear swung from side to side, causing chains of bright flashes. The creatures burned in whole packs, filling my experience crystal. There were some resource losses — I established experimentally that one stone spear could slay a hundred monsters before it wore down and broke. Afterwards, there was a rollback effect that felt as if my body had been struck by weak lightning. *Heal* only helped for a few moments, getting rid of the first sharp pang of pain, but didn't eliminate the unpleasant aftershock.

Nevertheless, the result was achieved: the creatures forgot about everything else. The capital, their other human victims — all this seemed trivial compared to me. They were eager to finish off the small gnat that had become such a thorn in their side, but this gnat had a painful bite.

At one point, I even threw away the now useless tables and created a second spear. Operating two turned out to be an order of magnitude more difficult, however, my speed in destroying the Wave monsters increased twofold. The experienced crystal absorbed the deaths of the creatures with a pleasing regularity.

Crafting another spear, head still buzzing until my concentration was restored, I used my remote intercom,

"Tell me, my cunning student, who decided to watch the terrible battle from afar, drinking cheap and tasteless wine, do you have any desire to join in?"

"Is it going that badly?" Kimal Sarento asked. I could hear the concern in his voice. "The dark aura was ineffective?"

"It was. As was magic. And the mithril armor is likely to be pierced by any blow. I haven't tested it, but to be honest, I don't really want to. But I'm doing alright, everything is under control."

"Nevertheless, you want me to join you."

"Yes, I do. In fact, you don't even have to join. If you want, you can sit out the entire battle in the capital. But there are major loot drops to be had here. Hold on a second..."

The creatures were encroaching from all sides. From the point where they had breached the Wall, they had spread out considerably and now had a broad front as they made their way toward the Kaliman capital. But as soon as the monsters realized that I had come out into the open field, they began to surround me from all sides, forcing me to constantly pivot. Both spears were slashing wildly, slicing through the creatures by the dozen, which in reality did very little. The thing about any Wave was that the beasts were spawned immediately before being sent to the portal. So all my heroism near the walls of Olro was pointless. Until I reached the leader and closed the portal through which the creatures were flowing, they would keep on coming. This was why I constantly pushed forward, allowing the monsters to surround me.

Another batch of spears was destroyed, and swallowing a wave of nausea, I allowed myself to relax for a few seconds. Even the fastest creatures needed time to orient themselves and begin a new attack. I had a few moments.

"Alright then, don't come. But you should know that killing the creatures gives you a fascinating little item. It's called a magic stone experience crystal. With its help, you can increase the level of your stones infinitely. Level fifty-one is not the limit, my leisurely student. The only limiting factor is how many beasts you destroy."

"Didn't you say that magic doesn't work on them?"

"Standard magic doesn't. But as far as I know, your *Chain Lightning* is no longer standard magic. After it began its journey to level fifty-one, it left the influence of the Light. There are so many creatures here that the experience for killing them drips into the experience crystal like a full-flowing river. The *Author* skill rocks."

"Got it. Open a portal for me?"

"I can't do that. I'd have to jump to Olro, find you, and jump back to this point. That's five to ten minutes, which the city simply can't spare. These things are too fast. I'm surprised that it took them two days to get here. Go on foot. We're not that far from the city."

"Okay," groaned Kimal Sarento. "In an hour they promised to give me the documents, as soon as I receive them, I will send them straight to you."

"In an hour I'll be able to open a portal to Olro," I said. "But an extra hour of fighting means that many more experience stones. But if you don't want to, I won't force you. More for me."

"My mother warned me that my mentor was a sly fox and that I shouldn't mess with him, but I didn't believe her. I thought she was slandering you. I'll be there in twenty minutes!"

Kimal Sarento made it in fifteen, face red with exertion. The creatures behind me exploded and flew into flaming chunks. Those that were still pressing down on me even stopped to look up. Apparently, they had thought the creatures of Chaos immune to any sort of magic. Surprise!

"What are we standing here for? Who are we waiting for?" Kimal Sarento was clearly enjoying himself. Once again he had the chance to unleash the full power of his magic, and to see a visible effect. It must be nice to realize that you are the strongest mage in this world and to prove it to others with such deeds.

"Did it give you an experience crystal?" I asked, forming more spears from the stones under my hand. As practice had shown, the stronger the material from which I crafted my weapon, the more durable it was. But the rollback when it was destroyed was worse. It even got so bad that I threw up on three separate occasions. There must have been some sort of fatal error in the syntax of the sentence I had crafted, but without proper education, I couldn't see it. I urgently needed to sit down and have a talk with the sixth-generation neural network. As soon as I had the book, I would. Self-improvement had its place, of course, but you couldn't get far with it. I needed examples. Lots of them.

"Why would I need it? My stone is already leveling up! And much more effectively than with the lithoids! I needed to kill tens of thousands of those to level up. But looky here — I've already made ten percent of the progress! Enough, my lazy mentor, stop pestering me! I'm working!"

Judging by his satisfied expression, Kimal Sarento was experiencing a euphoria that few in this world could. He was mowing through ten beasts at once, so that the main problem that arose was mana. After all, not everyone had a *Praxis* stone.

About two minutes later, Kimal Sarento drank the first mana elixir and reported the total number of remaining vials: forty-nine. Another ninety-eight minutes of unbridled bloodshed.

At some point, we had cleared all of the surrounding monsters in the area and could run forward uninhibited. Gradually, the stream of approaching beasts began to dwindle out. While before we were surrounded from all sides, the further we ran from the city, the less were surrounding us from behind. They huddled in tight formation, as if they could push us back, but we used this to our advantage. I kebabed ten creatures at once, and those who managed to avoid my weapon were taken out by lightning.

I almost didn't notice when Kimal Sarento fell behind.

On the way we came across a cart abandoned by refugees, on which we found some metal sheets. Using them as a source for my spears, I received a truly formidable weapon that did not collapse even after it speared through a thousand beasts. I knew that it was only a matter of time before this one was broken too and that the rollback would be brutal, but I didn't want to think of such unpleasantries while my spear was still flying.

Suddenly, I realized that Kimal Sarento was nowhere to be found. The terrible realization that one of the monsters could have devoured and digested him by now made me turn around and freeze, afraid to even breathe.

I was almost overwhelmed with horror as I saw Kimal Sarento kneeling about thirty meters away and, despite the distance separating us, I could see his blanched face. He was grabbing his chest with his hands, from under which an incomprehensible light was bursting out. As if someone had shoved a bright lamp between my student's ribs, so brilliant that it was capable of illuminating the space even during the day.

Dash brought me straight to his side, and, just in case, placing my hands on his shoulders, I used several *Heals*.

It didn't help. Kimal Sarento continued to

stand on his knees, clutching at the light pouring from his chest.

"Don't you die on me!" I shouted, but I had to tear myself away, as the Wave continued to come. Both my spears returned to work, and for some time I even forgot about the man. The onslaught was too furious, as if imbued with extra strength. Did they really think they could win? One of the metal spears pierced a dozen creatures at once and dissipated. It was as if a barrel of oil had exploded in my head. Bright circles swam before my eyes, I almost turned inside out, my legs buckled, and I completely dissociated from reality for a while. The monsters, the trials and strife, and even death itself faded into the background as my body endured the punishment for using the *Author* skill without proper training.

But I wasn't giving up yet. Yes, I felt awful, but I retained some part of my conscious mind and cast *Heal* to bring myself back to the waking world. It didn't help immediately, and by this time, from what I could tell, my second spear had also evaporated and the second wave of pain caught up with me. When I could finally perceive my surroundings once again, my first thought was that my brain had melted. Kimal Sarento stood a step away from me, stretching his arms in different directions, and from each of them one chain lightning broke off at a time. And this was not some thin strip of pure energy — it was a powerful stream, striking more than thirty creatures in one blow."

"Are you awake?" he asked. "What took you

out?"

"Improper phrasing when forming a spear. The denser the material it is made of, the worse the effect after it breaks. Where is all this lightning coming from?"

"A level fifty-one stone. Consumes much more mana, but the effect is much more powerful. Rest for now, this is my fight. With my now level fifty-two stone. Actually, you could run back to Hearth for mana elixirs. I'll need a few thousand vials, with how much this drains. Incidentally, my exhausted mentor, does it seem like the stream has begun to pick up again?"

The density of the Chaos Wave was truly impressive. They were rushing toward us in a solid block, sometimes crawling over the bodies of their slower comrades. Kimal Sarento's lightning tore the monsters apart by the dozens, even hundreds, but this had little effect on the overall number. They continued to run towards us, again from all sides, wanting to quickly finish what they had started. I didn't know what the Inquisitor expected, sending me to fight these monsters alone. How was I supposed to destroy them all? If it weren't for Kimal Sarento, I would have been crushed like a bug an hour ago.

"I wasn't kidding about the elixirs," he reminded me pointedly. "I have a little over twenty left. With such a heavy onslaught, they'll last about ten minutes, no more."

"Understood. On it," I somehow got to my feet, keeping my distance from Kimal Sarento. The lightning in his hands was too intimidating.

Finding the necessary line in the *Author* skill, I was about to activate it, when my gaze caught on strange movement within the ranks of the advancing army. It was moving forward in rows like a great steamroller.

Kimal Sarento could see the battlefield as well as I, and as soon as this steamroller entered his effective radius, he threw a bolt of lightning at the center.

The explosion scattered the Chaos spawn, and in place of the huge steamroller, a new monster appeared.

It looked like a badly dented ball, into which someone had carved a huge mouth with sharp teeth that occupied almost half of the body. You could safely say it was a giant, rivaling a six-story building in height. At least, that's how it looked in comparison to the beasts we had already encountered.

But the most peculiar and fascinating feature was the portal deep in its mouth from whence creatures covered in small scales with disproportionately long limbs continuously leapt out. Predictably, *Analyze* had nothing to say about this being, but everyone knew perfectly well what was standing before us.

The leader of the Wave. Familiar, but extremely unwanted sensations awoke within my body — my blood began to boil in my veins. The aura of *Tainted Blood* instantly enveloped both me and Kimal Sarento, almost smearing us into pancakes. It was hard to fight when your body wouldn't listen to you and all your organs wanted to jump through your skin.

Two chain lightning bolts flew at the enormous orb at once, but all it did was destroy the small creatures circling around their leader. The fifty-first level magic had no effect on him at all. Although...

"An *Integrity* bar appeared above the portal!" Kimal Sarento screamed in an inhuman voice. "Help! The elixirs can wait!"

I didn't need to be asked twice. I extended my hand, forming spears from the earth, and felt an unpleasant metallic taste in my mouth. My body couldn't handle the attack, so I had to play the equally important role of pouring *Heal* into myself and Kimal Sarento. It didn't rid me of the *Tainted Blood* effects, but it stitched all my cells back together and stopped me from decomposing. I instantly started to boil again, but each use of the spell granted us two or three seconds of adequate control over our limbs. An eternity by current standards.

A menacing roar was heard off to one side and Kimal Sarento sharply extended his hand in that direction, stopping the creatures that continued to attack us. The other hand was directed towards the leader. *Chain Lightning* did not harm it in any way, but it evaporated the new creatures being spawned from the portal instantly, before they could enter our world. The *Integrity* of the portal fell slowly but surely, and it was that moment that the Chaos creation decided to deal with us, once and for all. It rose up on several dozen stocky limbs and rushed towards us with the inevitability of a tsunami.

All the events that followed occurred so quickly that I hardly had time to process them.

First, both of my spears lodged in the creature's mouth and, as they touched the portal arch, swept it away like tissue paper

Second, the portal collapsed, but it didn't go quietly. It exploded, forming a fireball in the creature's mouth.

Third, two *Chain Lightnings* scattered the remainder of the creatures pressing in on us from all sides.

Fourth, the blast reached us before it did the Wave leader, sending us flying. The mithril armor handled the damage, but could not hold us in place.

Fifth, space was filled with the deafening roar of the wounded creature. It accelerated in an attempt to catch us mid-air and devour us.

Sixth, several tables appeared next to me, spaced about a meter apart. This was all that my agitated consciousness could create in this short period. Except that this time the legs were not facing me, but towards the creature rushing after us.

Seventh, and, it seemed, last — the huge, misshapen orb caught up with us and stopped abruptly, crashing into a cluster of tables. It seemed that something with such mass would break through my flimsy creations, but not so. Somehow my tables held the monster back. I finally crashed to the ground, rolled a few times, but immediately jumped to my feet.

"The beast is mine! Take the small ones!" I yelled at Kimal Sarento and began to form table after table, covering the creature of Chaos with them. First one side, then another, a third, above, below, behind — the tables appeared one after another in the air and crashed leg-first into the creature, forming a single structure. I couldn't completely destroy the creature. As soon as I did this, *Tainted Blood* would become a part of me, and the two Chaos beings that had settled in the Hearth would become my masters forever. But I couldn't just leave the monster like that. Even without a portal in its mouth, it was dangerous to human civilization. However, five days in the cage of the Kaliman Empire and the threats of Emir Hadji gave me a rather interesting idea: locking the beast in an impenetrable fortress from which it could never escape and putting it completely out of my mind. Even if it died of starvation, I would already be far away and be unlikely to receive *Tainted Blood* because of it. *Author* was just fine for me, and I didn't want to lose it to gain such an inconvenient ability. An aura that had no lesser effect on me than my opponents.

"It's impressive," said Kimal Sarento ten minutes later. While he was busy pumping his magic stone to level fifty-three, I was building a fundamental structure around the creature of Chaos. Tables were all well and good, of course, but after the issue with the spears, I didn't have much hope for my creations. In the list of examples, I found something that looked like bricks, after which I began laying out a hollow cube with walls five meters wide. At first, things went quite slowly, but after I learned to copy sections of the wall I'd already created, my speed increased tenfold. The ancients were real masters of space management. I set the last brick in place at almost the exact same time as the last beast was destroyed. Nausea rolled over me again — the tables that had previously held the ball in place had collapsed. However, this did not affect the final structure in any way. The bricks could hold the creature indefinitely. The huge cube didn't even wobble, even though I knew perfectly well that the monster was raging inside, eager to break free. And what pleased me most of all, the *Tainted Blood* aura had almost disappeared. Sure, my pupil and I were still affected and I had to cast *Heal* every two or three seconds to restore our bodies, but it would certainly go away sooner or later. We just needed to wait. And heal. Where would we be without healing magic?

"Did you reach level fifty-four yet?"

"I need literally a few hundred more," he complained. "Too many..."

Kimal Sarento didn't have time to finish speaking — the air flickered nearby, incarnating into the Inquisitor. From the look on his eternally stoic face, he was annoyed. For some reason, he didn't want to admit that he was furious.

"You're doing everything wrong!" the Inquisitor thundered, forcing me to fall to the ground. The *Tainted Blood* had still not cleared from my body, so this could have easily destroyed me. I popped *Golden Dome of Protection* out of my magic field and it got a little easier. I even managed to sit up, but I didn't have the strength for more. Three *Heal*s for myself, three for Kimal Sarento, who was already starting to stagger from the tearing pain and weakness, after which I looked at the Inquisitor.

"Mission accomplished. The wave has been stopped."

"You did it wrong!" the Inquisitor barked again, but this time I didn't turn into a spineless sack. The Inquisitor's voice had no effect on light humans.

"I did it exactly as I was told. You demanded that I stop the Wave — I stopped it."

"You were supposed to get the Tainted Blood! Remove these walls and finish what you started! One blow is enough. The creature will not resist!"

"No. I fulfilled my duty. The Wave has been stopped."

"You dare to contradict me?" The Inquisitor loomed over me and seemed ready to sweep me away with one wave of his hand. I looked sternly into the eyes of the Chaos spawn, who considered himself the will of the Light, and he didn't even notice when one of my hands fell to the ground. The air shimmered and I embodied two spears, aimed directly at the Inquisitor.Slowly, emphasizing each word, I repeated,

"I. Fulfilled. My. Duty. The Wave. Has. Been. Stopped."

With an elusive movement, the Inquisitor flew a few meters back and a sword appeared in his hands, emitting a bright light. Trying to keep my cool, I rose to my feet. I was tired of being afraid. Tired of groveling. Tired of living in the vain hope that today Chaos would not turn its eye toward me and decide to kill me. My tried-and-true tables materialized around me, forming an additional layer of protection. I wasn't going to retreat.

"I'll cover you." Kimal Sarento stood behind me, stretching out his hand towards the Inquisitor. Lightning danced in the mage's palm — I had never seen such a visual effect before.

"You will be punished, Archduke Valevsky!" the Inquisitor proclaimed and extended his sword towards us. A thick beam of light shot from the tip, but I managed to place one of the tables under it. It began to crack at the seams, filling with an inner light, threatening to explode, but my protection gave us a few extra moments of life, which we took full advantage of. Both my spears and Kimal Sarento's *Chain Lightning* flew at the Inquisitor. The spears struck the creature of Chaos and disappeared without a trace, leaving me befuddled, but I was not going to stop there — another set of spears was soon to follow. The table still flew apart, but the beam of light ran into the next table I crafted. Then the one after that. Then the one after that. And then into a brick wall that I had created in the image and likeness of the prison for the Wave leader. The Inquisitor was unable to destroy it. Realizing that my spears were not doing much harm to the creature of Chaos, I began my new favorite pastime — I began to build a wall around the Inquisitor. Yes, he could teleport, but would he be able to do it from a closed circuit?

He could. In fact, he didn't even have to teleport — with one swing of his sword turned my creation into a pile of useless stones, which almost instantly transformed back into earth. However, this allowed me to take a break, once again *Heal* from *Tainted Blood* and build myself additional defensive tables. The Inquisitor was strong, was a zero-orbital being, but the magic of the ancients somehow allowed me to resist him. Realizing that he had no chance at a distance, the Inquisitor raised his sword and walked towards us, wanting to finish us off in hand-to-hand combat. He paid no attention to my spears or Kimal Sarento's magic. For such a high-level being, our attempts at attack looked ridiculous.

"Stop! You are using too much power!" another voice rang out. The Interrogator appeared a few meters away from the Inquisitor. My shield stone automatically returned to its place. I would rather lie on the ground from the Inquisitor's voice than turn into a puppet of Skron because the Interrogator addressed me. Kimal Sarento, who had been standing next to me all this time, thought exactly the same. In any case, he began to back away, so as not to fall under the hot hand of the Chaos spawn playing the hand of darkness.

"He dares to contradict me!" The Inquisitor was clearly angry. However, since he was not addressing me, I managed to maintain an upright position. I may have fallen to my knees, but that was minor. The main thing was that I didn't lose consciousness.

"He has completed our task. The wave has been stopped," the Interrogator took my side. "You will not be able to punish Archduke Valevsky without wasting too much energy. This world is already out of balance, there is no need to detonate the charge of the ancients. We can overlook this moment."

"Everything is under control!"

"So under control that I had to come here myself, using borrowed power. Open your eyes, Inquisitor! You are allowing personal feelings to control your actions. This is unacceptable."

"He must receive *Tainted Blood*!"

"Are you willing to risk everything for this? How much energy and personal presence are you willing to withdraw from the zero orbit to force Archduke Valevsky to accept what you expect from him? Judge for yourself, Inquisitor! Be impartial!"

"He dared to contradict me! He dared to attack me!"

"Nonetheless, we must let it go. Archduke Valevsky has proven that he's able to solve problems on his own. Remove the beast. Hearth has won this battle. We must acknowledge and accept this. Balance is more important than our desire."

The sword in the Inquisitor's hands flared up once again and went out. The Supreme Being of the Light looked at me for a while, as if wanting to burn a hole through me, and then disappeared without further ado. The seething in my veins disappeared with it. *Tainted Blood* had left us.

The interrogator turned towards me. "Today you have won, Archduke Valevsky. But this does not mean that we will forget our defeat. The moment will come when the balance will be restored and we will ask you to answer for all the times when you contradicted us. Proceed to the next phase — you will go to Pharapho. The second-orbital power must appear in this world as quickly as possible. We acknowledge that you have fulfilled all our demands and the price for calling the Inquisitor has been paid. From now on, we work as partners."

With these words, the Interrogator disappeared without even casting a portal.

I wanted that power. Kimal Sarento came over and we stared at the now useless pile of bricks for quite a while.

Finally, he grinned and clapped me on the shoulder. "Hard times are coming, my revolutionary-minded mentor! Our uninvited guests are extremely vindictive and will definitely remember everything we did today. But you can't even imagine how glad I am that we did it! I don't care about the consequences — this is how the masters of the world are born! And today, my great mentor, you have come a lot closer to this goal. You can't even imagine how much. You have been recognized as an equal by the Inquisitor and the Interrogator. They have retreated...Okay, enough singing your praises, we must get to work. Open a portal to Olro — it's time to receive a well-deserved reward for our suffering. We suffered, right? Now let others suffer! The game called life goes on!"

End of Book Nine

Want to be the first to know about our latest LitRPG, sci fi and fantasy titles from your favorite authors?

Subscribe to our **New Releases** newsletter:
http://eepurl.com/b7niIL

Thank you for reading *Condemned!*

If you like what you've read, check out other sci-fi, fantasy and A LitRPG series published by Magic Dome Books:

NEW RELEASES!

The Selected
A LitRPG Action Adventure Series
by Vasily Mahanenko & Yuri Vinokuroff

Nanomachines
A Progression Fantasy Adventure Series
by Nikolai Novikov

The Afflicted
A LitRPG Apocalypse Adventure Series
by Konstantin Zubov

The Dark Summoner
A Portal Progression Fantasy Series
by Andrei Tkachev

The Last Paladin
An Action & Adventure Progression Fantasy Series
by Roman Savarovsky

The Other Side
A Progression Fantasy Adventure Series
by Rodion Korablev

The Dark Healer
A Historical Progression Fantasy Series
by Alex Toxic & Nadya Lee

Me and My Demons
A Portal Progression Adventure Fantasy Series
by Oleg Sapphire & Alexey Kovtunov

The Banned
A LitRPG Adventure Series
by Michael Atamanov

How I Built a Magic Empire
A Portal Progression Fantasy Series
by Konstantin Zubov

The Order of Architects
A Portal Progression Fantasy Series
by Oleg Sapphire & Yuri Vinokuroff

The Hunter's Code
A Portal Progression Fantasy Series
by Oleg Sapphire & Yuri Vinokuroff

The One Who Changes the Future
A Dystopian Portal Progression Fantasy Series
by Boris Romanovsky

An Ideal World for a Sociopath
A LitRPG Apocalypse Adventure Series
by Oleg Sapphire

The Healer's Way
A Portal Progression Fantasy Series
by Oleg Sapphire & Alexey Kovtunov

The Last Portal Jumper
A LitRPG Progression Fantasy Series
by Konstantin Zubov

The Dark Healer
A Historical Progression Fantasy Series
by Alex Toxic & Nadya Lee

Lord of The System
A LitRPG Progression Fantasy Series
by Alex Toxic & Furious Miki

A Shelter in Spacetime
A LitRPG Apocalypse Series
by Dmitry Dornichev

The Coming of God of Death
A Portal Progression Fantasy Series
by Dmitry Dornichev

The Village
A LitRPG Progression Fantasy Series
by Dmitry Dornichev & Alexey Kovtunov

Condemned (Lord Valevsky: Last of the Line)
A Progression Fantasy LitRPG Series
by Vasily Mahanenko

Living Ice
A Portal Progression Fantasy Series
by Dmitry Sheleg

Ghost in the System
An Apocalypse LitRPG Series
by Alexey Kovtunov

The Goldenblood Heir
A Portal Progression Fantasy Series
by Boris Romanovsky

Law of the Jungle
A Wuxia Progression Fantasy Adventure Series
by Vasily Mahanenko

Crossroads of Oblivion
A Portal Progression Fantasy Adventure Series
by Dem Mikhailov

More books and series are coming out soon!

In order to have new books of the series translated faster, we need your help and support! Please consider leaving a review or spread the word by recommending *Condemned* to your friends and posting the link on social media. The more people buy the book, the sooner we'll be able to make new translations available.

Thank you!

Till next time!

www.ingramcontent.com/pod-product-compliance
Lightning Source LLC
LaVergne TN
LVHW020725200726
843506LV00009B/620